APSIS FICTION

The Semi-Annual Anthology of Goldeen Ogawa

Volume 2, Issue 2 • Perihelion 2015

CONTENTS

author • illustrator • editor • book designer

GOLDEEN OGAWA

a HELIOPAUSE PRODUCTION

Apsis Fiction: The Semi-Annual Anthology of Goldeen Ogawa
Volume No. 2, Issue 2, Whole No. 4 (Perihelion 2015).
Published semi-annually by Heliopause Productions.

FICTION/Science Fiction/Short Stories

FICTION/Fantasy/General

First Edition 2014

ISBN: 978-06923127-6-6

State of the Orbit

If you, like me, do not pay much attention to cinema, you might be missing something remarkable that is happening. It's been happening since about 2008, when Marvel Studios released *Iron Man*, but it didn't become apparent to me until this April, when I saw *Captain America: The Winter Soldier* in the theater.

I am talking about how Marvel Studios has produced ten movies (as of this writing) existing in the same universe but with different stories and characters. It is called the Marvel Cinematic Universe, and you might already have heard of it. The ten related movies are the *Iron Man* trilogy, *The Incredible Hulk*, the two *Thor* and *Captain America* films, *The Avengers*, and *Guardians of the Galaxy*, with more on the way. Almost all the characters are played by the same respective actors, and references are made between films, even when no crossover characters appear (an example: *Captain America* is set during World War II and contains a character who is the father of the protagonist of *Iron Man*). The films are also famous for their easter-egg scenes, which usually tie in with the next movie in the MCU. These easter eggs began with a post-credit scene at the end of *Iron Man* that planted the seed for the story which became *The Avengers*, and can arguably be said to have culminated in *Captain America: The Winter Soldier*, which you must watch all the way past the end logos for the whole story.

These easter eggs, however, are probably some of the strongest threads tying the different films together. They give you a sense of a vast world (there's a reason it's called the Marvel Cinematic *Universe*) filled with stories that, even if they stand on their own, are still woven into a broader tapestry that contains a myriad of different stories, and by existing in this greater web, are made stronger for it.

The strengthening effect you get when stories build upon each other like this, in interconnecting blocks rather than a continuous line, is something that I greatly appreciate, as I try to do the same with my stories.

I can never take a story in isolation; I am always curious about how the events of that story reverberated out into its world, affecting people and places we didn't get a chance to meet. I like it when old friends show up in new stories, and we get to see how they've been getting on.

So although my stories can be sorted into three separate universes, they find a way to intertwine. This issue of *Apsis Fiction* features several such weavings of narratives—and two stories which rely upon each other to be whole.

While "The Stone Man" is a safe island in the chain of *Bouragner Felpz* stories, "The Withered Hand" results from events in a novel that has not been published yet. Not to worry, it doesn't spoil anything. It leads you into the bigger story that came before it, rather than the other way around.

"God, or Aliens," though fifth in the *Driving Arcana* saga, ties to the standalone short story that follows it: "Amar and Desta's Big Day Out," which fills the intentional gaps left in "God, or Aliens" and serves as the first stitch tying the universe of *Driving Arcana* to the multiverse of *Professor Odd.*

Therefore, a *Professor Odd* episode completes this issue of *Apsis.* "The Monster's Daughter" acts as the finale to the first season of the *Professor Odd* stories (of which there are six), and while referring to events from the previous episodes, it also provides a platform for another story—one that has yet to be told but that occurs in the world of *Bouragner Felpz.*

The cover for this year's Perihelion edition of *Apsis Fiction* features an illustration titled "Merman with Octopus," which, though not inspired by any stories in the collection, is relevant to the theme of "The Stone Man."

The coming perihelion (the time at which the Earth is closest to the Sun) will occur over the course of January 4th, 2015—wherever you are on the planet, I wish you a happy one!

—GOLDEEN OGAWA
California
September 2014

"The Stone Man" is another story in the Adventures of Bouragner Felpz *series, coming sixth in the second volume. (The first volume is available from Heliopause, and the preceding five stories have been published in* Apsis *volumes 1, 2 and 3.) Like the rest of the series, it concerns the exploits of the magician Bouragner Felpz, as told by his faithful companion Corianne Birch. It was written in September of 2013.*

The Stone Man

In the last days of 2317, leading up to Chandarmas, the whole of Kyreland was hit by a series of snowstorms. These were spaced such that we had a day or so of bright sunshine in which to enjoy the wintry scene, and before it could begin to wilt it would be renewed by another storm.

Snug in my rooms in the house between Kings Street and Bridgeton Way, I watched the snow flurry and cheerfully wrote seasonal letters of greetings from our fire-warmed sitting room.

It was from this happy pastime that I was roused by a banging on the front door. Being between housekeepers at the time (the much-lauded Mrs Bryce having retired that fall and moved to live with her niece in Burrock on Reid) I was obliged to climb out of my chair and tramp down the stairs, in no fair frame of mind.

Much of my sour mood vanished, however, when I opened the door to find my old friend Milky standing on the threshold—Milky, whom I had first met as a thieving street urchin, and whose adventures during Felpz's absence still remained a mystery to me. Now a solidly middle-aged man, lean and weathered but bristling with energy, he made his living—when not running errands for Felpz—as an antiques dealer and wood worker. Although he was bundled tight against the winter weather in a thick coat and hat, I recognized his scarred hatchet face at once.

My exultations of surprise and delight were, however, abruptly cut short when I saw what he dragged behind him.

It appeared to be a heavy burlap sack, of the sort used to deliver presents, but instead of the hard shapes of packages, it was soft and lumpy with a familiar head of dark hair protruding from the top.

"My dear Milky," I cried, "whatever is going on—and what on earth are you doing with *Felpz?*"

For it was the head of Bouragner Felpz, my childhood guardian and current benefactor, that I had recognized, and it followed that the corresponding body must occupy the rest of the sack.

"A favor he probably won't thank me for," Milky grumbled. "'Tis a favor nonetheless. Can you get a fire going in the moss? He needs a good thawing."

By *moss* I assumed Milky meant our kitchen, which was something of a muddle—its usual keeper being gone and a succession of less-than-adequate housemaids having done it little good. It had, however, the advantage of not being separated from the front door by two flights of stairs, and so it was in the kitchen that we gathered around my newly lit fire, propping Felpz up in front of it across two chairs.

Two chairs were required, and the burlap sack explained, by Felpz being frozen solid. Stiff as a board he was, and breathing so faintly as I nearly thought him to be dead.

"Not this one, and not so eas'ly," Milky said with grudging admiration. "But he got right up to the wall this time. I should give him a good kick in the shins if they weren't hard as rocks."

"That's less than charitable," I said reproachfully. "What on earth drove him to this? And where did you find him?"

Felpz had been absent from home for the past couple of days, but since this was his standard behavior I had not bothered to trouble myself over it. Now I wondered if he had been out freezing while I sat snug and warm at home.

"In Cawmeadow's Park," Milky said. "He'd fallen across the path, and the shovelers didn't know what to do with him. Recognized him right enough and sent a man 'round to my shop, they as knowing me and knowing I was a friend of his. Well, I took an old sack and went to save everyone some bother and took him home. As for why he should do such as daft thing as to freeze himself I can't poss'bly imagine."

"Oh, I can imagine some possibilities," I said shrewdly, putting a kettle on to boil over the fire. Despite the soft living I had enjoyed since returning to live with Felpz, the skills I had acquired as a single mother continued to serve me well, and in no time I had us outfitted with cups of tea.

We were sitting thus, drinking companionably, when Felpz's rigid body gave out a convulsive shudder, and he coughed violently.

"Easy there Mr Felpz, sir," Milky said, holding his shoulders so Felpz did not rattle himself clean off the chairs. "Have a care or you'll ruin Miss Cor's lovely fire."

"Blast the wretched fire!" Felpz wheezed, and though his voice was wrecked and hoarse I could tell his faculties had not been damaged in the least.

"Good to have you back Felpz," I said, pouring him a cup of hot water. "Give this to him, would you Milky? If it spills I doubt it will do him any harm—he's still cold to the touch."

He was, too; there was even frost on the lapels of his coat and the tips of his boots. This did not prevent him struggling (with Milky's support) into a sitting position and grabbing the cup I offered him and draining it in one gulp.

"That's better," he said with a satisfied sigh. "Another, if you please, Corianne, and I will be fit as a fiddle."

More hot water was procured, and I poured him a cup of tea without asking. By this time Felpz was sitting up on his own with one leg resting on the other chair. Briskly he shook out his coat, and I saw the frost disappear in the blink of an eye. Color returned to his pale cheeks, and his lips—which had been frighteningly blue—were now healthy and red again.

"You may ask yourselves—*thank you,*" he said, accepting the proffered cup of tea, "why I should attempt to freeze myself overnight, for I admit it is not a pastime I normally engage in."

"Oh, we assumed you'd have some daft reason," Milky assured our friend. "Though we did hope you'd tell us about it."

"Verily, verily," said Felpz with good cheer, and Milky and I arranged ourselves in attentive positions accordingly.

"A few days ago—what was it? Wednesday? Yes. Wednesday I received a visit from a most precocious young woman. Maybe you remember Miss Sutherhand, Corianne? The clockmaker's daughter from Endless Street? Well, I shall explain for Milky's sake. Quite a character, Miss Hilaria Sutherhand. *Robust* I think they are calling women like her these days, with thick round glasses and a penetrating voice. I remember she drove Corianne and her writing clean out of the sitting room with it.

"As it stood, Miss Sutherhand had been put through a most trying experience over the last few weeks. She is of that age—you will remember, Corianne—when young women are most susceptible to losing their heads and all the good sense that is normally contained therein over handsome young men. In this case Miss Sutherhand had been under additional pressure from her family to marry, given that she is an only child and her father is old and frail. They subscribe to the ridiculous notion that a woman cannot inherit her father's business, you see.

"To this end they had been introducing her to a veritable parade of young men, and she in the infinite wisdom of youth chose a young sailor of pleasing build and manners who had recently retired from the sea and was looking for shore work and was eager to learn the craft of clock making. A fine match, or so her parents thought, and the man was invited to live under their roof—he having no family living—in the days leading up to the wedding. This, as Miss Sutherhand impressed upon me many times, is next Saturday. It was also during this time that events took a change for the macabre.

"At first all went sunnily: the man was everything he appeared to be and took readily to her father's trade and soon began doing work for him. This required that he spend a certain amount of time at their workshop, which is around the corner from the family's house, and necessitated that he walk home in the dark most evenings. Not a problem for this man—whose name I should say: Jethro Waterworth—who was strong and energetic.

"One evening, however, he was missed at supper, and Miss Sutherhand herself went in search of him—imagining, I suppose, that he had become entangled with a project at work and simply forgot the time. This was on one of our recent bad nights, when it was snowing so fiercely no one went out if they could help it. Miss Sutherhand, bundled up in all her coats and armed with a storm lantern, reached the shop successfully only to find it dark and closed. Perplexed, she turned to make her way home. It was on this return journey that she stumbled into a strange figure cloaked in snow.

"He stood outside her house, and Miss Sutherhand was afraid he was some poor soul who had frozen to death in the night. However, when she held up her lantern to his face she found it was her own fiancé—not merely frozen, but turned to *stone.*"

"Stone?" I echoed, bewildered.

"Yes, *stone,*" Felpz assured us. "Miss Sutherhand ran away inside and got her mother up, and together the two women went out to see what could be done. Yet when they arrived at the same spot they found no man—stone, frozen, or otherwise—and the snow already filling in the place where he had stood.

"There being nothing else they could do at that hour the women went back inside, but for understandable reasons they were unable to rest easy. Then, after midnight, there was a thumping on the front door and who should come in but Mr Jethro Waterworth, quite cold and hungry but apparently flesh and blood.

"He was greeted with joy and relief, and upon hearing of Miss Sutherhand's misadventure, laughed it off as a foolish mistake. Miss Sutherhand returned to her room, much upset by all this, and tried to put the matter out of her head.

"The next night, however, she was unable to sleep, and in her restlessness she went to her window. That night the snow was thinner, but the stuff upon the ground reflected the weak moonlight brightly. In this she saw clearly the shape of a man standing below her window, looking up at her. In her fright she shut the blinds at once and remained in bed until morning.

"Mr Waterworth, all this while, was dismissive of her concerns, putting it down to hysteria and bad dreams. He was also spending an increasing amount of time at the shop—sometimes even spending the night there. None of this helped Miss Sutherhand's mood, but she endured it, until something truly disturbing befell her.

"As she described it, she was woken from a fitful slumber by a draft on her cheek, and sitting up she saw her door open. Knowing it had been shut when she had lain down she took up a match and lit her lamp, crossing the cold floor quickly to shut it again. Before she did, however, she took a quick glance out into the hall.

"That was when she saw him . . . or it. She was a little confused on that point. She said it looked like a man all curled up on himself with his head on his knees. Even as she stared, this strange person moved and raised its head to look at her. From what I can tell, its face was that of Jethro Waterworth but streaked and speckled as a piece of granite. It stared at her with blank eyes and from its mouth came not words, but a grinding noise.

"Miss Sutherhand admits she did become hysterical then, and in her upset she dropped her lamp and struck her head hard on the door frame, causing her to lose consciousness. She came to in the morning to find herself lying in her own bed, and not even a scorch on the floor from where the lamp had hit. But Jethro Waterworth has not been seen since."

Felpz had become more and more animated during the course of his monologue, and by now nearly all trace of snow and frost was gone from his person. Even his clothes were clean and dry once more.

"That is quite astonishing," I said, gathering up our empty cups and refilling them with tea. "It does not, however, explain how you came to freeze yourself overnight."

"Doesn't it?" Felpz said in surprise. He took his tea and sipped it. "No, I suppose it does not. I'd have to give you an account of my own actions of the previous days for that to become clear. As I am already overdue for an appointment with Miss Sutherhand, I suggest you come along and hear the whole story. I would be grateful for some steady characters by my side."

Naturally I agreed on the spot, and after some grumbling Milky allowed himself to be led along as well.

The weather had turned while we sat by the kitchen fire, and now dark blue-and-grey clouds hung overhead like a cold blanket. Sharp flecks of snow danced through the air on fitful winds, and the streets were empty save for the most courageous of travelers.

This included our three heavily wrapped forms, as we made our way out to the street, where plowing from the night before had left it more traversable than the pavements to either side.

I had expected Felpz to employ the sort of travel magic he usually did whenever there was a walk of more than a few minutes ahead of us, but to my surprise the clock maker's residence was hardly a hundred steps from our own front door.

"The shop is around the corner that way." Felpz indicated the direction down the frosted street after he had rapped firmly upon the clock maker's door. "And you may be interested to note, through that alley behind us is the back of Cawmeadow's Park, where you discovered me this morning, Milky. Bear that in mind—ah, here is Miss Sutherhand."

The door had opened and a charming young woman appeared. In person Hilaria Sutherhand was rather more attractive than Felpz's ungenerous description led me to believe, and I'm afraid Felpz was mistaken in the assumption that her emphatic voice was what drove me from the room: for I was certain I had never seen her before in my life and must have been inexplicably absent when she first presented her case to Felpz.

In height she was a touch shorter than I, with light brown curls piled clumsily on top of her head. She wore thick-rimmed spectacles and an awkward checkered dress that only served to make her appearance more endearing.

"Thank the Lady you're here, Mr Felpz," she said upon sight. "Father's taken badly since this morning. It was the shock, I am sure. As I was truly shocked as well, but my heart is stronger than his."

Felpz, who had been on the verge of introducing us, paused.

"Beg pardon, my dear," he said. "Do you mean to say some new calamity has befallen you?"

Miss Sutherhand waved her hand, ushering us in. "It is past now, but you come at a ripe time. Mother!" she called up a flight of narrow stairs as we entered. "Mother! Tell Father it is only the magician. The magician and his . . . er . . . " she trailed off at the sight of Milky and myself, who must have appeared to her an odd couple indeed.

"Miss Sutherhand, my friends Mrs Corianne Birch and . . . "

"Edder Thorn, ma'am," Milky said, dropping a polite bow. Felpz took this interruption in good grace, however, and continued smoothly:

"They are here to assist me and witness the resolution of your problem."

"Resolution?" echoed Miss Sutherhand, with the air of someone who has long given up on such a thing. "You may be less confident after you have heard what I have to say."

"That is as may be," Felpz allowed, removing his hat and shaking the snow off it onto the doorstep. "But I fear we are in danger of getting our narrative out of order. Will you sit down, Miss Sutherhand, and hear of my progress first? It may shed some light on the matter."

"Whatever progress you have made I would be glad to hear," Miss Sutherhand said agreeably, and led us through into a comfortable parlor heavily decorated with tinsel and ivy wreaths. Everything was remarkably festive, and I belatedly remembered that, were it not for this upending of their plans, the Sutherhand family would be preparing for the double holiday of Chandarmas and their daughter's wedding.

Miss Sutherhand sat us down on big, comfortable chairs and set out a plate of soft, buttery scones while she poured tea.

"First I must explain for Corianne and Mr Thorn's sake," Felpz began, "that I approached the disappearance of Mr Waterworth as I would any other missing person. You remember, Miss Sutherhand, how I asked for a piece of his clothing? I was able to use that to follow his trail to the shipping docks, where it then vanished. I searched the place with every spell I knew and still found nothing. Perplexed, I did some mundane searching and discovered a surprising thing. No one there had heard of Jethro Waterworth, not even the record keeper whose job it is to record the personnel of incoming and outgoing ships. As far as the books are concerned, Mr Jethro Waterworth never set foot on Redling's docks.

"Naturally this intrigued me, and I tried the passenger yard across the river—but with no success. Eventually I resorted to combing the records of every ship that came in shortly before you first met Mr Waterworth. I used some very complicated and tedious magic to make a thorough search that would tell me if he had been on any of those ships—even in an unofficial capacity. The results were troubling: on no ship had Mr Waterworth arrived in Redling. But I did find a ship that had carried him *away* from Redling. The brig *Marilda* had employed a sailor by the name of Jethro Waterworth, until he was lost overboard in a storm off the coast of Handmark last year."

At this Miss Sutherhand made an involuntary motion of alarm, and Felpz nodded consolingly.

"Do not doubt that this Waterworth they presumed drowned and the one to whom you are engaged are in fact the same person. Stranger things have happened. The question was *how did he do it?* To find out I would need to speak with him—or at least set eyes upon the fellow. To do this I began with the presumption that, if he had true feelings for you, he would not be able to stay far away, and if I positioned myself accordingly I would be able to get a glimpse of him.

"To this end I set up my vigil in Cawmeadow's Park, where I have been for several days. I became so absorbed in my task, I admit, that I quite forgot to care for certain physical concerns and in the end caused Mr Thorn here some trouble and Corianne an unwarranted shock. It was a foolish oversight. Had I been attentive to my own condition I could have solved this matter already, but as it is I can only report partial success."

We all looked at him expectantly. He looked back at us, clearly relishing the attention.

"I have seen your fiancé, Miss Sutherhand," Felpz said. "I saw him last night, in Cawmeadow's Park. I saw him break the ice from beneath the surface of Throttle Creek and walk out of the dark water beneath, moving stiffly through the snow. You may ask why I did not accost him. I am ashamed to say that by that point I had allowed myself to become so chilled that I could not move. It was thus how Milky—er, Mr Thorn found me, and having now been thawed out I come to you only to find there has been a new development."

"Indeed," said Miss Sutherhand. From her perch on the settee she knotted her hands in her skirt anxiously. "And I believe what you say, Mr Felpz, outrageous though it might be. For it explains why, when I saw him last night, he was soaking wet."

Felpz actually started out of his chair in his eagerness. "He has been here? Last night? Did he leave anything?"

Miss Sutherhand, a little put out by my friend's enthusiasm, pulled her arms close in at her sides. "It is a queer thing you should ask," she said. "For he did leave something on the doorstep—mother would not let me touch it so I took a pair of tongs from the kitchen and left it in a washbasin."

"Really? Oh that is *most* gratifying," Felpz said. "But would you tell me the events in order? Spare no detail!"

Miss Sutherhand sighed, but she bore my friend's insensitivities with fortitude. "I have not been sleeping well," she said, "as you can probably imagine. Last night I found myself jolted into wakefulness in the early hours of the morning for some reason unknown. I lay in my bed for what felt like hours, tossing restlessly, until I gave up the fight and lit a candle, presuming to go downstairs and read for a while.

"Almost as soon as the light had done flaring I heard a pounding on the front door. It nearly shocked me out of my own skin, and woke Father and Mother as well. They made me stay upstairs while they went to answer, but I opened my window and looked out, and saw all that happened.

"When the door opened I saw by its light that Jethro was standing there, in a puddle of dark water and quite bedraggled. I saw him reach out imploringly to my parents, heard my mother scream, and then the door slammed shut on him. It was only in the morning when I could see he had gone that they would let me go out. It was then I found what he had left: a rough copper ring, so rusted it bristled with blue-green stubble, holding a whorled piece of shell. Under it was a note in such a scratchy hand that I could hardly recognize it as Jethro's. The ring Mother did not allow me to touch, but I have the note here . . . " She fumbled at a pouch on her sash and eventually produced a stiff, ragged piece of paper, which she handed to Felpz.

"'My dearest Hilaria,'" he read, a frown creeping over his brow. "'It was never my intent to cause you grief. Even if you can never forgive me, I beg you accept my sincerest apologies. I had hoped my nightmares were over, but as it appears *she* will not let me go so easily, I have chosen to take my cursed self away rather than allow it to stain your life. The water does not forget. Yours ever, Jethro.'" He turned the paper over, sniffed it, then felt along its edge with his fingers. Then, with a small, triumphant smile, he said: "I have you!"

"You have him?" Miss Sutherhand said. "Do you know what is going on?"

"I have what I fancy is a fairly accurate idea," Felpz said. "But I'd much rather hear it from *him.* Come, Miss Sutherhand, show me this ring he left—that shall dispell any remaining doubts. Then, I think, we shall pay Mr Jethro Waterworth a visit." He stood up suddenly, slipping the note into his pocket and gesturing to Miss Sutherhand.

Understandably confused, the young woman led us into the kitchen, where she took a bowl down from the counter and presented it to us.

There in the bottom was a ring matching her description. Felpz gave a little ejaculation of joy and snatched it up immediately. As he turned it before his eyes, I saw the bit of shell glint like mother-of-pearl. Felpz squinted at it, tapped it with a finger and then blew on it. He rubbed it briskly on his sleeve and, holding it out, we all saw how the copper now gleamed rosy with no sign of rust or discoloration.

"It was prudent of you not to touch it," Felpz said. "As it happens, however, there is nothing dangerous about *this* ring. In fact, I believe you should wear it. It may help our case."

"Our case?" Miss Sutherhand said, bewildered. But she took the ring and slipped it on her finger. She had to wear it on her index finger, because it was so large. "Won't you explain?"

"It is not I who need do the explaining," Felpz said. "Won't you take word up to your parents that you are going out—in company of friends, assure them. Assure them also I will have you back for tea, and that they can expect this whole matter to be resolved—one way or the other—by that time."

While Miss Sutherhand went pounding up the stairs to deliver this message, Milky and I waited with Felpz by the front door, each of us on edge with anticipation.

"Mr Felpz," Milky began to whine, then caught himself. "Are you planning something, Mr Felpz?" he asked solemnly.

Bouragner Felpz shifted on his feet and gave us a sidelong glance. "Well, perhaps I am," he admitted. "But can you blame me? The whole matter is far too fantastic to be resolved in the mundane way."

I was about to make the case that Miss Sutherhand might appreciate a mundane conclusion, but was cut off by the reappearance of that person descending the stairs in a flurry of skirts and coat.

"Mother has decided to stay with Father," she relayed. "I am in your hands, magician. Lead the way."

Felpz did, out the door and through the snow, forging a path to Cawmeadow's Park, with Miss Sutherhand striding by his side. Milky and I followed at a little distance, walking in their tracks.

As a place of recreation I do not care much for Cawmeadow; I find it gaudy and pretentious, but that may be the fault of my own bias. That day, covered in snow with the metal railings studded with frost it did present a certain chilly beauty, and it also had the advantage of being quite deserted.

The centerpiece of Cawmeadow is doubtlessly Throttle Creek, that once-infamous tributary of the Reid that has confounded watermen and agents of the law since the founding of the city. Where it flows through Cawmeadow, however, a good deal of effort has been made to clean up the bank and do what can be done to prettify its noisome flow.

When we approached it through the frigid park that day, I saw with some surprise that it had not frozen entirely over. Its center was black and white reflecting the snowy banks, while the deep current which prevented it from freezing was visible only as a slight roil on the otherwise smooth surface.

"Before we proceed," Felpz said, coming to stand at the very edge of the water and turning to face Miss Sutherhand. "I must ask you a question, and see that you answer it frankly."

"Indeed, sir," said Miss Sutherhand gamely.

"While I do not see why your fiancé should not continue to be as you knew him, agreeable and kind," Felpz said. "It is quite likely—almost certainly so—that he is not the man you first took him to be. You may—*will* certainly—find him much changed. With this in mind, do you still consider it in the realm of possibility that you should take him for a husband?"

Miss Sutherhand appeared understandably taken aback by such a question. She stiffened under her thick coat and regarded Felpz critically.

"You put me on the spot, Mr Felpz," she said. "I can hardly answer that without knowing what these changes are."

"Yes, yes of course," Felpz said, a little impatient. "I only ask, would you dismiss him out of hand?"

"I would hope not," Miss Sutherhand said. "Mr Felpz, what on earth is going on?"

Felpz raised a hand, one finger extended, and brought it around in front of him to point at the dark water of the creek.

"Magic," he said, "always complicates matters. If magic had not been put to use here, your current predicament would have been cleanly avoided. However, in this case, I feel justified that a little more magic will help smooth the way to a resolution."

He fixed his eyes upon Miss Sutherhand's hand then, on the copper ring she wore, and then transferred his gaze to the water. His pointing hand turned so that it was palm up, and he *beckoned* with it, moving his arm in a strong arc.

Even though we stood behind him, Milky and I both felt the pull, and I saw Miss Sutherhand sway forward on her feet.

"Good gracious!" she exclaimed, and then stopped to stare. We all stared, save Felpz of course, who only smiled in satisfaction.

From out of the water a dark shape appeared, sending ripples outward to lap at the bank. It moved towards us, slowly rising, and I soon recognized it as the head of a man, dark grey and speckled, glistening wet.

He must, I reasoned, be walking along the bottom, for as he approached the shore, slowly his shoulders emerged. Then he bent forward, as if taking a step, and all at once the rest of his body surged upwards, the water sluicing off sopping wet clothes and raining upon the surface of the creek. He stood there in the shallows, among the broken ice, only his feet hidden beneath the surface, and stared at Felpz reproachfully.

In build he was a mid-sized man, not too tall or wide, and he wore what might have once been a good set of coat and trousers, but which were now draggled and ripped. His skin, everywhere it showed, was the shiny, dark, speckled grey of wet granite, his eyes polished orbs with black holes bored in them. His hair was a delicate filigree of stonework, and his mouth as it opened revealed similarly grey lips and teeth.

Miss Sutherhand, to her credit, only let out a small gasp, and staggered a little. The stone man's head swiveled to face her, and his features contorted into a look of concern. He made an involuntary movement, as if to take her hand, and at that she stumbled backwards and would have fallen in the snow had Milky not read the scene and come forward to steady her.

"Easy there, miss," he said, leading her in the direction of the nearest bench. I saw his meaning and went over to dust the snow off it.

"That was hardly fair, Felpz," I said reprovingly. "You could have given the poor girl *some* warning."

Felpz gave a little shrug, as if conceding this point, but he only said: "She would have needed no warning had Mr Waterworth here given her an honest account of his . . . hmm . . . curious predicament."

The stone man—Mr Waterworth—still with his feet in the creek, raised a hand and coughed. "You may scold me all you like, stranger," he said. His voice was a little raspy and hard, but not unpleasant. "Now you see me for what I am, could you blame me?"

"Oh . . . oh, Jethro." Miss Sutherhand, sitting on the bench, clutched her arms around herself and shivered a little. Milky took off his coat and draped it over her shoulders, but Miss Sutherhand pushed it off. "Jethro, what on earth has *happened* to you?" she asked.

Mr Waterworth gazed back out of his stone eyes unhappily.

"Come, Mr Waterworth," Felpz said gently, extending a hand. "Sit down and give us a full account of your history, and I promise to do all I can to set matters right."

Waterworth looked skeptically at Felpz, and did not move.

"I'll stay here, if you please," he said. "The water is . . . it helps me stay . . . er . . . fluid."

Felpz nodded assent, and went to stand a little way between Waterworth and the bench where we had gathered.

Jethro Waterworth hung his head and shuffled his feet, sending more ripples splashing up onto the shore. "I tried to tell no lies," he said. "I still think of myself as a man, even if I'm not much of one any more, and a man ought not to tell lies.

"I was a sailor, true enough, and worked aboard the *Marilda* five years. Maybe you've already found that out, and if you did, you know I was lost overboard in a storm last year. This is true, and if I left it out of my original story it was only because I wished it had never happened. But I will tell you now how it did, and how I came to be here . . . like this.

"The water was dreadful cold when I hit it—colder somehow than the stinging wind and rain I had already endured—and as it closed over my head I fought to claw my way back to the surface. But it was as though the waves were pounding down on me, and with all my clothes now soaked and heavy I began to sink.

"I've never been a particularly religious man. Is that an odd thing in a sailor? Perhaps. In that moment, however, I did pray. I prayed to whatever merciful god looks after drowning sailors desperate to be saved. I felt myself sinking farther; the light was gone entirely, and in the darkness I lashed out. My hand brushed something soft, and I felt something smooth with sharp pricks in it—like a cat's paw—close around my arm. I thought it must be some sea monster come to eat me—they have some mighty big ones up north—but then a low greenish light bloomed around me, and I saw it was not a monster at all, but a *mermaid.* She had a cloud of yellow hair that floated around her face, and though her hands were webbed and her skin mottled like that of a fish, she was in other respects perfectly humanlike—at least above the waist. Below it I caught a glimpse of fins and scales and some wicked-looking spines.

"She whispered to me through the water, asking if she should save me. Unable to speak at this point I nodded fiercely, and she drew me into her arms and pulled me down. My world went black, and I thought I was a goner."

Jethro Waterworth clenched his fists, making a grinding noise. "I should have been a goner," he said bitterly. "She *didn't* save me, not in any meaningful way. She took a fancy to me for some reason, and decided she would keep me—like a child finds a pretty crab or other creature on the beach, and thinking what a nice addition it would make to their home takes it with them, away from its rightful place in the world. Only the mermaid, knowing I would die and rot otherwise, turned my flesh to stone and my blood to water. So I awoke at the bottom of the sea, unable to breathe—but not *needing* to breathe—and before my eyes the darkness took form, and I found myself shackled to a rock on a vast and desolate landscape, while above, the mermaid and her kin swam like sinister birds, soaring on the currents of the ocean. They laughed at me when they saw my confusion and fear turn to anger, and though I found I could speak now, no matter how I shouted and pleaded with them to let me go they would only giggle and wag their fingers.

"They were not intentionally cruel," Jethro Waterworth allowed grudgingly. "They brought me food—freshly slaughtered fish, mostly—but I found that in my new form I could not eat. They took my disinterest for disdain and eventually the food stopped. My clothes slowly frayed and rotted away, and then they dressed me after their fashion: in plates of shell and rope woven of seaweed. Sometimes my mermaid—the yellow-haired one who had captured me—would unhook the chains that secured me to the rock and take me for walks along the ocean bottom. This seemed to delight her, but for me the abyssal plane looked all the same, and it only served to remind me how complete my isolation was.

"I thought at the time I must have spent aeons on the ocean floor, and that my existence would stretch out forever into this dim and bleak monotony. It came as something of a shock then, when on the return from one of these walks we found, waiting for us at my crag, a person I had never seen before. Like the mermaids he was half fish, but recognizably masculine. Also, the pattern of scales which decorated his tail continued up over the rest of him, and his face was fierce and alien, covered in spines and little fins. His tail too, rather than being smooth and shimmering like the mermaid and her sisters, was ridged with spines, and there were tendrils coiling around his underside. And though he was the most unnatural creature I have ever seen I could also tell that he was unspeakably angry.

"My mermaid saw it too and shrank away from him, her hair going slack and limp. The merman shouted at her fiercely in their language. He seemed to be admonishing her. He pointed at me several times with one spiny hand and made slashing motions with his arms. The mermaid, after meekly accepting this tirade for some minutes, eventually spoke up, and it appeared she was just as angry as he. They argued together, floating in the water over me, for what felt like a long time. Then the merman, clearly out of patience, darted down and raised an arm as if to strike me. Surprised and terrified I cowered away from him, but my mermaid dove in between us and the merman held his blow.

"She spoke again, pleadingly, and after a while the merman went away, muttering something threatening. Then my mermaid turned to me, and I saw there was a strange coloration around her eyes, as though she had been weeping. She embraced me with her smooth and prickly arms, kissed my cheek, and then undid the shackles from my leg. Then, grasping me under the arms she lifted me off the ocean floor and swam with me, farther than we had ever walked. We passed over deep trenches and mountains of rock. Eventually we came to a cliff where the water was lighter, and there she set me down. She stroked my hair lovingly and murmured something in her own tongue, and then she was a flashing streak disappearing into the murk.

"As you can imagine I was entirely at a loss for what to do. For many days I sat at the edge of the cliff, pondering whether to throw myself off it. Not needing food or sleep, I felt in no hurry to make a decision. After a time, however, I became aware that the murky light surrounding me dimmed sometimes, even when it was clearly day upon the surface. Straining my eyes I found I could make out dark shapes passing overhead, impossibly far above me. It took me some time to recognize their shape, as in my previous life I had never seen them from such an angle.

"They were ships, I tell you. Ships! And they passed with such frequency that I guessed the mermaid must have left me right in the middle of one of our shipping lanes. For the first time since I felt myself plunge into the icy water a hope flared in my chest, and I got to my feet and began following the shadows along the ocean floor.

"It was a long and weary walk. I later estimated that I must have walked along much of the coast of Kyreland, down past Gaela, and right up to the mouth of the Reid. I trudged over deserts of sand, and crept through strange canyons carved of rock. I climbed, steadily, and the floor became thicker and siltier. I began to come across pieces of debris, and the unmistakable detritus of human beings. I passed one or two sunken vessels, gutted and crawling with fish. At last I reached a place where all the dark shadows of the ships converged, and here I felt a change in the water, a heady sweetness that made me feel drunk. It quite took me off my feet, and I lay in the sands feeling the tides wash over me, slowly burying me, until at last my head cleared a little, and I found the strength to dig myself out. I suppose that must have been my body adjusting to the fresh water, though I couldn't imagine what it was at the time.

"I continued following the ships, walking up the bottom of the river. Now more than ever I had to navigate between discarded pipes and wire fencing; I passed many a rusting bicycle and once the corpse of an animal.

"Though the water was much shallower here, and I could even see the surface glittering above me, I still did not leave the water. Since I had given up all hope of seeing land again, now that it was a distinct possibility I found I was terrified of it. I continued walking upriver, until I found myself at the docks of Redling.

"There I stayed, hunched under a pier, until at last I summoned up enough courage, and one night I walked up a boat ramp and out of the water for the first time in what felt like years.

"I cannot tell you the horrible, bittersweet joy that filled me, to see my city as I had left it, but through stone eyes that saw through the darkness as easily as you see by sunlight. I could not return to my family like this, nor could I go back to work. Then I thought of returning to the water, and I could not bear it.

"Now without fear of any mortal disease I visited the lowest parts of the city and there acquired clothes. I learned to paint my face and hands so that in passing I appeared human. I found work, for in this vast metropolis there is work enough for someone with a strong back who asks no questions, and eventually saved enough to go to a witch whom I knew of old who makes a living off enchanting sailors. I put my case before her, and though she couldn't break the curse the mermaid had put on me she gave me a spell that would make me appear human. This I took, and under its guise I set about starting a new life for myself. I had not intended to fall in love or take a wife, but when I found Hilaria it was as though all the cold water in my veins turned to steam, and I felt warm for the first time in ages."

Jethro Waterworth hung his head, looking a bit like a kicked dog. On the bench, Miss Sutherhand clutched her breast, one hand covering the finger that wore the copper ring.

"It was foolish of me to think I could ever have a happy, normal life. As you discovered, if I remain out of water for any length of time I feel my muscles stiffen and my body freeze. The first time it happened I was horrified, for I could see all that happened around me, but could not move myself an inch. Hilaria found me once in this state, and it was crushing to see how she recoiled. Eventually I managed to break myself free, and through supreme force of will I staggered to the nearest body of water and threw myself in. Almost at once my body came to life again, and I was able to return. But I had to keep going back to the water, otherwise I would freeze up again. To make matters worse, not long after that, the spell the witch had given me began to wear thin, and when I went to her for a new one she was unable to help me. Apparently her spells are not the sort that you can simply recast if they wear out.

"Needless to say I was utterly distraught, and argued within myself back and forth over what I should do. I had thought I had decided I would tell Hilaria the truth, but when I came to her I found I had not the heart, and I sat in the hall outside her room cursing myself and my wicked life. I had no idea I had woken her, and to my horror I looked up and met her eyes as she gazed out into the hall. I cannot tell you how distraught I was to have frightened her, and when she hit her head on the door frame as she fell I cursed myself harder than ever. But I caught her lamp before it reached the floor, and I carried her back to bed before taking myself away. I decided I should leave her, and take myself and my curse out of her life. But I could not go without a word, and so I left her a note and my ring—the one piece of my old life the mermaid hadn't taken from me. I had thought I would return to the river, perhaps find myself a secluded spot in the country and leave myself out to dry . . . "

He rounded on Felpz accusingly. "But now *you* come and drag me from the water! Who are you to think bringing up my sad past will solve anything? Can you break the mermaid's curse? Can you give me my life back? For I tell you now, I want nothing of the one I have!"

Felpz, who had listened to the man's appalling story in silence and with gravity, endured this outburst serenely. He drew in a deep breath and looked the stone man over with a critical eye, folding his arms and cupping his chin in one hand.

"My dear Mr Waterworth," he said mildly. "While I can appreciate the trials you have been through, I cannot help but feel you have not given Miss Sutherhand the credit she is due. Certainly *she* should have some say in whether her marriage should be called off. Have you not seriously considered that, even though she has acted in fear and alarm, *you* have also been acting in a frightening and alarming fashion? If what you say is true—and I see no reason why it should not be—then you have nothing to be ashamed of and everything to gain by accepting this new life that has offered itself to you."

Jethro Waterworth glared at Felpz, then cast a beseeching look at Miss Sutherhand.

"You must understand," he said, grinding his hands together, "I *cannot* ask that of her, not in my current state."

"By refusing to ask," Felpz said, "you are robbing her of the chance to say *yes.*" He looked over at us where we sat on the bench, and shrugged. "I realize this is not what you may have had in mind, Miss Sutherhand, and I certainly do not wish to put you on the spot, but if you remember my earlier question to you: *do you* still think it is within the realm of possibility?"

Steadying herself on Milky's arm, Miss Sutherhand rose shakily to her feet. Slowly she walked through the snow to the water's edge, where she reached out and hesitantly touched the stone man's cheek. She turned to Felpz, a frown creasing her forehead.

"You are said to be the greatest magician in this country," she said, a little accusingly. "Even *you* cannot turn him back?"

"The thought had occurred," Felpz conceded. "And had it been that simple I would have done it already. But the more I see of you, Mr Waterworth, the more I think you are better off like this. I believe you had already drowned when the mermaid cast her spell on you, and I fear that if I turned you back you would revert to that state: a dead, drowned man. Not something either you or Miss Sutherhand would find at all agreeable. As for the difficulty you have remaining out of water . . . I think it is merely a problem of lubrication. *Drink* more, Mr Waterworth. I know you have gotten out of the habit of it, but I think you can manage a dozen glasses a day. A dozen glasses of water will do the trick nicely, I believe."

Jethro Waterworth blinked at Felpz. He turned and blinked down at Miss Sutherhand, who was scrutinizing him through her glasses.

"Well, Jethro," she said, and by her tone I could tell she had got herself under control once more. "You've made about as big a mess of this as possible, and by rights I should cast you off. Not for being made of stone, mind, but for being such an utter *coward* about it. I should give you a sharp slap, I think, but that I imagine it would hurt me more than you."

Jethro Waterworth hung his head, and made a motion as though he were going back into the water, but Miss Sutherhand caught him by the sleeve.

"I did not say I *am* casting you off, you great fool. Come back with me, we'll get you changed into some dry clothes, and if you can stand to come upstairs and explain this—*calmly,* like a gentleman—to my parents, we'll see if we can't keep our appointment on Saturday."

And taking him by the arm, she led him out of the water. Pausing as she passed Felpz she tipped her cap to him. "Thank you for finding him," she said briskly. "It is not the outcome I would have wished, but at least it is not outside the realm of possibility."

Wandering over to stand by Felpz, Milky and I watched them go: the straight-backed woman and the drooping, dripping man, as they walked arm in arm through the snow.

"Do you think they'll make a go of it?" Milky asked, putting his coat back on.

"I hope so," I said. "I rather think he's a better man than the one I married. What do you say, Felpz?"

Felpz, who had been gazing into the depths of Throttle Creek, looked up at us and shrugged. "I don't see why not. There have been stranger couples, after all."

I wish I could tell my readers that Miss Sutherhand and Mr Waterworth did go on to marry, but as this is a true account I cannot tack on whatever ending I like. In fact Miss Sutherhand's parents did not take the news nearly as well as their daughter had, and Mr Sutherhand died of a heart attack not long after. Following this calamity Miss Sutherhand and Mr Waterworth were obliged to postpone their nuptials indefinitely, and it would be almost three years before Felpz received a small parcel in the mail, attached to which was a brief note saying that the clock maker's shop on Endless Street was changing its name to Sutherhand & Waterworth's, after the marriage of Miss Hilaria Sutherhand and Mr Jethro Waterworth. In the parcel was a beautifully carved pocket watch with mother-of-pearl lining and a note from the new couple, thanking Felpz for his assistance.

"'You will be pleased to know,'" Felpz read aloud to me, "'that the watch is fully waterproof. Jethro made certain of it.'"

"How thoughtful," I said, turning the piece over in my hands and thinking back to that cold winter day. "Though it might serve you better were it proof to freezing."

Felpz laughed, taking the little clock and swinging it by its chain. "Well," he said, "rest assured I do not intend to *test* it any time soon."

Coming seventh in the second volume of Bouragner Felpz *stories, following "The Stone Man," "The Withered Hand" grew from one of my earliest ideas concerning the* Felpz *series, almost ten years ago. Since that time it has put out tendrils and wound itself into the overarching mythos of those stories, though it reads perfectly well on its own. It was written in October 2013.*

The Withered Hand

When I turn to my notes concerning the macabre incident of the withered hand and the incredible events that followed, I find it was in the autumn of 2321. How long ago that seems now, but at the time I was so well bundled in current matters that I hardly noticed the passage of time. When I did it was with increasing alarm that I found myself advancing steadily towards the midpoint of my sixth decade. I had at times in the past considered myself *old.* At twenty I felt old in comparison to myself at fourteen; at thirty I felt old in comparison to myself at twenty-three; at *forty* I thought of myself as an imposing and ancient matron. When I discovered I had vaulted clean past fifty—an age I now think the very picture of youthful energy—I no longer wished to think of myself as old, and only acknowledged my age inasmuch as I complained at length about any physical inconvenience affecting me. This, however, became more and more difficult, due to interference from my friend Bouragner Felpz.

Whenever I complained about any of the frequent indispositions attendant upon a woman of my age, Felpz would suffer nobly for a week—and then the attacks of discomfort would cease abruptly. When I began to complain of the arthritis in my ankles he put up with it for all of two days, and then my joints inexplicably improved. And I had only mentioned offhand how my near vision was not what it had once been, when the very next day a package arrived for me containing a pair of thick, ugly, round glasses, which rendered my vision sharper and more accurate than it ever had been.

I am sorry to say I was unreasonably annoyed by this. Having had to bear with persons older than myself airing the grievances of their age all my life, I now considered the one advantage to my slowly failing body to be the privilege of complaining about it. But I did not wish to seem ungrateful to Felpz, who I knew was behind all my miraculous recoveries (one does not live with a magician for the better part of twenty years and not become aware of the signs). The conundrum made me irritable in a way that physical discomfort never could and was therefore beyond Felpz's ability to correct. I regret to say we took to snapping at each other relentlessly, and anyone privy to our private interactions would have wondered why we still suffered to live together. Indeed, the state of our combined tempers was as dry as tinder, and I fear a conflagration would have been kindled had not the events I alluded to in the first paragraph taken place.

They were heralded, as many of our adventures were, by an unusual letter. It came with the morning post on a chilly autumn day, and I noted its presence between a parcel from my daughter and the paper purely by reason of it slipping from between the two and onto the stairs as I brought the mail up to our rooms. Picking it up I was surprised to find that it was hardly more than a scrap of soft, grey paper folded over upon itself. Its front was almost entirely covered in penny stamps, as though the sender had not been sure of the postage required, and all it bore for an address was: *to le Viole Magicien du Felhass,* which was such a queer mishandling of Felpz's name—and his original, lesser-known one at that—that I marveled at the letter being delivered at all. The writing was sloppy and spidery, with many slips and slides as if the writer had not been in full control of his quill.

Such was my fascination with this curious piece of post that I brought it straight to Felpz, completely forgetting the argument we had been in the middle of when I'd stormed out to bring in the mail. I found him at his bench, which took up the better part of his workroom. This place had, in my early days, been the only area of our flat off limits to me, but when I returned to live with Felpz as a grown woman he generously offered to give me a tour, and I had been welcome in it ever since. Save lately, when we were at each other's throats, and he retreated into it in order to escape me. This had doubtless been his motivation on this occasion, and he reacted to my presence in his retreat of magical artifacts and oppressive clutter by letting out a cry of frustration and turning perfectly invisible.

"Felpz, you must see this," I said, hardly noticing the absence of his visual form and heading unerringly to the one empty spot on his bench where I knew him to be sitting. "It must be the queerest letter you've ever received and I know I shall die of curiosity if I don't learn what's in it." So saying I stretched out my hand, holding the grey paper gently between two fingers, as if offering a nut to some exotic bird with a powerful beak.

Felpz faded back into view bending forward to peer at the letter. Gone was any trace of sour temper, and he seemed wholly enthralled by the sight of the writing. He brought his hands up swiftly as if to snatch the paper from my fingers, but then stopped himself and let me place it gently in his waiting hand. With careful fingers he folded back the edges and flattened the letter over a silver plate on his bench, this being the closest thing to a clear area. He leaned forward and read what was written there with narrowed eyes, then shut them entirely and breathed in a long, deep inhalation. Then he picked the letter up, held it before the light, turned it upside down, and finally took a corner into his mouth and nibbled at it. Taking it from his mouth he looked at it in some perplexity, a line of worry creasing his brow.

"I know the owner of the hand that wrote this," he said at length, softly and uncertain. "But I do not know how he should come to write me such a thing."

"What is wrong?" I asked. "What does it say?"

For answer Felpz handed me the limp sheet of paper. I took it, and had to look twice in order to find the words in such a wild and raggedy hand. It appeared they said:

Old friend, please help. Come at ons.

And below that an equally ragged and spidery drawing of a manse, surrounded by a shaky scribble that seemed to suggest greenery and a garden.

"What on earth could they mean by that? 'Come at ons?'" I mused, passing the letter back.

"I expect it was meant to be 'Come at once,'" Felpz said, and he tapped the drawing on the bottom with his thumb. "There, it seems, is the place the writer wishes me to go. It is certainly not *his* house—that I should recognize."

"It could be any number of country mansions," I conceded.

Felpz waved a hand sharply. "No, it is one in particular, one where I am needed urgently. Corianne, do bring me that frivolous volume of illustrated houses that Mrs Bryce sent us last Chandarmas."

I knew the book he meant precisely, and went and fetched the thing from where it had lain, brick-like, at the foot of my writing desk all summer. It was a marvel of a tome indeed, with entries on all the large and majestic houses of Kyreland and Torland, with huge glossy photographs of each, and until that day had been perfectly useless. I laid it heavily on a hastily cleared corner of Felpz's workbench, and he laid the letter, without opening it, face down upon the cover.

The magic he did then was quiet and subtle, and I felt it only in the rising of the hairs on the back of my neck and a faint chill in my spine. He simply held his hand flat, palm down, over the letter and the book, and shut his eyes for a few moments. Then he lifted the letter and, opening the book flat, held the edge of the letter up to the edge of the pages. Immediately they began to fly across, as if whipped by a strong wind, and then abruptly stopped and lay still again. Felpz brought his free hand down on the open page with a triumphant smack.

"Asterly Hall," he said, pointing. I leaned forward and saw there the accompanying photograph for that entry, and found it indeed bore a striking resemblance to the drawing on the letter. It might have been difficult to tell—the house being in many ways a typical Warken mansion—except for the singular detail of the windows, which were arranged in a diamond orientation rather than a square one, and this detail had been preserved in the drawing—though when I had first seen it I thought it due to a quirk of the artist.

"Odd," said Felpz, and I could not tell whether he was relieved or frustrated at the finding. "Really it is the *oddest* thing."

"What is?" I asked.

Felpz looked up at me in surprise, as if he had forgotten I was there.

"It is only that, unless my magical sensibilities are wildly out of whack, the person who wrote me this note should not be at Asterly Hall."

"Yet it seems clear they wish you to go there," I observed.

"Indeed," said Felpz, his brow furrowing. Then, as if the cogs in his mind had finally aligned and engaged the rest of his body, he stood up abruptly, slipping the note into his breast pocket and reaching for his coat—which he'd lain casually over the back of his chair. "The only thing will be to *go* and *see,*" he said, shrugging the garment on. It was a rich violet today with a delicate magenta filigree pattern around the collar and in the lining. This was in contrast to the dull greyish purple—nearly navy—that the very same coat had been yesterday. The changes his clothing went through was something I had come to accept about my friend, but this change seemed to indicate a fundamental shift in his mood; where before he had been bored, lethargic and a little displeased with the world in general, now he was excited and interested in something, and this in turn excited and interested me. Bending low over the book I noted the address of the mansion.

"It is only just outside Briarford," I remarked. "We can have a bite of breakfast at Webley Square and take the Dartfordale Regular from Peddlefield and be there before noon. I'll pack you an overnight bag, however, just in case this turns out to be something more involved. I know how things like this can distract you." I gave him a firm pat upon his shoulder as I slipped away, leaving him unable to respond before I was out the door and busy assembling our travel things.

Felpz was uncharacteristically mute on the journey out of Redling. Had it not been for the vibrancy of his clothes I would have thought him melancholy, if not outright depressed. He kept touching the pocket of his waistcoat where the letter was stored, as if to assure himself of its presence, and stared out the window with a blank, vacant expression.

All of which, I felt, was rather a pity, it being one of our glorious fall days, with the trees like bonfires of gold and orange and red, their leaves lying in drifts beside the tracks. The sky was alive with birds, and in the fields the sheep and cows and horses were looking exceptionally soft and fluffy in their new winter coats. The few clouds were high, unobtrusive white things, providing no impediment to the bright slanting sunlight.

We reached Briarford easily enough, and I was a little taken aback to find it a much more bustling and urban place than I remembered from my youth. Though farms and fields still separated it from the metropolis of Redling, the Great Kyrish Railway had brought the throbbing pulse of the city to this small hamlet, and we emerged from the station to find ourselves on a street lined with busy shops and offices, loud with the clop of shod hooves as horses pulling everything from sleek black cabs to huge hay wagons trotted past. One such cab pulled up to a stop right beside us, and a distraught young woman tumbled out. She was wearing a neat black dress with a black collar and matching black hat—but of the modern sort fashioned out of felt after men's hats, with only a modest bundle of rooster tail feathers affixed to the band. She saw us and, clutching at her breast, staggered over.

"Oh, thank goodness you are here," she said. "I do hope you were not waiting long; you understand Asterly Hall is very upset at the moment. I had no idea his will would be so particular. If you'll come this way . . . "

She trailed to a stop, for Felpz had raised a hand and was taking off his hat.

"Madam, I'm afraid you mistake us. We are bound for Asterly Hall, but we have no knowledge of recent events there. Whomever you presume us to be I assure you we are not them."

The woman appeared to trip, even though she was standing still. "What? Then you are *not* the solicitors?" She sounded rather accusing, as if we were doing her a disservice by not being what she expected.

Felpz and I looked at each other, and I had to repress a laugh until I remembered that I was wearing my sharp new traveling coat and, if the color of Felpz's costume were ignored, we made a very dignified and respectable-looking pair.

"No, madam, we are not," Felpz replied with perfect gravity. "I am Bouragner Felpz, a magician from Redling, this is my friend and confidante Mrs Corianne Birch. I recently received a communication suggesting all was not well at Asterly Hall, and I am here to discover why that is and to improve matters if I can. If some calamity has befallen you, I would like to lay my services and expertise at your disposal—if the skills of a magician are something you require."

"A magician?" the woman said, and her face shifted violently. It was as though her nerves, already strung high, took a bit of a turn and veered off in another, no less unpleasant direction. "That is . . . most extraordinary. Unexpected. I should not know what to say. My grandfather died last night, you see, and this morning we are like an overturned beehive—his passing was not expected. Family matters have become more complicated by the minute, and I had to summon his solicitors up from Redling. That is who I was expecting to meet, but perhaps I missed their train. Oh, dear. But we *do* have need of a magician, sir, I believe that no matter what my brother says. Here, you take this cab back to the hall—he's been paid—and I will meet you there as soon as I have located Kellard and Mikkel. Tell Barrydew—that's our butler—what you are and that Miss Asten sent you. Try to avoid my brother if you can, but if you should meet do *not* let him turn you away until I've had a chance to speak with you."

Felpz took this outpouring with stolidity, and touched his brow to the young woman as she hurried past us into the station. With a shrug to me he put on his hat and approached the cab.

"Straight to the hall then, gentlefolk?" the cabbie said, tipping his cap to us.

Felpz paused with one foot on the running board. "Yes," he said. "But not up the drive. Leave us at the gate, if you please."

"Curiouser and curiouser," he said to me as we rattled off through the town.

"It is quite a quandary indeed," I agreed, with perhaps more cheer than was tactful. Felpz raised an eyebrow at me.

"You are enjoying trampling through this tangled web?" he asked.

"I look forward to watching you unravel it," I replied primly.

Felpz smiled, but it was a tight smile and gone almost as soon as it had formed. "I hope I can bring this to a satisfactory conclusion," said he, and glanced sharply out the window. "I fear . . . no. No, I will not dwell on that. No use fearing the worst without concrete evidence. First, we must see what Asterly Hall has to say."

Asterly Hall turned out to be a large and rambling estate not far from the bustle of Briarford, but the gate the cab dropped us at was clean and modern and stood open. Far from walking up the wide gravel drive, however, Felpz immediately veered off through a thicket, and we ended up approaching the residence from across a field of neatly manicured lawn. When I expressed surprise at this choice of route he held up a hand to silence me and marched on. In this way we passed through a small grove of brilliant orange-and-red-leafed trees and eventually arrived at the back of the house, where we surprised a footman and a housemaid smoking in the rear courtyard. By the way they guiltily hid the ends of their cigarettes I assumed they mistook us for someone else, but upon seeing we were strangers—and well-dressed ones at that—they became even more flustered.

"If you'll 'scuse my saying so sir, ma'am, but I'm afraid you've got the wrong end of the house," the footman said stiffly as the maid hurried inside. "If you'll follow me I'll lead you 'round to the front."

"Not at all," said Felpz congenially, lodging himself firmly beside a cart loaded with empty glass bottles and clay jugs. "It was this end I was aiming for. You'll do me a greater service, young man, if you would inform your butler that a pair of visitors have arrived at the behest of Miss Asten, and wish to share a confidential word."

"Just so sir," said the footman, his creamy-pale face going poker blank. "If you'll step with me I'll take you in via the drawing room . . . " and he made a move as if to lead Felpz out of the courtyard.

"No, thank you," said Felpz, and a rather dizzying thing happened. Felpz was suddenly farther along the cart, and the footman, rather than leading us out of the courtyard, was walking away into the house saying, "I'll only be a moment, thank you."

"Felpz, what in the worlds—" I began, but once more Felpz silenced me with a gesture. He ran his hands briskly over the cart, lifted the lid of a jug and sniffed the contents. Shrugging to himself he went over to the waterbutt and peered inside. Shaking his head he replaced the lid and was just going to peek into a broken-down shed standing in the corner when again the rear door opened and a short, roundish person dressed in immaculate black tails and pinstriped trousers stepped out. Seeing Felpz engaged with the shed they cleared their throat disapprovingly, and I was obliged to step forward to introduce us.

" . . . and you are Barrydew then?" I finished.

"It is *Mister* Barrydew, if you please," said the odd little person. He had a highish, throaty voice, and I would have been hard pressed to put a sex to it had I not been given the preferred pronoun. "You'll forgive Jakob, but you must admit this is somewhat irregular. Err-*herm,*" he finished pointedly, and Felpz at last withdrew his head from the shed. There was a spiderweb stuck to one ear, which he flicked away impatiently.

"This is not the house I feared it would be," he said, as if he had not heard the butler arrive. "But that does not help me in my quest. Barrydew? Oh good, perhaps *you* can tell me what has been going on here."

"If Miss Asten sent you I assume you'll have been told more than I can say already," Barrydew said, tightlipped.

"It was more an accident of chance," Felpz said with a wave of his hand. "I was summoned here by a third party, and Miss Asten sent us along from the train station. She said we were specifically to speak to *you.*"

Barrydew looked at Felpz skeptically, then turned to me.

"A magician, you say?" he said, unimpressed.

"One of the best in the country," I replied. "Have you never met one before? They are all a bit eccentric."

Barrydew gave a little wiggle about his shoulders that might have been a repressed shrug, or might just have been him settling his coat. "Come inside then," he said. "If you won't at least go around to the drawing room, you'll have to come in through the downstairs."

He made this sound as if it would be some hellish ordeal, but the corridor and pantry we passed through were very neat and clean, if a bit plain and worn—but the good, honest wear of a place well-used. I caught sight of a pair of inquisitive eyes gazing up at me from waist level, and turning I saw a mousy little girl with a wild head of brown hair and an even darker face staring back at me. Aside from this vision, however, we saw no one else, though I could hear the thumping and hammering of feet running about floor above us. We climbed a set of stairs and passed through a narrow passage before emerging into a light, tasteful room decorated with sofas and draperies in soothing moss green.

Barrydew crossed at once to the only other door and pulled it gently shut, then he checked out the window and finally came back and ushered us into chairs.

"I believe they can spare me for two minutes," he said, swiftly and quietly, and in tones far different from the ones he had employed in the courtyard. "The facts, magician, in the extreme brief, are these: Miss Asten's grandfather, Lord Asterly, passed away yesterday evening. And in the time since I laid him out then and this morning when the doctor arrived to sign the death certificate, his left hand has gone missing."

Felpz, who had been examining an arrangement of autumn branches set in a vase beside the sofa where he sat, looked up abruptly and fixed the butler with a penetrating stare.

"Gone missing," Felpz echoed, but not as a question. It was as if by repeating the words he was driving the facts further home inside his brain. "His left hand . . . " he murmured. Then, with a full-body convulsion, snapped to his feet and paced to the window. He pulled aside the drapes and checked behind them, as if he expected to find someone hiding there.

"Yes," said the butler tightly. "Gone clean off at the wrist, leaving a fairly well healed stump. It was no prosthetic hand, I assure you: I saw the man use enough cutlery with it."

"No," said Felpz, and there was a bubble of excitement in his voice. "A prosthesis would be problematic. But a real hand . . . and a *left* hand . . . "

Whatever he was about to say was interrupted as the outer door—the one Barrydew had shut upon our entering—cracked open and the footman, Jakob, put his head in. "Flares up, Barrydew, his young lordship wants you urgently."

"I must go," Barrydew announced. "Pray, do not leave this room. I will send Miss Asten in directly when she returns." And with a swish of fine black coat-tails he was out the door, leaving the footman to close it behind them.

"How very *peculiar,*" I murmured in their absence. I turned to Felpz and found him standing by the window, his cheeks flushed with color, practically hugging himself in relief and joy.

"Not at all," he said distractedly, when he noticed me looking. "This sort of thing happens all the time. The trick will be figuring out *how,* and where the wretched thing has got to."

"The what?" I said.

"Why, the *hand* of course—the missing *hand!*" He fairly leapt over to the nearest bookcase, and began running a finger along the spines on the shelf. "I may be getting ahead of myself. Better to familiarize ourselves with the history of this land and family. We may be dealing with a more entrenched servitude than I hoped. A history of the family's lands and titles, if you please," he said, very firmly, to thin air. Then, a moment later, he pulled an old volume off the shelf that had not been there before. "Thank you," he said, flipping through it as he walked back to the sofa.

We were in the moss-colored room for almost an hour, during which time Felpz summoned several more books relating to the family's history, and I grew hungry. Eventually he gave a deep sigh of satisfaction and leaned back, holding a battered old journal in his hands.

"You have a great gift of patience, dear Corianne," he said, gazing up at me from where he sat on the floor, surrounded by books.

"Hardly a gift," I replied. "I fought for it dearly. Are you able to shed some light on the matter now?"

Felpz raised a hand, one finger extended, as if requesting yet more patience, but he said: "First, allow me to walk through the history of this estate, as it has been presented to me by their own records—partly for my own benefit."

"I am all ears," I said readily.

"Good. Then I shall begin by saying that there was nothing particularly of interest about the Earls of Asterly up until a century ago. Then one of them, through a combination of bad luck and personal vice, managed to lose the greater part of the title's wealth. The hall and lands remained, but with no money to run and maintain them, they fell into a sad state. It was into this low point in the family's history that the previous Earl, one Wallard Asten, was born. Things are a bit muddled here, but it appears that in his youth he was able to locate and dig up what is referred to only as 'Halliard's Legacy,' and used it to restore the monetary wealth of his family. When he came into the title he expanded his affluence further by the traditional means of prudent book-keeping and sensible investments. He married, had one son, who in turn married and sired two children. The son died unexpectedly some twenty years ago, and Lord Wallard was, for the better part of their lives, the primary caregiver to his son's children. These are undoubtedly the Miss Asten and her brother who currently reside beyond—" he waved a hand at the door. "What interests *me* is 'Halliard's Legacy' . . . " he set aside the journal and pawed through the books until he came to an ancient red tome with peeling gold leaf on the cover.

"According to this compendium of Asten ancestors," he continued, opening the book, "'Halliard's Legacy' refers to one Halliard Asten who, in the 2140's, acquired what is described only as 'a great treasure' and buried it on his home lands. The writers of this useful volume assume it is gold, which seems to be borne out by the use to which Wallard Asten put it some hundred years later, but I think it was something else entirely. Something altogether more powerful and dangerous than gold. Because Halliard Asten, it is said, acquired his treasure . . . from *Amstrass.*"

I confess this pronouncement did not evoke quite the realization and awe in me that Bouragner Felpz desired. I was still too caught up in the mystery of the disappearing hand, and could not fathom what connection it had to the turn in a family's fortune or to the mythical vampire, Amstrass. I began to point this out, but was interrupted by the door banging open violently and a young man striding into the room.

He looked enough like Miss Asten—wavy chestnut hair and high, aristocratic cheekbones—that I guessed this must be the promised brother, the new Lord Asterly, and made to get to my feet. The young man paid me no attention, however, and aimed his assault purely at Felpz.

"What is this, sir? I ask you! It is entirely impertinent and disrespectful—do you not know we are a household in *mourning,* sir? I'm afraid I must insist you *leave,* immediately."

Felpz looked up at the boy serenely from within his circle of books. "I answer to Miss Asten," he said calmly. "It is by her request that we are here. Hers, and an old friend of mine. Until affairs are settled to their satisfaction you will find me quite immovable."

He spoke frankly and without rancor, which only served to enrage the man further. It was quite a stroke of luck, then—or perhaps it was Felpz's magic; the timing was so spectacular that I imagined it was so—that Miss Asten herself entered the room. She was breathless and a little flushed, and carried in her wake the butler Barrydew and two dour-faced lawyers in black. I saw the footman Jakob behind them, his face a contortion of confusion as he was drawn into the room as well.

"Reginald, that's quite enough," Miss Asten said shrilly. "I still live here—they are my *guests.*"

The young lord rounded on his sister. "Hickory," he said, the figurative steam rising from his ears almost visible to the naked eye. "If this is more nonsense concerning your midnight hallucinations—"

"But they were *not* hallucinations, as you well know!" the young woman returned hotly.

Barrydew came over and began neatly picking up the books Felpz had piled on the floor. "If you're done with them, sir," he said deferentially. "And a word of warning; they may be at it a while."

"As long as they do not block the door," Felpz said pleasantly, still sitting cross-legged on the carpet.

More people were filing into the room as the two siblings argued. Behind Jakob came the little dark girl I had glimpsed in the kitchen, and behind her a wide, matronly woman in a dirty white apron. An old man with wavy, white hair who looked like a valet squeezed in behind her, followed by the housemaid whom we had surprised in the courtyard, and finally a rail-thin woman in a tidy tweed dress.

"Right," said Felpz, standing up. Immediately the volume of the arguing voices dropped sharply, and into the relative quiet he said: "Is that everyone?"

No one answered. They all stared at him with varying degrees of confusion and—in the case of Lord Asterly, the footman, and the housemaid—anger. Felpz took it all in with his same bluff pleasantness, and clasped his hands modestly behind his back.

"First, allow me to introduce myself, as some of you may yet be unaware . . . " he began.

"This is most—" Lord Asterly said, and then his mouth shut with a snap as Felpz's beam-like focus turned on him.

"I am Bouragner Felpz," my friend continued, as if he had not been interrupted. "You may already know the name. I am a magician of some means, and I was summoned here by *this note.*" He reached into his breast pocket and removed the folded piece of soft grey paper. Holding it delicately between two fingers he presented it to the crowd as he went on. "Which I am certain none of you wrote, by the way. Yet it indicates that someone in this house is in distress, and so I have called you here: Everyone who has knowledge of the goings on relating to the writer of this note: I would request you tell me everything you know, as that will allow me to resolve the matter in the most timely fashion, and allow you to get back to your peaceful, ordinary lives." He said this last with an arch look at the Asten siblings, who gazed back unlovingly.

"First," said Felpz. "I already know about the late lord's escapade in his youth and Halliard's treasure. I have also been informed that, after his death, his *left* hand has gone missing. What I wish to know, now, is whether anything extraordinary relating to his left hand was noticed while he was *alive.*" His eyes scanned the crowd invitingly, and I felt the pull of the magic he was using to encourage anyone with such knowledge to come forward and share it.

At first there was no response, but then the tidy woman in the tweed dress exchanged a look with the footman and the housemaid, and took a cautious step forward. "Mrs Beller, sir," she said, her voice deep and dry. "Housekeeper. The young lord and lady will forgive me saying this, as it was not to be common knowledge beyond the family, but the late lord was *left handed,* sir."

Felpz nodded encouragingly. "It has been known to happen to the best of us," he assured the woman. "Personally, I believe there ought to be no shame in it."

"That's most generous of you," the housekeeper said, her own hands folded tightly together in front of her stomach. "But I mean to say, he *wrote* left handed. Signed his letters left handed. Why, we had to make sure all the maids knew to set his place mirrored from what was proper, for he even *ate* left handed."

"And that is all?" Felpz said, a hint of disappointment in his voice.

The housekeeper exchanged another look with her fellow adult servants, but it wasn't until the aged valet nodded firmly that she replied: "That is all we *saw,* sir. All we saw."

"But there was more to see?" Felpz asked, and again cast his gaze over the assembled crowd.

This time it took longer, but at last there was a nervous shuffling, and the dark little girl, eyes wide in fear, made her way to the front of the crowd. With her wild dark hair she looked almost like some fey child, and she glanced about at the surrounding adults, clearly in awe of them.

For his part Felpz went down on his knees so their faces were even. Gently he said: "And who are you?"

"Pattiny, m'lord," she said, her voice small and lisping.

"I am no lord, not any more," Felpz replied, a small smile flitting about his mouth. "But it is no matter. What did you see, Miss Pattiny?"

Pattiny looked around again, and I saw both Barrydew and the white-haired manservant staring at her sternly. Clearly the poor girl was intimidated by them, but then the matronly woman in the apron, who I assumed was the cook, came forward and patted her on the shoulder.

"You g'on and tell the magician, luv. He'll understand."

Pattiny swallowed, twisting her boney, dark hands in her skirts.

"I din't *see* so much," she whispered. "Not as awake I din't. I could never *see* it with my eyes open. Only dreaming, like, with them shut."

Felpz nodded. "That is true to its nature," he said. "Nothing to worry about."

"I always thought it was some sort of spider," Pattiny admitted. "So I tried to kill it at first. Mighty big it was too, for it knocked over a vase in Miss Asten's room. But it weren't no spider m'l—sir. It only had five legs, an' I know all the spiders have *eight.* I saw it in a dream once, and it came and climbed up my window trying to get out. I tried leaving my window open after that, and from then on it would come down to the kitchens at night and help me with the washing up."

"During which time you never saw it?"

"Not as I see you," the girl said quietly. "But I saw the things it moved, and it left tracks in the flour."

"And this happened . . . ?" Felpz trailed off.

"A year," Pattiny said in her brief way. "At least a year."

"Pattiny here starting speaking of it to me about eight months ago," the cook supplied helpfully. "Goodness knows I never saw anything, but I don't doubt her word. Our Pattiny has always had a special touch about her."

"Thank you," said Felpz respectfully, getting back to his feet. He turned and looked at Miss Asten, who was staring at the girl with her mouth slightly open.

"You saw it too!" she cried suddenly, her hands flying to her face. "Why didn't you speak up *sooner?*"

Pattiny looked terrified at this, and backed away into the cook's skirts as if to hide herself in them.

"She did, ma'am, she *did,*" the woman said. "But who listens to the nattering of a simple kitchen maid? Why, I only believed her because I walked in one evening and saw the dishes dancing in the sink, as if held by an invisible hand, and Pattiny here giving it directions as to the proper washing. Gave me quite a turn it did, but I believed. Oh, never doubt *I* believed."

"Barrydew!" cried Miss Asten, rounding on the butler. "Why was I never told this?"

Barrydew, his arms full of books, pursed his lips and looked deferentially at the young Lord Asterly. "I was given to understand," he said in a pinched voice, "that the late lord wished his peculiar shortcomings kept an utmost secret."

"*Grandfather's* shortcomings?" Miss Asten gasped. She turned to Felpz. "Magician," she said. "The reason I wanted you here was this! For the past year I have been plagued, like Pattiny, with strange visions and half-dreams of a disembodied white hand that crawled along the floor and battered at the windows. I would have dismissed them as nightmares but that one morning I woke to find handprints fresh upon my window frame. It is a *hand,*" she said, turning to Pattiny. "The five legs you saw were *fingers.* Very long and boney ones too, quite like spider legs. And the hand itself was all withered, and the skin wrinkled and dry. Sometimes it even appeared bluish, so I never associated it with my *grandfather's* hand . . . until last night, that is."

"And what happened last night?" said Felpz, his voice gone sharp as a knife.

"Oh, don't tell me this is all about that silly dream of yours," Lord Asterly began, but his sister turned on him.

"For the last time, it was *not* a dream, Reginald!" she more or less screamed, and the two lawyers drew back in surprise.

"Please tell me," said Felpz, his soft voice cutting through the clamor and bringing silence with it. Miss Asten checked herself and took a deep breath.

"Last night grandfather died," she said, a little shakily. "It was not entirely unexpected, him being so old, but it was still a shock, you know. Why, I had thought the old man would live forever. It was quite upsetting, anyway, and it was near one in the morning before I was at last abed. Once there I found it impossible to sleep, but lay restless with my eyes closed. And I dreamed, or thought I dreamed, in the way a nervous mind does, while still being partly awake. I heard the creak of my door open, and a skittering of nails on the wooden floorboards, and I smelled something . . . hard to describe now that it is day and I am surrounded by living souls. It reminded me of wet grass and night sky, and put me in mind of old books—the sort with spines so stiff they are fused shut.

"All this I thought of as a dream, but I was rudely awoken by the feel of cold, twig-like fingers gripping at my face, and I opened my eyes to find my vision blocked by a dark object. I believe I screamed, and pulled at it with my own hands. It came off easily enough and landed softly at the foot of my bed. I sat there, feeling the cold air rush in at my back and my heart thudding in my chest, and as surely as I see you now I *saw,* for it glowed ghost white and pale blue in the dark, a withered, disembodied *hand.* It lay there, twitching, for some moments, before it righted itself and, like a spider, scuttled off into the darkness.

"I struck a light and called for Flowers, my maid, and when she came we made a thorough search of the room but found nothing." Miss Asten raised her chin in defiance at her brother, and looked upon Felpz. "Yet come morning we discovered Grandfather's own hand had gone missing! That would have been enough to send me on a search for a magical consultant, only I had to deal with his solicitors, who were needed on account of his will not being entirely complete."

"I quite understand," said Felpz. "Thank you for being so frank, Miss Asten. You have been most helpful. And I am sorry to hear of the fright you were given last night. If it alleviates your discomfort at all, know that I do not believe you were in any real danger."

Miss Asten did not look convinced, but Felpz had already moved on to the two solicitors, who were looking increasingly uncomfortable.

"Which brings me to you . . . Kellard and Mikkel, was it?"

The man cleared his throat ponderously. "Yes, yes, we are," he said. "I am Kellard, and I would like to say we have no knowledge of any of this strange business concerning missing hands. We are only here to deliver the missing portion of the late Lord Asterly's will."

"Ah," said Felpz graciously. "Can you tell me what is in it?"

Both the solicitors inflated indignantly.

"We are the custodians," said the woman. "We were involved in its drafting and would never violate a client's confidentiality in such a way."

"Indeed," said Felpz agreeably. "However, as the relevant heirs are present now, perhaps you would be so good as to read its contents—with their consent, of course."

The lawyers exchanged looks, but Miss Asten spoke up at once.

"If you think it will have some bearing on this mystery, then I would greatly appreciate this," she said. Her brother, however, looked troubled and reluctant. Kellard gave us a grave look and frowned.

"It was impressed upon us that the matter contained herein was of a most intimate and confidential quality, for the eyes the next Lord Asterly only," he murmured, glancing at the young man.

"If it had nothing to do with the matter of the withered hand," Felpz said relentlessly, "then you would not be standing here. As it is, whatever is contained in that missing portion has direct relevance on my investigation, so I must insist."

"Oh blast it, Kellard," said Lord Reginald, "give it here and let me read it. Perhaps it will get them to *go away.*" He shot the last words pointedly at Felpz, who received them in good grace and nodded, smiling.

The solicitors did not look best pleased by this, and cast disapproving glances at the servants—who seemed to be using the excuse of Felpz's magic to shamelessly indulge their curiosity—but they came forward, and the woman, Mikkel, laid a slim black briefcase on a nearby table. Kellard produced a key and unlocked it, gently lifting the lid and withdrawing a thin, paper folder. This he passed without opening to Lord Reginald, who briskly flipped it open. He made a little noise of surprise at finding a single sheet of paper contained therein, but held it up and, squinting rather, began to read.

"'To my rightful and legal heir, the next Lord of Asterly. You hold in your hands the last will and testament of Wallard Asten, seventh Earl of Asterly. In it you will find no provisions for land deeds, titles or other practical matters, but rather this concerns the most important artifact of the Asterly Title. That is the peculiar matter of Halliard's Legacy which I, Lord Wallard, did unearth and uncover in the year 2246. I have used it faithfully since that date to repair and restore the glory of the Asterly title, and I hereby call and command you to do the same. Use it well, and allow it to guide you in all things, and as surely as my life is testament, your lordship will be as successful as mine. I hereby entrust the legacy to you, that on my passing it will leave my body and become one with yours. This has been the ultimate will and testament, made by Lord Wallard Asterly, being of sound body and mind, on September the 18th, Year of our Lady, 2292.'"

The young lord looked up, a bewildered expression on his face. "Why this is most vexing," said he. "It does not help us at all with the problem of the missing bequeathment lists."

"I expect the problem there is entirely a mundane case of misfiling," Felpz said dryly. "However, that letter does bear directly on the matter at hand. You'll note the curious turn of phrase at the end: *'on my passing it will leave my body and become one with yours.'* Keeping that in mind, consider the mysterious loss of your grandfather's left hand, and the upsetting experience Miss Asten endured last night—not to mention the testimony of Miss Pattiny, and one cannot help but become aware of a great, nebulous web coming slowly into focus."

There was startled gasping from the servants, quickly hushed by the housekeeper, and slowly Lord Reginald lowered the letter, staring at Felpz aghast.

"Do you mean to say . . . that . . . that *hand* these women have been hallucinating—that was grandfather's *legacy?* And now it is coming for *me?*"

"That would be what is implied by that statement," Felpz said. "Although the fact that the hand went to Miss Asten first suggests that it might have its own ideas of who should be the next Earl of Asterly."

"Well," said the young man, the color rising in his cheeks. "I want no part of it. Sounds downright witchy to me. Hickory can have it."

"*I* don't want it!" Miss Asten proclaimed, eyes gone wide. "It frightened me half to death!"

"That is just as well," Felpz said mildly, gazing around the assembled room. "For I do not believe the legacy should go to *anyone* save its original owner."

"And how do you suggest we do *that?*" Lord Reginald said, somewhat accusingly.

"Oh, that should not be too difficult," Felpz said. "If you would leave matters *completely* in my hands, I can assure you the case will be settled and done before the sun rises tomorrow."

Relief flashed across the face of Miss Asten, but Lord Reginald narrowed his eyes suspiciously.

"How surprising," he said cynically. "The magician will make all our problems go away . . . for what fee?"

For the first time the good humor that had flowed in an undercurrent beneath Felpz's manner evaporated completely. Something hardened behind his eyes and he looked as close to being offended as I had ever seen him.

"My *fee,*" he said, dropping the word as if it scalded him, "is your quiet and docile cooperation, *Lord Asterly.* What I do, I do on behalf of an old, old friend—not for any reward a human peer could ever grant me."

I could see Asterly bristle at this, but for once he thought better of antagonizing my friend, and held his peace. His sister, meanwhile, came forward hopefully.

"Whatever assistance you require, I will be more than happy to provide," she offered graciously. "If only I could have some sort of an explanation of these extraordinary events as well, that would settle my mind greatly."

Felpz looked round at her; the cold fury melted away, and he smiled briefly. "A full explanation indeed, my lady," said he. "But as I can do nothing further until tonight, I suggest you put the matter out of your mind until then. Let us all meet again in this room, after sunset. Kellard and Mikkel, I need not keep you, but in addition to Miss Asten I will need you, Lord Reginald, and you, Miss Pattiny. You have been touched by this hand, and you would do well to witness this. As for the rest of you, let me detain you from your valuable work no further. Corianne, I think we shall walk back into Briarford and find a bite to eat—the colors are astonishingly bright this year—and return here by six, when, I hope, I will be able to give you all a satisfactory explanation."

This was, more or less, how events unfolded. We had a good luncheon at a charming inn in Briarford, and were back at the hall before sundown. The house had settled somewhat by then, and this time we entered properly through the front door—much to Barrydew's relief.

We gathered once more in the moss-colored sitting room, and in addition to myself, Felpz, Miss Asten, Lord Reginald and the girl Pattiny, I got the impression that a number of the staff were crowded around outside the door. Barrydew stood defiantly just inside it, his face blank as a poker player's, but Felpz only shrugged when he noticed, and set about clearing a space in the middle of the room—pushing chairs and sofas up against the wall and tucking the tables in between them. Barrydew and Pattiny tried to help at first, but eventually gave up when it became clear their efforts were not appreciated.

"I think our appetites are thoroughly whetted, Felpz," I said, once he had the furniture to his liking and we were all seated, facing the open area that had been cleared in the center of the room. "You did promise an explanation."

"Mr Barrydew, would you be so good as to turn down the lights?" Felpz asked. Then, as the butler obliged, he went on: "An explanation, yes. Thank you, Corianne. Well, as we have a little time I suppose now is as good an opportunity as ever."

He rested himself on the edge of a nearby table and crossed his hands. "The crux of the matter is this legacy. Corianne and I have recently familiarized ourselves with your family's history, and perhaps you remember the stories of Halliard's Legacy?"

"Indeed," said Miss Asten. "I was given to believe it was gold."

"As was I," admitted Lord Reginald. "Why, I dug up half the grounds as a small boy searching for it. Quite a tongue-lashing I got for that, too. Now you mean to say this mysterious, magical hand . . . *that* was Halliard's Legacy all along? What the Devil *is* it?"

"Something almost as far from a devil as it is possible to get," Felpz said mildly. "It is an object of great power and potency. That it came into the hands of a Kyrish Earl is remarkable indeed, especially considering it came from *Amstrass.*"

"You'll have to elaborate on that," Miss Asten spoke up. "For I always understood it to mean he found it on a journey to Svenia."

Felpz gave Miss Asten a disappointed look.

"Corianne, *you* know who Amstrass is, I pray," he said tiredly.

"Near enough, I should think," I said, and turning to Miss Asten I explained. "You may know her as the *Vampira d'Amstrass,* or the Red Vampire. She turns up all over the place in legends from that area, and even makes an appearance in some Kyrish literature. She's known for riding a giant stag and keeps a hellhound at her side. Though I must admit," I added, turning back to Felpz, "I always thought she was a myth."

Felpz nodded and smiled. "A myth, yes, and so much more. Never doubt, however, that she is very much a real person. How Halliard Asten managed to get the hand away from her is a mystery to me, though knowing her, it is possible she simply became bored of it."

"This hand," said Lord Reginald. "You said you know what it is?"

Felpz nodded assent. "It's a tricky matter to explain. Put as simply as I can manage, that hand is a piece of a *lamphra*. Lamphra, as I can see you do not know, are the lords of the great realm of Dream that lies between ours and oblivion. They are primordial creatures, not bound to any one shape; they also gave vampires many of their powers, along with their weakness to sunlight. A lamphra cannot appear in daylight except under special circumstances, which is why we are holding this gathering after dark. They do, however, possess many extraordinary powers, which your grandfather, as bearer of the hand, would have been able to use to restore the fortunes of his estate."

"And how do you know," the young lord pressed on, "that it was this hand that Amstrass passed on to Halliard Asten? Why should she have it in her possession?"

Felpz leveled a steady, dark look upon the young man. "I knew she had it because I was there when she took it," he said blankly, in tones that forbade further questions. Then he sighed and went on: "The hand of Halliard's Legacy once belonged to a particular lamphra I know rather well—hence my involvement in this matter. Being first in the possession of a powerful vampire, then locked in a box and buried, and finally affixed to the arm of a living human—I can only assume it drew on the life of Lord Wallard's own left hand in order to be visible in daylight, hence the disappearance of his left appendage entirely—the lamphra hand having completely consumed the human one. At the death of its human master it took the first opportunity it could to escape. Indeed, has been trying to escape for at least a year, according to Pattiny's testimony." Felpz nodded at the little girl, who shivered. "But on every occasion it found itself blocked by the power of that curious testament Lord Reginald carries. Although . . . " and now his eyes, dark in the dim light, swung to Miss Asten, "the fact that it went to *you* on the night of your grandfather's death seems to indicate it has a different notion as to who should inherit the Asten title." Felpz shrugged. "In any case, it took advantage of its limited measure of freedom to write a note to me, I being its closest ally. So I am here, with those who hold the power to free it, and the one who was closest to a friend it had in this house, and I have been calling the hand, gently, all this time I have been speaking. I feel it drawing close now, and provided no one does anything rash, we should not have long to wait."

Felpz's voice faded into silence, broken only by the sound of someone—I believe it was Lord Reginald—breathing heavily. Despite Felpz's optimistic words we waited in the dark and the quiet for almost twenty minutes before the monotony was broken.

Felpz uncrossed his hands, letting them fall to his sides in a low swish of cloth. Turning in his direction I saw him outlined against the dim glow of Barrydew's lamp, his head erect and his neck arched. He was staring very intently at a corner of the ceiling, and at once I cast my gaze in that direction as well.

"Can you see it, Corianne?" he asked, his voice low and unusually hoarse.

I strained my eyes, but at first could see nothing but the seam of the wall where it met the ceiling in a tight corner. I fancied I saw a tiny crack in the plaster there, but the light was so bad that even with my enchanted glasses I could not be sure.

Then, and I cannot describe how this set my heart pounding and my hands shaking, I saw a pale finger, as thin and knobby as an oak twig and the color of milk, creep out from the corner where the wallpaper met the plaster. It was soon joined by another, and another and another. They gripped at the wall, and slowly the whole hand emerged: veined and faintly blue-tinged, the thumb supporting the palm as the hand stood there, like an alien spider. It ended neatly at the wrist, where the skin was pulled down to cover the bones and flesh beneath.

Slowly it crept down the wall, climbing awkwardly on its five limbs. The nails looked chipped and torn, as if it had been through some hardship lately, and it walked with its pinkie raised, as if that finger pained it.

Still none of the others in the room reacted as if they could see it, though Pattiny's head came up, and she said: "Is here now."

"Yes," said Felpz, coming forward into the clearing and going down on one knee. "You have very good witchsight, Pattiny. Better trust it over your own eyes."

The hand was nearing the floor now, and disappeared behind the back of a chair. At once I began scanning the carpet, trying to catch a glimpse of it between the chairs and table legs.

Lord Reginald and Miss Asten—not to mention Barrydew—though they could not see what we did, were still following our gazes in the direction of the hand.

Eventually it emerged. Pale and timid as a newborn lamb, it rocked on its destroyed fingernails, and slowly crept forward into the clearing.

Felpz, now on both knees, held his own left hand out towards it, his fingers open and inviting. I had been impressed before at the spidery grace and delicacy of Felpz's hands, but in comparison to this withered thing they looked quite thick and meaty, full of blood and flesh. The disembodied hand was clearly something dusty and dry, shriveled and discarded like the shell from a molting insect.

Yet on it came, growing slightly transparent in the light, and when it reached the tips of Felpz's outstretched hand it seemed to hesitate. Then, almost unbelievingly, it slid first one and then another finger over Felpz's palm, until it was pressed against his in a bizarre handshake. Felpz's fingers closed around it and he stood up, the withered hand held limply in his own.

The hand must at that point have become visible to Miss Asten and Lord Reginald, for they shot backwards in their seats and exclaimed. Barrydew's face twisted in alarm, but he was master of himself a moment later. Pattiny, however, leaned forward, a look of fascination on her bluff, dark countenance.

"Now comes your part," Felpz said, turning to the Asten siblings. "The hand has chosen you, Miss Asten. Do you accept it?"

"No!" cried Miss Asten, bringing one of her own up to cover her mouth. Then, seeming to realize how this reaction could have a negative effect, she cleared her throat and added: "I would not wish to take advantage in such a way."

Felpz nodded, and turned to Lord Reginald.

"You are the legal heir," he said. "The hand is still bound to you, as long as you keep that testament. Do you wish this?"

Lord Asterly looked at the hand in outright horror, thinking, no doubt, how it had consumed his grandfather's own hand.

"Not at *all,*" he said, his voice a little strangled. "If only I knew how to break that testament!"

"Fire is the standard method," Felpz said. "But in this case, I think if you simply broke the words, that would suffice."

"Break the *words?*" Lord Asterly said, but his sister had already reached into his coat pocket, where the testament had lain, folded, and taking it out she began to rip it to pieces, carefully shredding it so no word remained intact. Miss Hickory Asten, I thought, would probably become the true lord of Asterly Hall, title or no title, just as the hand had implied.

There was no noticeable change in the hand once she had finished, the testament lying in shattered leaves at her feet, but Felpz smiled and gave her a little bow.

"Now what?" the woman asked briskly. "Now what will you do?"

Felpz seemed surprised she should ask. He closed his right hand protectively over his left, and I saw the withered hand curl, like a satisfied cat, against his palm.

"I will take the hand," he said, as if this should be obvious, "and return it to its rightful owner."

Barrydew drove us back to town, and though Felpz insisted we go at once, Barrydew and I found ourselves waiting on him in the drive. When he did appear, it was from around the side of the house, having clearly just come from the kitchens.

"Remarkable girl, that Pattiny," he said, climbing in beside me. "You'll do well to heed her words, Mr Barrydew. Particularly after she finds her name."

Barrydew gave him an odd look, but said nothing. He flicked the reins, and the coach lurched forward into the night.

I was surprised, once we reached Briarford, to find that there were not one, but two trains to Redling that night. Felpz and I boarded the earlier of these with time to spare, and soon we were on our way home.

The adventure of the night, however, was far from over. Felpz, though he seemed altogether less nervous than he had been on our journey of the morning, was in no way relaxed.

"I confess," he said, gazing pensively out into the passing night, "I was not certain it was not Madgrin *himself* who was confined within that house. Such things have happened before. It was one such instance that resulted in his loss of this . . . " he patted the breast of his coat, beneath which the tips of the hand's fingers were just visible.

"Madgrin?" I repeated, puzzling at the odd-sounding name.

"The lamphra in question, and a very old friend," Felpz said. "One of the better dream lords, if a trifle too kind for his own good. It is him I intend to summon tonight. If you can bear with me a little longer Corianne, you may find the interview a pleasing finale to the day's events."

As you can imagine, the prospect of meeting such a mysterious person served to keep me well awake for the duration of the journey home, and upon reaching it I sat up with admirable fortitude while Felpz assembled the necessary items for the summoning. These were surprisingly simple, consisting only of a candle and a long mirror he pulled out of the closet and propped against the wall.

"Ordinarily I would go to *him*, but events of recent years have made it difficult for me to reach his house. However, with sufficient effort on my part he should be able to find *me* with little to no trouble. Do you just sit there, Corianne, and have a little more patience yet."

At this point I was pleasantly full of patience, warming myself by the fire with my feet propped up. Felpz could have taken the remainder of the night to perform his spell, and I would not have cared. As it happened, the magic worked perfectly and immediately, but without the intended result.

I remember it like this: Felpz stood before the mirror and lit the candle. He brought it to his face, staring intently at the glass through the flame. Then he gripped the base of the wax cylinder in one hand and threw it at the mirror. I could not suppress a flinch at this, as I fully expected the flame to bounce off the glass and burn the carpet. Instead, however, it passed clean through the surface of the mirror as if it were made of water, and I saw it travel in a graceful arc into the reflection of the room. This had gone suddenly dark and dim and a bit twisted, and with a jolt I realized it was no longer a reflection of our sitting room at all! Gone were the comfortable maroon carpet and the gentle drapes, scuffed armchairs and the litter of books and papers that persisted no matter what I did; in their place was a dark and lonely corridor made of stone slabs, with a pricking around the top that suggested a starry night sky. The candle I could still see, hanging as if in midair, until I realized it was held in the hands of a dark shadow, who stood in the corridor looking back at us—though they remained invisible, cloaked in the dark and masked by the light of the flame.

For a moment nothing happened. Then there was movement in the mirror, and the shadow grew suddenly larger. The surface of the mirror rippled, like the surface of a dark pond disturbed by a stone, and the candle re-emerged, now held in a small but robust hand, white as marble but tinged blue at the tips. A moment later the shadowy figure stepped out of the mirror, coming fully into our view at last.

My first thought was surprise: in all his references Felpz had clearly stated that Madgrin was *male,* yet the person who stood before us now was obviously a woman. Or at the very least, woman *shaped.* She stood about a head shorter than me, with such a round, full face that her cheeks turned her eyes into smiling crescents. She wore a simple, loose dress made of flowing, velvety fabric that draped around her rotund figure and swirled at the bottom, hiding her feet. Her hair was a tangle of gold and silver, and her lips were sky blue. Lit from below by the candle she carried, it was difficult to tell her age: she might have been ancient, or she might have been hardly more than a girl. There was a confusion of movement behind her, and I saw that her shadow did not keep the shape of the body that cast it, but writhed about, sometimes sprouting great, creeping spider legs, sometimes throwing up the head and flying mane of a horse, sometimes a slithering whip like a snake's tail. She brought with her into the room a smell like that of fresh grass after a summer rainstorm, and under that a dry, musty smell of old books.

She looked about the room with pleasant expectation, and when her eyes landed upon Felpz her face burst into a wide smile.

"My dear magician!" she cried, and blowing out the candle, she tossed it aside and threw herself at him. Felpz, surprised yet clearly delighted, laughed as he caught her up into his arms and swung her round. This caused her shadow some excitement, and I saw the silhouettes of horse, spider and snake all thrown against our wall in turn.

"Badgrave," said Felpz, setting the unusual woman down again. "You were not the one I was expecting, but I am glad to see you nonetheless. Please do not tell me your being here means the old master has got himself into another pickle, it would entirely ruin my night."

"Not in the least, not in the least," said the woman Badgrave, settling her garment. I noticed that now she stood still again, her shadow gathered as a lump around her feet, shooting curious tendrils out towards me and Felpz. "He is beyond well, only I was the nearer when we heard your call, and it is easier for me to cross the bounds these days." Her voice was light and airy, pleasant to listen to even though she had a strange lilt to her words that suggested an old accent that had not quite let go yet.

"I am glad to hear it," said Felpz heartily. "It is fitting enough, however, that you should play a part in the return of this, being as you were also present at its taking." As he spoke, Felpz reached inside his coat and removed the withered hand, presenting it to Badgrave.

The woman blinked and stared at it, a look of wonder crossing her bluff countenance.

"By Grimby's boots," she breathed, taking the hand reverently in both of hers. "Yes, I remember that day well, as I do this hand. I see Amstrass was not very careful with it after all. I do hope it did not cause much trouble."

The hand, I noticed, was the exact same blueish white as Badgrave's complexion, and as soon as it was placed in her hands it came to life, crawling up her arm and twining itself into her trailing mane of hair. Badgrave hardly batted an eye at it, merely stood still while the hand got a good grip on the strands of silver and gold.

"Hardly any," Felpz said, watching the antics of the withered hand with amusement. "Indeed I think it might have done some good. I'm afraid it was the hand itself that suffered most, in the end."

"Well, all that is over now," Badgrave said, patting gently at the hand currently knotted in her hair. "I shall see it gets back to Madgrin, though what he will do with an extra hand is beyond me. Still, I'm sure he will find some use for it."

"I have no doubt," said Felpz, giving her a bow.

Badgrave turned to leave then, but caught sight of me. I had remained mute in my chair the whole time, feeling that this meeting of old friends should not be interrupted. Now, however, I felt a strange thrill course through me, and cleared my throat to introduce myself.

There was no need, however. With a crooked sort of smile, Badgrave said:

"You must be his storyteller! Corianne, is it not? I have heard much of you—that is, I have heard much of your stories. Very fine things they are, too." She came forward and shook my hand. "If it is not too forward of me to offer, I find myself upon the verge of settling down into a house of my own soon, you see, and as such I will be in need of a staff—particularly a *librarian.* If that sounds at all appealing to you, please consider it an open invitation—after you are finished here, of course."

She beamed at me, radiant and blue, squeezed my hand—hers felt like the cool caress of river water—and then sailed back through the mirror, taking her oddly twisting shadow with her.

The lights in our room flared brighter upon her leaving, and I saw now the mirror was back to its ordinary self. A gentle murmur from the window suggested that the earliest of risers were getting about their business, and checking my watch I was astonished to find that four hours had passed.

"Felpz," I said, my voice weak in my throat. "Who on earth was that?"

"That was Badgrave," Felpz said, smiling fondly at the mirror, as if he could still see into that dark and stony corridor. "Another lamphra, though a young one—comparatively speaking. You could say she is the daughter of Madgrin."

"And she will return the hand?"

"As sure as you can be of anything," Felpz said, and there was a note of pride in his voice. "Trust nothing but that Badgrave will look after her old master."

"It is as well," I said, levering myself out of my chair. "For she seems to have taken the remainder of the night with her."

Felpz waved his hand dismissively at this, and wandered off towards his own rooms. "Lamphra have a different handle on time than we do. Never fear, where once they take they give back in dreams."

There was a rustling, and the sound of pouring water, and I guessed Felpz was readying himself for bed despite the imminently rising sun. I went over to where the candle had fallen and picked up the extinguished stub. Puzzling over the magic I had seen done, I went on to puzzle over Badgrave's words to *me*.

"Felpz, whatever did she mean by *'after I have finished here?'*" I called out to my friend.

Silence fell in the next room, as though Felpz had frozen in his tracks. Slowly his head reemerged, and he stared at me, wide-eyed. "I beg your pardon," he said. "*What* did she say?"

"You did not hear?" I asked.

Felpz shook his head. "Her words were for you, I only caught the general intent."

"It was the most curious thing," I said, punctiliously setting the candle on a bookshelf. "She offered me the position of *librarian* in her new house, provided I was 'finished here.' Whatever did she mean by that? Do take me seriously, Felpz, I am not joking." For Felpz, upon hearing my words, had burst out in delighted laughter.

"I have never been more serious!" he cried, darting back into his room. He emerged moments later, now dressed in a brilliant lavender suit with matching top hat and mauve boots. "Do you fancy some breakfast, Corianne?" he asked, his face aglow with cheer. "The Caison Patisserie will be opening soon, have I never treated you to their croissants? Their eclairs are the most marvelous things as well. Yes, we can let Caison serve us breakfast for supper and then dream the day away, content in the knowledge that all will turn out well in the end. Take my arm, Corianne, and come along."

Seeing I would get no solid answers from my friend, I nevertheless accepted his arm, and set aside the words of Badgrave as a mystery to be solved at a later date. I contented myself with the knowledge that the immediate future held fresh baked goods and the promise of sleep. Which was, I thought, as much as anyone could hope for.

AUTHOR'S NOTE

The characters of Madgrin and Badgrave, and indeed Felpz himself, all appear in the novel Lucena In the House Of Madgrin, which explains in more detail how Madgrin came to lose his hand in the first place, and why Badgrave's shadow behaves the way it does. It also sheds some light on the curious offer Badgrave makes to Corianne, and why the news of it makes Felpz so happy.

Bouragner Felpz will return in
"The Moonfoot Problem"

As a part of the Driving Arcana *saga, "God, or Aliens" comes fifth in the first volume (or "Wheel" as I am calling them). The preceding stories have been published in* Apsis *volumes 1, 2 and 3, with the first three also available in* Driving Arcana: Rotation One *(from Heliopause). It was written over the end of October and the beginning of November, 2013.*

God, or Aliens

Green River Campground, outside Roosevelt, Utah

The Basin Elementary Second Grade Nature Camp Trip was, in Amar Dresner's opinion, a big letdown. He had been camping before and enjoyed it thoroughly, but that had been with his family, in the summer. It had been rather full of bugs and dirt, but his dad had taken him on wonderful, ranging hikes and let him light the campfire.

Now it was March. It was cold. They would not let him go for hikes off the well beaten trails, and Miss Matthews would not let him anywhere near the campfire. Once it was alight she had the class gather round and gave them metal skewers with which to roast marshmallows. In the ordinary way Amar liked a roast marshmallow as much as the next seven-year-old, but found that when he went to roast one himself it came out burned and blackened and tasting mostly of charcoal. His classmates laughed at him when they saw his sorry, black lump of a marshmallow. Amar thought this was singularly unfair of them, since theirs were not much better.

He raised his hand and asked to use the bathroom.

"Of course Amar," said Miss Matthews. "Sarah, would you take him?"

Sarah was an imposing seventh grader who gave the impression of having been roped into assisting Miss Matthew's class as a form of punishment. She was able to roast marshmallows perfectly, and looked across at Amar over the beautiful gold-and-brown melting lump on the end of her skewer with a sour expression.

"Yes, Miss Matthews," she said, in a voice which tiptoed up to the line of goody-two-shoes, but didn't quite step over it.

Amar got up, dusting off his jeans and carrying his skewer with him; he did not put it past his classmates to hide it while he was gone.

The bathroom was an outhouse a little way outside and uphill from the campground. Its door was covered in rude graffiti, and it smelled horrible. Amar had put off using it for as long as he could, hoping he would get a chance to sneak off into the shrubby woods, but Miss Matthews and Sarah had so far prevented him.

Now he walked up to the door, and stopped.

"Well, *go on,*" said Sarah, eating her marshmallow with delicate care and extreme relish. How Amar envied her that marshmallow.

"It smells bad," Amar said, hoping he could appeal to Sarah's sense of reason.

"*Yeah,*" said Sarah, swallowing the last of the marshmallow. "And the longer you take, the longer *I* have to stand here and smell it. *Go on.*"

Amar went . . . but not into the stinking hut. Instead he darted around the side, slipping between the bushes, and pelted off among the trees. Heedless of Sarah's shouts, he skipped over half-seen rocks and stumbled over others. He was terrified, and exhilarated. He hit upon one of the well beaten trails, followed it for a few feet, and then spying a deer track leading off to one side, he took that.

There was a great pounding all around him: his feet, his heart, and the more distant pounding of Sarah's feet. Finding a small clearing he put his back to a tree and was just about to fulfill his original purpose when an enraged arm snaked around and grabbed him by the shoulder.

"Come *here* you!" Sarah snapped, dragging him out of his hiding place and back toward the campground. "What *are* you, a little savage?"

Amar kicked and screamed. Sarah called him a rude name and twisted his arm. That made Amar cry.

"Shut *up,*" she hissed in his ear. "You want to get me in *trouble?*" She pulled him roughly out of the bushes, and Amar found they were back at the outhouse. He must have run in a circle. Sarah pulled open the door and pushed him inside. Then she shut it and leaned her back against the scummy surface, panting. She fixed her hair, then she adjusted her top and jeans. In his flailing, the boy had grabbed the silver cross she wore around her neck and the chain it hung on had bit into her flesh. She adjusted it gingerly, cursing inwardly.

"Everything all right, Sarah?" Miss Matthew's voice called.

"We're fine, Miss Matthews," Sarah replied, dropping an extra dose of sweetness into her words. The little turd would probably go crying to teacher as soon as he got out, and she'd have to be on best behavior to win a word-off with him. Amar Dresner might be the only kid in Basin Elementary's second grade who wasn't peach and creamy white, but his mother was known to be a terror. She'd raised a huge stink when it came out that each student had been given a complimentary Book of Mormon upon enrolling in Basin Elementary, and made them change it.

"Muslim oppression!" Sarah's mother had cried.

Ayana Dresner was not, in point of fact, Muslim, but Sarah's mother thought everyone who was darker than a vanilla smoothie and didn't have a Biblical name was a Muslim, and the unfortunate tendency had percolated down a generation.

It had made a rather ugly impression on Sarah, who now felt a twisted sense of satisfaction in being able to strike back, as it were, through Ayana's son.

Who was, it must be said, not making a sound within the stinking building. Sarah gave him a good minute before she banged on the door.

"You finished in there?" she asked, keeping her voice down so she could use a tone that threatened trouble if this was not actually the case.

Silence.

"Amar?" she called, louder this time.

Still nothing.

"Amar, this is *not* funny," said Sarah, leaning on the door. "Finish your business and come *out*."

All she got was the scubby door's graffitied face gazing mutely back at her. Someone had scribbled an obscenity over a smiley face right in the middle. It made Sarah feel like the door was mocking her.

"Amar," she said, "I am going to count to *five,* and if you're not out here I am going to Miss Matthews. One."

Not a sound.

"Two. Three. Four . . . "

Sarah trailed off. She did not actually want to fetch Miss Matthews, for the topic of why Amar was hiding in the outhouse might come up, and the kid could make difficulties. On a whim Sarah tried the handle and found to her delight that it was unlocked.

"Five!" she cried with vicious triumph, and flung the door open.

For one horrible moment there was a blast of bright, multicolored light, and a snap of something that was both white-hot and deeply cold at the same time. It seared Sarah's skin and she fell back, throwing up her arms to guard her face. She hit hard on the dirt and yelped, then screamed in earnest as the pain from her hands reached her brain.

Abruptly the light shut off and there was darkness again; the air was the right temperature, and Miss Matthews was at her side.

"What is it Sarah? What happened? Oh my *god!*" There was a frantic beeping, and then the teacher's voice, shrill from fright and shock, said: "Yes, my name is Laurel Matthews, I'm at the Green River Preserve campground off 88. I'm with a student who has been badly burned. No, I *don't* know how, she wasn't anywhere near a fire—but it looks *really bad.* Yes, thank you . . . "

The words washed over and around Sarah, but none of them penetrated her mind, which was quickly becoming consumed by the blinding pain radiating up from her hands and arms.

It wasn't until later—*much later,* after the ambulance had arrived, and she'd been taken to the hospital—that she was made to understand that the reason the outhouse had been so quiet was that Amar Dresner had not been in it: he had disappeared without a trace.

Interstate Highway 15
Cedar City, Utah

STANDING IN HER JEANS AND BRA in front of the motel mirror, Selene Shields inspected the damage with the detached objectiveness of one assessing the usability of a piece of equipment.

The cracked rib she had acquired escaping from Death Valley had finally finished healing during the month they'd spent in Cedar City. Now the only signs of that struggle were the three thin, shiny black lines that began just below her neck and stretched down, across her back and over her shoulder in a wide arch, and the small pebbly scars on her left forearm. Experimentally she clenched and flexed the muscle there, taking deep satisfaction in the complete lack of pain. Really, the bruising had been almost as bad as the puncture wounds. Now, however, the skin was new and fresh, and Selene rolled her shoulders, delighting in the feel of intact skin stretching effortlessly over her bones.

She had to hand it to Clara; the woman knew how to suture a wound. In time, she fancied, these scars might fade away entirely. Quite unlike the sloppy job she'd done on her own leg five years ago—that one was still rough, and the skin pinched in around it—or the scuffed elbows and knees she had acquired from those funny shallow scrapes that never bled, but left the nastiest-looking scars behind. Selene examined one of her elbows now, idly running a finger over the darkened and mottled patch of skin. What had that been from? The strange night in Death Valley? Or more recently, in the drains of Las Vegas? Or was it from sometime much earlier? Selene couldn't remember. She had layered the scars on her elbows, one on top of the other, over the years.

It was all so much superficial damage in the end, she thought as she pulled her shirt on. Banged up elbows might look gnarly, but they didn't stop you doing your job. And if you weren't being paid for how you looked, why worry about the marks at all? Selene had long since given up caring about the aesthetics of her physical appearance beyond keeping it clean and in clothes that were not too dirty or worn out. With this in mind she bundled her hair back into a lumpy braid and tied off the end with a piece of leather shoestring, pulled on her work shirt, and strode out into the main area of their room.

To her surprise, she found Jill awake and seated at the little desk with her laptop open, a plate containing the best food the motel's complimentary breakfast could provide pushed over to the side. She was sipping an orange juice and had the little frown between her eyebrows of someone whose computer was not magically giving them exactly what they wanted.

"You're awake," Selene said.

Jill looked up, and her face broke into a triumphant grin. "Slept through the *whole* night," she said. "Woke up around one AM to use the bathroom but went right back to sleep again. *No dreams,*" she added. "I'm catching up on email and then Clara says she might have found us something."

"Glad to hear you've managed to return to the ranks of the pleasantly diurnal," Selene said dryly, coming over and taking a piece of thin brown toast off Jill's plate and smearing it liberally with all the little jam samplers. "What sayeth the emails?"

"Spam and junk, mostly," Jill said. "Lots of requests for interviews from sketchy magazines—some vampire website wants me to write them a blog. I *told* Okedo not to give out this email, but I suppose they got it from the college or something."

"Any news from the good professor?" Selene asked, her mouth full of toast.

"Not as such," Jill said, snatching the other piece before Selene could grab it. "They've been trying to figure out how the chimera mother worked—remember when you killed her, all the others keeled over? And none of them tried to regenerate? Why did that gland cease to work?—but so far nothing conclusive. It's hard, as the subjects are all dead and staying that way."

"Tough life," Selene said.

Jill adjusted her glasses and looked Selene over critically. "Not as tough as yours," she said. "How's the rib?"

"I can't even tell which one was broke," Selene said proudly, thumping her side for emphasis. "So, what has Clara got?"

"Nothing online, as far as I can tell," Jill said. "She's been over in the lot all morning, running some sort of scanning algorithm."

"Running a what now?" Selene asked. Jill had a way of applying inscrutable sciencey-sounding names to perfectly ordinary spells that made them unrecognizable to Selene's ears.

Jill screwed up her face in distaste. "She called it the Savannah Circle or something like that. I made her explain. Essentially it's a scanning algorithm, using sticks and stones balanced on top of each other to sense disturbances in the fabric of our world . . . " she trailed off as Selene waved a hand.

"Yeah, yeah," she said. "I know what a Savannah Circle is. What did she find?"

"She wouldn't say," Jill said without rancor. "Apparently, the first result wasn't definitive enough. She's running a refined search now. You want to finish that?" she asked, seeing how Selene was eyeing the plate of food. "Then we could go meet her. She's set up in that empty lot just around the corner."

Under a pale blue sky streaked with thin, high clouds, the mountains rising blue and white beyond the low houses and trees of the city, Clara Nordstern leaned against her motorbike and pulled the collar of her leather jacket tighter around her neck against the wind.

Anyone passing on the road might have seen her: a tall, leather-clad figure in black with a black motorcycle parked in the middle of an empty lot covered in scratchy dead grass. They probably would not have seen the careful series of stone cairns with sticks balanced at their tops that were arrayed in a circle around her. The stones had been hard to come by; she'd been obliged to use bricks, pieces of cinder blocks, and chunks of old concrete in places. It was close enough. The irregularities in her ingredients did not explain the extraordinary reading she'd got. It had been so extraordinary that she hadn't been able to tell Jill. Not right away. Not until she'd confirmed it.

Now, as the little pendulum she'd hung from a branch propped in a hollow at her feet—out of the wind—swung gently to a stop, she looked up to find Jill and Selene both approaching down the edge of the road.

Clara shook her head violently, and Selene put a hand on Jill's arm to stop her. Clara liked that about Selene; she could understand her in a way few people did. And she was good at explaining things to Jill, which Clara *hated* with a passion. She felt as though the woman was judging her, but Selene always made things sound simple and obvious and got Jill to leave her alone. Like now.

Clara watched the little pendulum swing to a halt, its smooth motion going slower and fainter with each successive pass. And then . . .

It did it again. A sharp jerk to the northeast, stretching so that the string it hung on was parallel to the ground. Then it was back to its almost still, minute motion.

It was against all the proper laws of physics and the theories of gravity and momentum, and Clara knew seeing it would have sent Jill into fits. She being unable to accept the easy answer: magic.

Low grade, rudimentary, simple magic, but magic nonetheless. Clara liked this sort of magic; it was practical and it worked, and it didn't cause any lasting harm to the order of the world.

Reaching down she stilled the pendulum and began walking in the direction it had pointed. Like this she came eventually to the small cairn of stones set in the northeast extremity of the circle.

It was no longer a cairn. The stones had tumbled outward as if blown by a small explosion, and the stick had been shredded. Clara frowned and rubbed her chin. When at last she'd made a decision she looked up and beckoned to Jill and Selene, who still waited patiently by the side of the road. As they made their way over, Clara bent and picked up one of the scattered stones. She couldn't feel anything through the thick glove she wore, but bringing it close to her face, she sensed warmth and a faint smell of something. Maybe ozone.

"Whaddaya got?" Selene asked cheerfully.

Clara looked up, her eyes wide and clear and icy blue. Her angular face opened in honest bewilderment.

"I don't know," she said.

* * *

The fresh paper of the map crackled as Clara spread it out over the hotel bed. Using pillows and one of Selene's boots, she carefully weighed down the corners so it was pulled flat.

"You know, we do *have* Google maps," Jill pointed out.

"Your screen isn't big enough," Clara said. She had produced a pen and was making little notations on the paper, beginning with their current location (Cedar City) and working her way up and to the right. "The field stood for the state of Utah. The affected cairn represented the Uintah Basin. I need to see the towns and how they relate to the whole. *These . . .* " She drew a broad circle in the upper right-hand corner of the map. "One of them is the town affected."

"Duchesne . . . Myton . . . Roosevelt . . . Vernal . . . " Selene read out. Jill promptly looked them up on her laptop. "But what is *going on* there?"

Clara pulled up a chair and sat in it, leaning back to survey the map.

"A bent stick means a malicious nature spirit. A broken stick means demonic activity. A blooming stick means increased magical activity."

"And *your* stick?"

"Stripped of bark, shredded, the cairn stones scattered."

Selene's eyebrows wagged and she let out a low whistle.

"It suggests something unusual, something drastic. Something big."

"No kidding."

Jill made a little sound like "*Oh!*" and looked up. "Something big, like, 'boy disappears from class camping trip in bizarre freak accident, one injured'? *That* kind of big?"

The two hunters turned to stare at her. "I expected something a little more . . . drastic," Clara said.

"No, no, wait until you hear the rest," Jill said, raising a hand for silence. "'Amar Dresner, 7, of Basin Elementary, has been missing for two days since he disappeared from his second grade camping trip. Sarah Wightman, 13, is still in the hospital from burns sustained in a freak accident. According to eyewitness reports, Ms. Wightman had been supervising Dresner in using the campground restroom, when her teacher, Laurel Matthews (38, of Roosevelt) heard screaming. Upon reaching the scene she found Wightman with severe burns on her arms and hands. Wightman was hospitalized at the Unitah Basin Medical Center, and a search of the surrounding park was unable to locate Dresner. No signs of foul play have been found, but local authorities are treating it as a possible kidnapping. Any persons with information pertaining to the case are encouraged to contact the Duchesne County Sheriff's department at . . . ' number number, number number . . . " Jill trailed off. "And if that's not enough, there's an interview with this Sarah Wightman girl. *She* says she opened the door of the outhouse to check on the kid and saw a bright, blinding light right before she was burned. There are a bunch of posts on alien conspiracy blogs saying this is a case of alien abduction." She looked up expectantly to find Selene rolling her eyes.

"Alien abductions are *never* worth the trouble," she groaned. "It's *always* only so many pranksters or government airplanes or flat-out delusions."

"Yet, there is my stick," Clara said. "You say this occurred near Roosevelt?"

"Green River Nature Preserve," Jill said. "Just off Highway 40."

Clara nodded. "I'll go check us out," she said.

Sarah Wightman lay in a haze of pain and confusion. Her burns were slow to heal, and they were puzzling to the doctors. She had not been allowed to see her hands, but from the deep aching pain she felt under the bandages, she knew they must be very bad. Her arms hurt too—everywhere she had been burned hurt—but not in the same way. It was almost a relief when, on the third morning after the incident, she woke up and couldn't feel her hands at all. But when she told the nurse, the man blanched and fairly ran out of the room. Doctors came pouring in. They gave her more painkillers and then took off her bandages. Sarah got one glimpse of her right hand—it looked like a mummy's hand, gray and mangled, with chunks missing from the fingers—and screamed. They gave her sedatives then, and after that she didn't remember much. Eventually her mother came in, crying, and hugged her and stroked her hair. In her still groggy state the words bubbled up in Sarah's mind and out her mouth before she realized she was speaking aloud.

"It's my own fault," she said, muffled against her mother's bosom.

"Sorry sugar?" her mother said.

"My fault," Sarah repeated. "'M being punished. I did a bad thing, so I'm being punished."

"You did nothing wrong, sugar," her mother said. "This is all a horrible accident."

"No, I did," said Sarah, stronger now. It seemed important that she get it out. "I was being mean. So I'm being punished."

"Jesus loves you, sweetheart," her mother said. "He'd *never* punish you like this."

"You love me," Sarah pointed out. "You still hit me with a ruler that time I broke granny's vase."

She felt her mother still. In the stillness and the silence things became perfectly clear in Sarah's mind. She pulled back and looked her mother in the face. "This time, He's going to take my hands. You watch and see."

EXTRAORDINARY BURNS GOD'S PUNISHMENT TO TEEN FOR BULLYING (*Tearful Mother Claims*) read the front-page headline of the garishly colored newspaper insert. Jill lifted it by the corner from where it lay in the center of the breakfast table as if it were a rotten animal carcass.

"What," she said, wrinkling her nose, "is *this?*"

"Propaganda rag," Selene said cheerfully, sliding her plate piled high with eggs and bacon onto the table. "They can be useful if you read between the lines."

"Or misleading," Clara said. She had Jill's laptop open, her own breakfast of oatmeal and fruit remaining untouched.

They would have been standouts in the comfortable, western-style diner, except that word of the unusual incident had apparently drawn a crowd of disaster tourists and UFO hunters that made Jill, Clara and Selene look comparatively normal. At the next table over sat a fat white man and his equally large, white wife, both of whom wore denim jackets with little green alien appliqués on the back. A trio of young hispanic men who would have ordinarily been written off as farm workers stood out with their crisp clothes. They also had the better part of a telescope laid out on their table. A pair of weatherbeaten older men who would have been white had they not been so thoroughly tanned hunkered in a corner. They wore evidently hand-decorated t-shirts so well worn there were holes around the collars. The shirts had slogans printed on them in fading dye: one said "Ask Me About Aliens" while the other read "I Had a Wife but Her Planet Needed Her More."

Jill had been able to spot the locals easily enough by the dirty looks they were shooting at all the obvious intruders. By comparison, the trio of women at the table by the window—even if one of them was exceptionally tall and dressed in black biking leathers and one was *actually* black—were refreshingly mundane. Selene had also made a point of tipping the cashier when she'd paid for the breakfast buffet, and that was enough to secure the congeniality of the entire staff.

"Coffee?" asked a perky freckled waitress with blond pigtails. Her name tag said Fay, and she looked like an out-of-place elf. "Oh, here, let me take that—someone must have left it," and she reached out and plucked the offending paper out of Jill's unresisting hand.

"We were actually kind of curious," Jill admitted, indicating the headline. She waved her hand at the proffered coffeepot, but Selene held out her cup gratefully.

"What? Rebecca Wightman's tearful interview?" Fay said, filling Selene's mug with practiced ease. She made a face. "Tasteless, I call it. With her daughter still in the hospital and everything. And the poor Dresners—that's the parents of the kid who's gone missing—have to sit back and read stuff like that when they've actually *lost* a kid. I ask you, who's really being punished? So are you ladies on a road trip then? Plan on staying here long? Roosevelt's not usually so full of . . . um . . . well, so upset. You know." She rolled her eyes at the diner.

"I can imagine," Jill said tactfully. "We might stick around a while."

That brought a smile to Fay's open face. She happily stood and chatted at them about this new park that just got renovated and that band that was playing at a local bar the coming weekend. She seemed singularly unwilling to leave their table, and when Jill cast around and saw some of the looks the other patrons were giving her she found she hadn't the heart to make the poor woman leave.

The upshot was they left breakfast with little knowledge of the contents of the rag, but a lot of minute details about the daily goings-on in Roosevelt.

"Where to now?" Selene asked, pulling open the driver's door of Arcana. The big Ram truck completely filled the parking space outside the diner, but the locals seemed to give it an honorary resident card based on the fact that it could obviously haul a fully loaded four-horse trailer without breaking a sweat. They got friendly waves from passing traffic just by standing next to it.

"I want to see the campsite where the incident happened," Jill said, climbing in. "I doubt it's been thoroughly examined. Do you think we'll have any trouble getting at it?"

"If we do," Selene said with a shrug, "I can probably handle it. You coming, Clara?"

Clara had wheeled her motorcycle around and now stood astride it, looking up something on a pad of paper.

"If my presence is not required," she said diffidently, "I would like to speak to the missing boy's parents."

"That sounds like a good idea," Jill agreed. "We'll meet back here for lunch then and compare notes."

Clara nodded, putting the pad away and pulling on her helmet. Her motorcycle, with its spike of black anodized aluminum mounted above the headlamp, barked roughly as she accelerated onto the road.

The Green River campground was crowded with tents and RVs, and here they found the bulk of the pilgrims. These had erected a clear zone around one of the outhouses—a big, blockish wooden structure with graffiti on the door and a pervasive stench—more secure than any police line. It had a constant sort of honor guard comprised of picture- and note-taking enthusiasts, who were quick to pull anyone back who was getting too near. A bemused sheriff's deputy sat in his truck nearby, reading a paperback and occasionally checking texts on his phone. Jill pulled Arcana up behind him and got out.

"What do you think you're doing?" Selene asked, catching her elbow.

"I'm going to ask permission," Jill said, all open innocence. "What? It's worth a try!" she said in response to Selene's look of doubt.

"For you, maybe," she grumbled, and remained steadfastly in the truck while Jill climbed down and went around to the deputy's door.

"Hi," said Jill cheerfully to the man in the truck. He looked young for a deputy, comfortably large and brown-haired, and he was reading a Stephen King paperback. Jill thought he looked more bored than anything else.

"Hello," he said, blinking at her rather. "You need help?"

"I'm Jill Hamilton of UCSC," Jill said briskly, handing him a small white card. It was one of a batch of several dozen she had ordered during their downtime in Cedar City. It had her name on it and two numbers: her cell phone, and Professor Okedo's office phone. Since Jill had been able to ship him some small but incredible samples, her old professor had become increasingly willing to swing whatever weight he could muster in her favor.

The deputy inspected the card dubiously.

"I'm a field researcher," Jill breezed on. "I'd like to document the site of the disappearance you had here a few days ago, and my assistant and I would also like to take some samples."

The deputy blinked at her. "You mean the outhouse?" he said.

Jill nodded.

"You do know we don't think the boy *actually* disappeared from there," he said, gently, as though breaking an unpleasant truth to a child. "We did have that thing taken apart and put back together again: the kid's never been in there. His babysitter probably told a lie to cover up her mistake—or she's too out of it on pain meds to remember. She got burned pretty bad. I'm just here to make sure no one does anything stupid."

"Yes, so I heard," Jill said briskly. "Well, if you have no objection, I'd like to take some measurements, photographs, and minor samples."

"Wait what," the deputy put down his paperback at last and gave her a good look. "What *samples?*"

"Wood scrapings," Jill said. "Swabs. That sort of thing. Nothing that would damage the integrity of the structure."

Back in Arcana, Selene had her face pressed against the steering wheel in embarrassment. In the deputy's truck, the man gave Jill an incredulous look.

"Do you want a sample of waste to go with that?" he said. "You know, in case someone's taken a magical dump or something?"

"I don't think that will be necessary," Jill said, perfectly serious.

The deputy gave her a long, hard look, as if weighing the chances of her being crazy with the chances of her being a *harmless* crazy. He must have settled on the latter, for in the end he shrugged and said: "Well I don't see why not. At least you're more polite than half the other loonies here." He slid down out of his seat, throwing his book onto the passenger side and offering Jill her card back.

"Keep it," said Jill. "You might need it later."

With a shrug the deputy slipped the card into his pocket. "Deputy Rich Gordon," he said, extending his free hand. "Just don't be offended if I don't call."

"Wouldn't dream of it," said Jill, taking the hand. "C'mon Selene, bring my case, would you?" she called back to the truck.

Selene, who was watching the scene unfold with annoyed admiration, shook her head as she grabbed up Jill's briefcase and hopped down out of Arcana.

The crowd of pilgrims did not welcome the presence of Deputy Rich Gordon in their midst, and turned downright resentful when he lifted the yellow tape and ushered Jill and Selene under it.

"Why do *they* get a closer look and *we* don't?" someone young and male called out.

"Field researchers for UCSC," Deputy Gordon called back, grinning a little. "And they asked nicely."

"*See?*" whispered Jill.

"Yeah, yeah," said Selene, pushing the briefcase into her arms. "Only because you got a softie this time."

Jill ignored her. She set the briefcase down on the steps of the outhouse and began taking pictures.

The outhouse was the solid wooden type with a deep cesspit below. It sat on a concrete base and had a heavy shingle roof with a skylight and a ventilation shaft. It also smelled so bad Jill had to consciously breathe through her mouth in order not to get sick to her stomach. From the reports she had read, the missing boy had been reluctant to use the bathroom, and now she understood why.

With a gulp she opened the door and had Selene come and hold it that way. Inside was a single pit toilet, a urinal, and a small sink with a cistern of water above, a little bottle half full of liquid pink soap clamped to one side. There was a roll of paper towels, a trash bin, and strips of wet toilet paper on the floor. It smelled, if possible, even worse.

It was also obviously, painfully, *normal.* Just to be certain, however, Jill went to the toilet and lifted the lid. Taking a small flashlight from her pocket she cast its beam down into the depths. It illuminated a shiny pile of brown muck with bits of white paper and a couple of cigarette ends. She let the lid fall closed with relief and went to leave.

She stopped in the doorway, resting her hand on the frame, only to freeze when she felt something *give.* Turning abruptly she saw that the wood beneath her hand, which she thought had been painted gray, was actually disintegrating, like ash disturbed after a fire. She took her hand away, and little flecks of door frame floated free with it.

"What in the world . . . " she murmured, and turned to have a closer look. Now she saw that the line of gray began abruptly midway through the door frame—at about the place the closed door would have rested, Jill thought—and ran all the way around, up and down both sides and across the top and bottom—except the concrete there, which had been scorched black. Jill ran her finger across it, and though it was firmer than the wood, it too gave way with a little scraping.

"Deputy Gordon," Jill called, and the man—who was chit-chatting with one of the sightseers—looked over and waved. "The girl who was burned," Jill went on. "It happened *here,* didn't it?"

"Around here, yeah," said Deputy Gordon agreeably.

"No, I mean, *right here,*" Jill said, gesturing to the door frame.

Deputy Gordon frowned at that and walked over. "What did you say?" he said, quietly now.

"This wood," Jill said, pointing at the line of gray, "and this concrete," she tapped her foot, "all show signs of having been exposed to extreme heat. Of being *burned.*" She looked intently at the deputy.

Deputy Gordon cleared his throat awkwardly and glanced around. "I didn't want to say so here," he said, leaning in, "because we've got enough UFO-seekers already. But, we're not exactly sure *how* Sarah Wightman was burned. *She* says she went to open the door to check on the Dresner boy, and then she was burned. But her teacher didn't *see* any fire."

"But the girl *was* burned?" Jill asked.

Deputy Gordon gave a little shudder. "Oh yes," he said. "Yes, she was. Is. It's very bad, actually."

Jill looked around at the little line of scorching, and frowned. "*Huh,*" she said.

Selene obligingly leaned forward and inspected the line of black, scorched wood. It ran all the way around the interior of the door frame, just where the door itself would rest when closed. On the side of the hinges it had scorched neatly between the door and the frame, leaving a mirror of blackened wood on the edge of the door itself. Selene nodded patiently as Jill showed her how the scorching started cleanly on the inside but then flared outward, leaving flame-like streaks.

"And all this means . . . what?" she asked eventually.

"*I* don't know," said Jill excitedly, taking a panorama of the door frame with her phone. "This is the part where you lend your expert opinion."

Selene looked critically at the door and shook her head. "Sorry," she said. "I got nothing."

"Really?" said Jill, lowering her phone. "*Really* nothing?"

"Really nothing," Selene repeated, rolling her eyes emphatically in the direction of Deputy Gordon.

Jill, bless her, had learned enough to take the hint, and finished up taking samples and documenting the area without insisting on an explanation there and then. When she was done she thanked Deputy Gordon politely, nodded to the bitter-looking pilgrims, and led the way back to Arcana.

"So, what *do* you think happened?" she asked once the doors were safely closed.

"Honestly, I don't know," Selene said, putting the truck in reverse and backing carefully out of the campground. "Looks to me like someone opened some kind of portal there. Big one too, considering the burn. If there *was* fire then I suppose it could have been a demon. They go in for that type of thing. Don't think it was, though; demons leave behind a rather noticeable smell, and this place, well . . . "

"It smelled *horrible,*" Jill pointed out.

"Yes," allowed Selene. "Horrible and *normal.* Demons, they leave behind this residue which . . . well, it don't smell like no outhouse. Just as well, really. Demons are slippery bastards and a royal pain in the butt."

"Perhaps Clara will have some ideas," Jill mused.

"One can always hope," Selene said, checking both ways before turning onto the highway.

While Jill and Selene had been investigating the door of the outhouse, Clara's bike came to a purring halt outside a generous two-story house with oak trees, now covered in tiny green buds, lining the street beside it. Its windows were shuttered, but a bright blue SUV sat in the driveway, which Clara had to edge past in order to reach the front door.

After ringing the bell she waited upward of a full minute before there were footfalls from inside and the door cracked open. The face on the other side was as dark as Selene's, though at a slightly higher elevation. Clara took a step back, holding her helmet modestly at her side.

"Mrs. Dresner?" she asked, bowing her head slightly.

The face on the other side of the door frowned. "Who sent you?" it asked. There was a gruffness to the woman's voice and a puffiness around her eyes that told Clara she would have to tread very, very carefully.

"My name is Clara Nordstern," she began, and considered the words she would use next. "I am here to find your son," she said at last.

Mrs. Dresner glared at her through the cracked door, her brows creasing an impressive ridge between her eyes.

"You with the police?" she asked.

Clara shook her head. "No," she said simply. "I'm a . . . an independent investigator."

"Uh-huh," said Mrs. Dresner. "And how much do you charge?"

Clara shrugged. "You? Nothing."

She waited. Mrs. Dresner was a fine looking woman, and gave her a cold, imperious stare. Clara bore it patiently.

The door creaked as it was pulled open the rest of the way.

"Wipe your boots before you come inside," she said by way of invitation.

The house looked to have been a neat and tidy place that had recently suffered some catastrophe. Books and articles of clothing and shoes were scattered everywhere, and a child's playset was spread across the living room. Understandable, Clara thought, as she carefully stepped over a pair of pink sneakers and toward the kitchen, where Mrs. Dresner was running water.

"Tea? Coffee?" she asked as Clara entered. "I only have instant."

"Just water," Clara said. "I do not wish to put you to any unnecessary trouble."

"*Huh,*" said Mrs. Dresner, pouring Clara a glass and putting the kettle on to boil anyway. She took down a mug and a packet of instant coffee, which she shook viciously before pouring the contents into the cup. "So, how are you going to find my son?"

"I am not sure, yet," Clara said truthfully. "First I must find out where he has gone. This has turned out to be a difficult task. I was hoping you might help me determine whether any similar incidents have occurred in the past."

"Similar incidents?" Mrs. Dresner asked, pouring the hot water. "Well, *no,* Amar's *not* gone mysteriously missing ever before."

"Granted," Clara said with a nod. "But has he ever . . . well, has he mentioned anything to you? Bizarre stories, tales of improbable adventures? Does he have any imaginary friends?"

Mrs. Dresner gave Clara a cold look. *"No,"* she said decisively. "And no imaginary friends either, except the ones he *knows* are imaginary. We try not to go in for that sort of thing. No offense," she added.

Clara, who knew just how dangerous imaginary friends could become if allowed to run rampant, shrugged. "None taken. Does he have any friends with whom he plays complicated games of make-believe?"

Mrs. Dresner turned right around and frowned at Clara.

"What does this have to do with finding out what's happened to him?" she asked, a slight trill to her voice suggesting a steel trap, ready to spring.

"It could have quite a lot to do," Clara said plainly. "Or, nothing. I am merely collecting information, at the moment."

Mrs. Dresner narrowed her eyes and wrinkled her nose. Then she cast her eyes down and sighed heavily.

"The truth is," she said, going to lean on the counter. "Truth is Amar doesn't *have* many friends. Not any that he plays with outside of school. The closest you could say would be his sister, and they do get up to flights of fancy now and then. They built a fort out in the living room last week and insisted it was a castle." She stopped and swallowed hard.

"I see," said Clara, glancing in the direction of the living room. "And . . . where is his sister now? May I speak with her?"

"Desta?" said Mrs. Dresner. "She's up in her room. But I've been trying to keep her calm about all this. I don't want you upsetting her."

"I will do my utmost," Clara said. "Do you wish me to fabricate soothing lies or simply conceal the truth?"

Mrs. Dresner gave her a sharp look. "Just don't tell her her brother's *missing,"* she said. "Josh and I have made sure she thinks her brother's still on his camping trip. She's only *five,"* she added, seeing the look of shock on Clara's face.

Clara's phone rang. Clara excused herself, while Mrs. Dresner called upstairs: "Desta? Desta darling, there's someone here who wants to talk to you!"

"What did you find?" Clara asked. She listened intently to Jill's answer, covering one ear against Mrs. Dresner's repeated calls.

"Say that again?" Clara asked, watching keenly as Mrs. Dresner went upstairs. She followed at a safe distance.

The calls were becoming annoyed now. Doors opened and shut upstairs.

"Desta? *Desta* come out! Desta, you stop hiding this minute! Desta? *Desta where are you?*"

Clara reached the landing and saw Mrs. Dresner, eyes bulging in alarm, come out of the master bedroom.

"I can't find *Desta,*" she gasped, more shocked that anything. "I left her in her room, but she's not there . . . she's not *anywhere . . .* " The woman ran down the stairs, still calling for her daughter.

"What's happened?" Jill's voice asked.

Clara stood in the doorway to the girl's room. It was decorated with blue cloud wallpaper and there was a model castle on the bedside table. The window was shut, fastened on the inside, and it was entirely deserted.

"Explain what you found," Clara said grimly. "Very, *very* thoroughly."

"It's what I *haven't* found that bothers me most," Jill said, scratching her head.

They had regrouped back at their motel, as Mrs. Dresner had been less than enthusiastic about suddenly entertaining more guests. They had left her standing in the drive talking animatedly on the phone with her husband, and gone back to their base for Jill to run tests on the samples she had collected. These had turned out to be singularly disappointing.

"As far as I can tell," Jill said, pushing dishes of wood scrapings and ashes about. "These are all perfectly normal. They show regular molecular structure—as far as I can tell with my field microscope—apart from damage sustained by the burn. But the *pattern* is all *wrong*. You don't get sheets of fire appearing and disappearing at the drop of a hat—or the opening of a door!"

"No signs of sulfur?" Selene asked.

"None!" cried Jill. "Wait, why sulfur?"

"The fact that there is none rules out the possibility of this being a demonic abduction," Clara explained. She dipped one shoulder suggestively. "Unless, of course, it's a very special demon."

"So essentially it's inconclusive," Jill said, leaning back in her chair. "What I wouldn't give for a high-purity, germanium-crystal detector."

"A *what* now?" said Selene.

"To check it for radioactivity," Jill said. "There could be something going on here that I simply don't have the equipment to test for."

"There is *obviously* something going on here that you don't have the equipment to test for," Selene drawled.

"I don't see you offering any options," Jill snapped.

"Honestly, I'm as stumped as you are, sister," Selene said with a shrug. "Doesn't feel like a demon. Or a fairy. *Or* a mundane kidnapping."

"I want to see the girl who was burned," Jill said, frowning. "There may be evidence in her injuries that the doctors have missed."

"And how are you gonna do *that?*" Selene said, trying—and failing—to mask a sneer. "Just walk in the front door and *ask?*"

Jill looked up and adjusted her glasses. She raised her eyebrows in an expression of perfect innocence.

To Selene's astonishment and Clara's bewildered amusement, this was exactly what Jill did. And it *worked.* The doctor in charge of Sarah Wightman—an overweight, pink-faced man with neat gray hair named Carlston—spent almost half an hour on the phone with Professor Okedo back in California before he would let Jill into his office, and even then he insisted they all sign confidentiality agreements before ushering them into chairs, but then he laid a folder down in front of Jill with a *smack* and said:

"*There.* You take a look at that and see if it makes sense to *you.*"

With an air of a child opening a Christmas present, Jill flipped open the file and began going over the reports, photos, and x-rays within.

It was not a sight for the faint of heart. Jill had to clench her teeth and force herself to think as analytically as possible when she found the pictures that had been taken upon Sarah Wightman's admittance. The burns *were* horrible, the skin blistered and hanging off the muscle and bone beneath, vividly red and white except where it had been singed purple.

"It was a close thing she didn't lose both hands," Dr. Carlston said, leaning forward. "But we were able to successfully debride the wound and excise the dead tissue. We transplanted skin from her thighs to serve as a graft, and *that* appeared to be working well, but . . . "

"But what *then?*" Jill said, flipping through the pages.

"Her arms rejected the grafts. The flesh had necropsied to a greater extent than we thought—well, that's how it first appeared."

"I'm sorry?" Jill said.

The doctor sighed and flipped through to a couple of horrific photos. They each showed a hand, practically skinless save for a few patches of pale white flesh that hung limply off them. The muscle and tendon visible beneath were all a dead, gray color.

"That was *healthy* flesh when we first treated the burns," he said, slapping the paper. "It was healthy, with *no sign* of burn or necropsy."

"A slow burn?" suggested Jill.

"She's not a *tree,*" said Dr. Carlston. "And that's not *burn* damage either. I took a biopsy and ran it through every test we have. The cells *are dying,* but not from burns."

Jill held up a glossy printout. The hand there looked almost like a piece of preserved cadaver—not like a living thing at all.

"Spontaneous cell death?" Jill asked.

"Not *exactly* spontaneous," said Dr. Carlston. "The effect is definitely localized to the area of the most severe burns. But it *is* spreading."

"Are the hands still attached?"

"For now," said the doctor unhappily. "But a double amputation looks likely at this point. We can't have it spread to other parts of her body, and we're risking a systemic infection as it is. I've explained all this to her mother but . . . " He made a frustrated sound in his throat.

"Understandable," said Jill, setting the picture down. "And... I'm not sure an amputation would stop it at this point."

Dr. Carlston began gathering up stray sheets, a look of horror growing on his face. "Why is that?" he asked.

"I believe Sarah Wightman was exposed to something—I don't know what yet—which severely injured her. It may have caused other damage—somewhat like radiation poisoning—that was not immediately apparent. I would encourage you to find out *why* these cells are dying, and try to find a way to stop it, because if my hypothesis is correct, you will begin to see spontaneous necropsy all over her body."

Dr. Carlston leaned back in his chair with a sigh. "And what makes you think that?" he asked.

"Habit," said Jill. "I have a habit of imagining the worst possible outcome. Now, may I speak to Miss Wightman herself?"

This turned out to be more difficult. They had to acquire her mother's permission to do so, and at the description of the woman Selene promptly excused herself ("I'll hurt your cause more than help it, I *promise* . . . "), and Clara decided she wished to have another look at Desta Dresner's room.

So it was that Jill was alone when Rebecca Wightman bustled into the waiting room. She was a large sort of woman: her midsection bulged out over the line of her tightly belted jeans, and her western-style suede vest had silver studs on it. Her hair was improbably yellow and buttery, and she wore a lot of very colorful makeup. So even though she was actually rather short, she gave the impression of being much taller. Jill didn't know whether to be impressed or disconcerted.

"Mrs. Wightman," Jill began, but didn't get any farther.

"You're the doctor from California," Rebecca Wightman announced, only the subtle upturn at the end of her sentence suggested that maybe, possibly, what she had just said might have been a question.

Jill opened her mouth to correct the woman, but found she had wandered into deep water with this one, and the current was strong.

"It's about time they gave me someone new: that man Carlston is a *butcher.* Did they tell you he wanted to cut my Sarah's arms off?"

"So I heard," Jill said. "Mrs. Wightman, I wanted to speak with your—"

"I'm sure *you'll* be able to sort this out," Rebecca Wightman said, now clasping Jill by the hand. Hers sported long red nails, Jill noticed, and a silver bracelet with a large silver cross hung from one wrist.

She extracted her hands as quickly as politeness allowed and then clasped them protectively behind her back.

"Mrs. *Wightman,"* Jill said sternly. "What I really need is to speak with your daughter. *Would* you allow that?"

Rebecca Wightman blinked eyes with mascara so heavy it had clumped together on the individual lashes, and pulled away from Jill.

"Yes, yes of course," the woman said. "I'll just tell her you're on your way, and you can go get *changed."* She made a disparaging gesture at Jill's tidy, plain street clothes, and bustled off.

Jill rolled her eyes at the receptionist, who had witnessed the entire interaction. The woman gave her a shrug and a nod, as if to say: *yes, that is what* I *have had to put up with for the last week. Just roll with it.*

Sarah Wightman lay propped up on pillows in a monstrous hospital bed, hooked up to an IV and a heart monitor. She was staring vacantly off into space when Jill entered, following Dr. Carlston into the little room. Rebecca Wightman, who had been sitting fretfully at her daughter's side, jumped up at the sight of them. If she noticed that Jill had done nothing to alter her appearance she didn't say, but said instead:

"There's no need for *him* to be present," jerking her head toward Dr. Carlston.

Dr. Carlston sighed and went over to check the clipboard hanging from the foot of the girl's bed.

"Hello Sarah," he said, quite gently and kindly. "How are you doing?"

"Mrs. Wightman," said Jill, very seriously. "You need to know that I am *not* a doctor. I am a scientist. I wish to understand what is happening to your daughter, and hopefully from that understanding I will be able to develop a successful treatment plan. But I *need* Dr. Carlston in order to conduct my research."

Whatever Rebecca Wightman was going to say in response was cut off by a little sound from the bed: Sarah had spoken. That is, she'd tried to speak, and coughed instead.

"I'm sorry, I didn't catch that, sugar," her mother said, shoving past Dr. Carlston as she rushed to her daughter's side.

Sarah Wightman, however, was not looking at her. She was staring over the blankets at Jill, her eyes very wide and unfocused.

"You said you were a scientist?" she asked in a small, dry voice.

"That's right," said Jill, smiling encouragingly. "I research extraordinary phenomena . . . like this." She gestured awkwardly at the two bundles of white wrapping that were all she could see of Sarah Wightman's hands.

"Oh," said the girl, sinking back into her pillows. "Then you won't find anything here."

"We'll see about that," Jill said, unable to help the grim edge that crept into her voice.

"No," said Sarah Wightman, listlessly shaking her head. "No, you won't find anything. It's my punishment from God, you see. God is beyond science."

Jill frowned.

"Now Sarah, you know you've done nothing wrong," said Dr. Carlston as Jill circled around the bed to stand beside the girl's head.

"Why?" she asked, and when Sarah Wightman rolled her head to look at her she continued: "*Why* is your god punishing you?"

To her surprise Sarah Wightman pursed her lips and began to cry. Immediately her mother and Dr. Carlston began shushing her, but Jill just listened. Through the sobs, the girl was speaking again.

"B-because I p-put him in the bath-r-room," she choked. "I p-pushed him in when he-e didn't w-want to g-go. And when—when I tried to check on him it *burned* me."

"The door to the outhouse *burned* you?" Jill said, attempting to puzzle out the discombobulated admission.

"I took him to the bathroom," Sarah Wightman whispered. "He ran off into the woods. I chased him. I was angry. I grabbed him. I think I *hurt* him. I put him in the bathroom. He didn't want to go. I pushed him in there anyway. He was quiet. He was *too* quiet. He took too long. So I tried the door to see if I could check on him. And it burned me."

"The door did?" Jill asked.

"The *light,*" hissed Sarah Wightman. "The light *inside* the bathroom!"

"There was light inside the bathroom?"

Sarah Wightman nodded.

"What did you see?"

"Just the *light,*" said the girl. "Just the *light.* I thought it would burn my eyes out, so I . . . "

"So you threw up your hands," Jill finished, letting her gaze travel down the limp arms once more. "Thank you, Sarah. You've been very helpful. A word, doctor," she said, beckoning to Dr. Carlston.

Once out in the hall and a safe distance away from Rebecca Wightman's withering glare, the older man turned to her and said:

"Now, Miss Hamilton, I'm as good a Christian as anyone in this town, but there's some things you just can't go believing at the drop of a hat. The girl is traumatized; *clearly* she is fabricating a story. There's no *knowing* what went on that night."

"Actually, the evidence supports her statement," Jill said simply. At the doctor's incredulous look she explained: "I found traces of fire—*very hot* fire—around the door of the outhouse in question. *Something* burned there, from the inside flaring outward. What she says about the door—or the *doorway*—burning her, looks to be true. Now, I've taken some samples of the burns at that site. I'd like to compare them to a sample from *her* damaged tissue. And I'd like to use the strongest microscope you have. Also, I need to check for any radioactivity. And . . . I'd like to have a sample from an *undamaged* part of her body, for control. I don't know yet what I'm looking for."

Dr. Carlston frowned and leaned toward her. "That would be . . . extremely irregular," he said.

"This *entire incident* is irregular," Jill agreed fervently. "Now, will you call a nurse to take the samples or shall I?"

Selene lay in the back seat of Arcana, her duffle bag full of weapons lodged behind her head and one arm thrown over her face. She was drifting on a pleasant cloud of sleep, secure in the knowledge that it was broad daylight, and that she was in the middle of a concrete parking lot with many cars to provide cover, and a fully functioning hospital nearby, no less. Then her phone rang.

It was a new phone, purchased for her by Jill on the grounds that her old one was cracked and unreliable and probably water damaged. In reality Selene thought it was because this new phone had a camera and the ability to send pictures over the cellular network, and Jill just wanted another person who could document supernatural events. She'd tried to buy Clara one, but Clara—who did not like having a cell phone in the first place—refused on the grounds that her phone was still new and undamaged, thank you very much. Selene thought, if given the chance, this phone might have changed Clara's attitude. It was slim and black and had a shiny, vibrant display whose keyboard changed from numbers to letters depending on what you wanted. It also had a wide variety of ringtones, some of which were so musical and soothing that they did not immediately sound like ringtones.

One of these was playing now, and Selene listened to it for several moments before she realized it was her phone. Slipping a hand into her pocket she pulled it out, and had a moment of discombobulation when she automatically tried to flip it open and discovered she couldn't. Then she blinked at it, and remembered she had to slide her finger across the bottom half instead.

"Yellow?" she said, pressing the phone to her cheek and rolling onto her back.

"Any word from Jill?" Clara's voice said on the other end.

"Nah, not yet," said Selene. "Though she's been in there long enough, I think she probably managed to see the girl. Where you at?"

"Desta Dresner's room," came the answer.

"Oh. Find any scorch marks?"

"No," said Clara. She sounded a little irritated. "There is nothing. Only . . . "

"Only what?"

"Her boots are missing."

"Her boots."

"She had pink rubber boots," Clara explained. "She always kept them by her bed. It was this . . . thing she liked to do. They're gone."

"So wherever she is, she's got protective footwear," Selene said, suppressing a yawn.

"Whatever came and took her, gave her time to put on her boots," Clara said.

Selene's phone made an impatient *beep, beeeeeep* noise, and she took it away from her head to see a flashing display that said "Boss Jill Calling . . . "

"Hold on a sec, Clara," she said, and with a little smugness she put the other woman on hold, and then pressed the little "merge" button that had appeared on the screen.

"Say hello to the boss, Clara," she said, putting the phone back to her ear.

"Selene?" said Jill. "Selene, I need you to . . . *what* Clara?"

"Yes, I'm here," said Clara, sounding a little confused.

In the truck, Selene grinned, then felt bad, and covered her mouth with her fist.

"Jill, Clara was just telling me that wherever Desta Dresner went, she's got her favorite pair of pink rubber boots," Selene said. "Clara, anything else you want to tell the boss while I have her on the line?"

Silence—from both ends—and then Clara said: "No," and hung up.

Boop, boop, boooop, said the phone.

"Selene, Selene are you there?" Jill asked, sounding urgent.

"Yeah, yeah," said Selene, smiling a little guiltily. "What's up?"

"I need you to bring me the samples I took from the outhouse this morning. They're in my case marked *evidence,* and you'll see them labeled with today's date."

Selene pulled herself up using the back seat as a handhold. "On my way, sister," she said, then paused. "Wait, just where are you?"

It turned out Jill was in the hospital's pathology department, and it took Selene almost half an hour to navigate her way past what felt like dozens of unfriendly receptionists and through as many doors with "private, no entry" signs on them. It was exhilarating, in a way.

She found Jill seated behind an elaborate machine made of tubes and pipes with little knobs. To Selene it looked like some sort of bizarre robot, but Jill was manipulating it with as much calm detachment as if it were a coffeemaker.

"What you got?" she asked, setting the tray of little bottles on the counter beside Jill.

"A few skin cells from behind Sarah Wightman's right ear," Jill said, not looking up from the eyepiece.

"Oh, that's exciting," said Selene, pulling up a stool and sitting on it.

"It *is,*" agreed Jill with total seriousness, "when you compare it to the cells from the palm of her right hand. Are those the samples from the outhouse? Give them here . . . "

She took a bottle labeled "door frame" and popped it open, taking a new dish from a stack to one side and, with a pair of tweezers, transferred a single splinter from one to the other.

"So . . . you *found* something?" Selene asked, scooting closer.

"Maybe . . . possibly," said Jill, sliding the new dish under the microscope. She peered in, adjusted the focus on the machine, slid the dish around, and then peered some more. Then her whole body went stiff and she made a little sound of indrawn air and the word "*Yes . . .* " slipped out.

Pushing back from the microscope she spun to face Selene, the pupils of her eyes blown wide behind her glasses. "I *thought* so, but this proves it—well, pretty much."

Selene frowned and wagged her head. "Proves *what?*" she asked.

"These . . . muscular tissue cells," Jill pointed at a slide with a few flecks of gray between two pieces of glass. "The ones from Sarah Wightman's hand. They are exhibiting a strange form of cell death. I can't see any sort of damage—not from a virus or infection or *even fire*. They're just . . . dead. Not just dead, but disintegrating too. These skin cells . . . " she placed her hand next to another slide, "from behind her ear, are perfectly normal and healthy—as far as I can tell. But *these* . . . " She slid forward to the dish that held the blackened door frame splinters. "They *do* show damage from extreme heat, and of course any cells within the wood had died a long time ago. But they *also* show the *exact same* disintegration process."

Selene blinked at her. "And . . . this tells us . . . what?"

"Well, that Sarah Wightman is telling the truth when she says she was burned by the open door," Jill said. "Her testimony is supported by actual physical evidence."

"Okay," said Selene, hooking her feet behind the legs of the stool and resting her elbows on the counter. "Does this tell you *what it was* that burned her?"

"Nnoo . . . " said Jill, stringing the word out uncertainly. "Only that it was something very *hot* and with some highly unusual properties. But I have some ideas about that, too."

"Oh," said Selene, straightening up. "Let's hear 'em."

Jill swiveled around on her stool and clasped her hands between her knees. She pursed her lips and looked very hard at Selene. "I was thinking. About what you and Clara said about demons. You don't think this is a demonic abduction—but I'm thinking it's safe to say that whatever burned Sarah Wightman also took Amar and Desta Dresner."

Selene nodded her head. "Demons are tricky though," she said. "I mean, it *could* be . . . but it would be the *weirdest* demon I've ever seen. It doesn't feel like any demonic possessions or abductions I've witnessed. Put it that way."

"Fair enough," said Jill, and took a deep breath. "Well, if it's not a demon . . . what about an *angel?*"

Selene leaned back on her stool and let out a long breath.

"There *are* angels, aren't there?" Jill pressed. "It follows, if there are demons."

"*Yeee*aahh . . ." said Selene, letting the word out in heavy sigh. "Angels . . . that's a really . . . *distorted* area. Depends on what *kind* we're talking about. There are tons, you know. The Abrahamic angels are what most people think of when they *say* 'angel,' but those usually turn out to be fravashi or Amesha Spentas. Devas and garuda have also been mistaken for angels. And then *within* the Abrahamic angels you get this really complicated hierarchy that's always given *me* a headache. You could ask Clara to explain—she probably knows more than me."

"But . . . could it be possible that an angel abducted Amar Dresner and burned Sarah Wightman?" Jill pressed. "I remember something about angels burning people."

"Those are eyes you're thinking of," Selene said. "Abrahamic angels are known to burn out the eyes of anyone who looks at them directly." She shrugged. "It's worth considering. Though I should warn you; angels are harder to deal with than demons. There's not much you can do but put your head down and wait for them to finish their business and move on."

"But there would be a way to test for angelic activity?" Jill asked. "Or . . . I don't know . . . some residue we could sweep for?"

Selene made a noncommittal shrugging motion. "We could run a Celestial Gunn Sweep—that should tell us if an angel manifested in this plane within the last week or so."

Jill nodded. She had been nervously fidgeting with the dish of splinters, and now she took a new one and filled it with splinters from a different bottle and placed that under the microscope. "None of this tells us what we can do for Sarah Wightman . . . what the *hell?!*" She shot to her feet so fast she sent the stool skidding backward. Selene caught it before it could tip over into a glass-fronted cabinet full of bottles and syringes.

Jerking the dish out from under the microscope she slid the old one in, checked it, then checked it against one of the slides. Then she picked up the new dish of splinters again and thrust it under Selene's nose.

"The bottle this came from? *Where was it?*"

"Er," said Selene, going a bit cross-eyed. "Right next to all the others. Why?"

"This," said Jill, wagging the dish, "doesn't *match!* There's no sign of the cellular disintegration!"

"Er . . . good?" said Selene.

"No, no, *bad,*" said Jill. "These splinters were *also* taken from the outhouse door frame. They *should* show the same type of damage as the others. But they *don't.* Unless they've been tampered with somehow. But the only difference I can think of is *where* they were placed within my case. So . . . *what was next to them?*"

Someone else might not have been able to say at once, but Selene had solved enough problems by noticing little things that did not fit to make her memory unusually strong. She also had good reason to remember what had been next to the little bottles of door samples.

"Er . . . " she said, unsure how Jill would react. "It was the . . . um . . . the bottle Johnny Bathory gave you. Y'know, the one with his . . . um . . . blood?"

Jill's eyes widened and her brows dropped, and Selene could almost see the gears turning in her mind. She was half expecting the woman's next words by the time they were spoken.

"I need it," Jill said. *"Now."*

"Gimme me a minute." Selene raised her hands defensively as she backed off her stool. "I can't *teleport,* you know."

Selene's phone rang as she was hiking across the parking lot.

"Yellow," she called into her phone.

"I'm back at the hotel," Clara's voice said. "Where are you?"

"Running errands for our very own mad scientist, of course," Selene said, unlocking the truck and climbing into the back. This time she grabbed Jill's entire briefcase, mentally scolding herself for not having done so in the first place.

"Now . . . ungh . . . now she thinks it could be *angels,"* Selene said, tucking her phone against her shoulder. It was too thin and slippery, however, and nearly fell out immediately.

"Angels," repeated Clara's voice.

"Yeah . . . so . . . think you could round up the ingredients for a Celestial Gunn Sweep? I mean, *I* don't think it's angels but at this point who knows. Oh, and be ready to explain to her the difference between angels and fravashi and stuff."

"There is no difference," Clara said promptly. "They are all the same thing called by different names."

"Really?" said Selene, sliding back out of the truck, briefcase in one hand, phone in the other. "That makes things *much* simpler. I'll tell her. Thanks."

"Selene?" Clara said, and this time there was a note of concern in her voice. It made Selene pause before shutting Arcana's door with her foot.

"Yeah?"

"I fear wherever Amar and Desta Dresner are, they are beyond our reach."

"Never say never, sister," Selene said, briefly setting the case down so she could thumb the lock button on the remote key. "Don't forget the ingredients for the Gunn Sweep, and remember: you can always hope for a miracle."

Clara made a derisive snorting sound and hung up. Selene shook her head as she slipped the phone into her pocket and began the long hike back to the pathology lab.

The frustrating thing about dealing with supernatural specimens, Jill thought as she compared once again the two splinter samples, was that there was clearly *something* going on—she just didn't have the instruments to measure it. As it was she was reduced to a sort of trial and error that was not only inefficient and time consuming, but also held enormous room for error. Yet when Selene arrived—carrying her entire briefcase this time, bless the woman—she noted with satisfaction that the sample of vampire blood was indeed right next to the slots where the bottles of door-frame samples had lain.

Carefully moving the disintegrating samples to the end of the counter, she pulled out the little bottle and set it on a dish of its own. Then she took a single splinter of affected wood and the slide of damaged tissue and set them on the dish beside the bottle, before putting the entire arrangement away on a shelf.

"It would be best if I knew how to isolate its effects," she grumbled. "But as I have no idea how this stuff interacts with physical barriers, I don't know what to use."

"Iron's usually a pretty good magical insulator," Selene offered.

"Iron?" said Jill, retrieving yet another dish. "Not lead?"

Selene shook her head vehemently. "Lead's actually a bit of a magical conductor."

"Huh," said Jill, taking an eyedropper and drawing out a tiny sample of blood, which she squirted onto the center of a new dish. Taking another splinter and a fresh sample of tissue she laid these directly in the blood, before immediately slipping it under the microscope. Pressing her eyes to the viewfinder, she carefully refocused the machine.

"Oh my god," she whispered.

"What's up?" she heard Selene say, and felt the warmth of the other woman leaning over her shoulder. It was only with distant attention, however, because of what was going on before her eyes.

The samples of wood and tissue, which she had ascertained *were* damaged before coming into contact with the blood, were rebuilding themselves as she watched.

Jerking her head back she removed the dish and went and got down the slate with the bottle on it. Removing the bottle she slid the slate, with the splinter and tissue samples, under the microscope. Here the change was not nearly so pronounced, but already she could tell some of the damage had been reversed. She looked over at Selene, her mouth slightly agape.

"The vampire blood," she whispered, "is acting as a regenerative agent. It's counteracting whatever is causing the disintegration."

Selene raised her eyebrows.

"Tell me *that* is a good thing," she said.

"It's *astonishing!*" cried Jill. "And yes, it is also a *very* good thing—certainly for Sarah Wightman. Here, could you bring me some of those sterile pads? Ask a nurse—*any* nurse. I want to test this on her *actual* hands."

* * *

Sarah Wightman was dozing, but in that shallow, unsettled way that was not true sleep. Her hands no longer hurt—she couldn't feel them at all—but now there was a slow ache spreading up her arms. It made her feel extremely tired. So tired she couldn't even be bothered to rouse herself when a crowd of people bustled into her room. Her mother was there, her mother would see what they wanted.

She watched in detachment as Dr. Carlston gently put her mother aside, and a nurse came forward and began changing the dressing on her hands. She noticed the woman with glasses from earlier, and a black woman with messy hair who she'd never seen before. She watched them fuzzily as the nurses gently re-wrapped her hands and arms, and her eyes lingered on the doorway after they had left.

"I would give it overnight at least," Jill told Dr. Carlston once they were in the hall. "Remember: you're not looking for *dead* tissue, but that particular disintegration pattern I showed you."

Dr. Carlston nodded, but he was frowning. "I don't understand," he said. "What exactly is in those bandages?"

"I can't say for certain," Jill said primly, and behind her Selene let out a silent breath. She would not have put it past Jill to say, with perfect innocent honesty: *"It's two-month old vampire blood diluted in saline solution brushed onto sterile pads,"* and expect the doctor to just *accept* it the way she did.

"You're getting better at this," she told Jill as they made their way out of the hospital for good.

"It was the *truth,*" Jill insisted. "I don't know if it's actually the blood that's doing it, or something *about* the blood that is reacting with whatever is in the damaged samples. It's too early to tell."

"Whatever you say, boss," Selene said agreeably.

"That's just the thing. I *can't.*" Jill sighed. "Where are we with Amar and Desta Dresner?"

"Still where we were," Selene told her, holding a swinging door open. "Clara found absolutely zilch—no burns, no nothing. So I had her pick up the ingredients for the sweep. We can start that as soon as it gets dark."

"Why—" Jill began, but this time Selene anticipated the question.

"Elementary magic, girlfriend," she said, "tends to work better in the dark. And don't ask me to explain it—that's just the way things *are*."

Jill pursed her lips, clearly biting down on a swell of skeptical remarks, but managed to contain them.

"Good," she said at length. "Then we'll have time to eat beforehand."

They ended up back at the same diner they had patronized for breakfast, this time sitting clustered around a little table in the back as Clara laid out the plan for the night. Fay was nowhere to be seen now, and the staff shot them a number of dirty looks as Clara shoved plates of food down to the end of the table to make room for her chart.

"The Celestial Gunn Sweep is a modified version of a seventeenth century divining spell first developed by Romani wizards," Clara explained as she laid out a burnished brass bowl filled with little glass bottles. "Originally it was used to detect the presence of a wide range of supernatural entities, but the Gunn brothers refined it in the 1970's to specifically target angels. They had many opportunities to perfect it, and it is still the best method to tell whether an angel has been or will be present at a given place for a short duration of time."

"Hold on a second," Jill said, chewing her overcooked steak and peering into the bowl. One of the bottles definitely contained lavender, and another rosemary. There was also a small tub of oil. "You said has *or* will? What does that mean?"

Clara looked pleadingly at Selene, who hastily swallowed her bite of cheeseburger and wiped her mouth on her sleeve.

"Angels don't exist in linear time, like we do," she explained. "They can drop in and out of our world as they please. They can *literally* be in two places at once—at least, that's what people who study the Brothers Gunn say. Truth to tell, there have been few confirmed reports of angelic activity since the attempted apocalypse of 1970—"

"There was an *apocalypse* in 1970?" Jill exclaimed.

"It was averted," Clara said.

"Anyway," continued Selene. "The thing about the Gunn Sweep is it scans for angels in the near vicinity—in the past, present *and* future. So you can use it to check and see if an angel is going to make an appearance, as well as seeing if one has been around lately."

"Or if one is standing right behind you," Clara added.

"Can they sneak up on you like that?" Jill asked.

Selene and Clara looked at her and nodded in unison.

"Behind you, beside you, in front of you, *in you,"* Selene said. "Angels can pretty much go wherever they want."

Jill pursed her lips and nodded. "Okay," she said, poking at the copper bowl. "How does this work?"

The night was dark and the sky scattered with stars by the time they set up at an empty campsite not far from the outhouse in question. It would have been best, Clara had remarked bitterly, if they could have run the sweep at ground zero, as it were, but Jill had felt this would be trying the patience of the volunteer officer who was currently keeping watch on the crowd of pilgrims—who were for the most part clustered around a bonfire and chatting happily—and so they set up at a prudent distance. They were still close enough, Selene assured her, to get an accurate reading.

"The sweep is actually pretty wide, space-wise," she explained as they laid out the bowl, and Clara began mixing ingredients. "It's just more specific the closer you are to the exact location."

"And how long is this going to take?" Jill asked.

Clara paused in the middle of sprinkling crushed rosemary into the bowl. "About four hours," she said after some thought.

"Four *hours?"* Jill exclaimed. She checked her watch. It was a quarter past nine.

"This is magic, hon," said Selene wearily. "Not . . . um . . . *magic.* I mean, it's not called a *sweep* for nothing. Think of how long it takes you to find a missing sock or bra in your bedroom, when your bedroom is a mess and that sock or bra may or *may not* be there, oh, and you also have to check the hours, days, and even *weeks* before and *after* that moment to see if it appeared in those times as well."

"Oh," said Jill, leaning back against Arcana's door. "That makes sense, then."

Clara dipped her fingers into the tub of oil and smeared a wide streak around the rim of the bowl. She wiped her hand on a black handkerchief and sat back on her heels.

"Would you like to perform the incantation?" she asked Selene deferentially.

"Why not all of us?" asked Selene. "It'll be more powerful that way. Do you have the English version?"

Clara nodded. She had produced a battered little book and was leafing through its pages.

"Here," she said, opening it and placing her finger in the middle of the spread. "You may read from it. I memorized it when I was eight."

"Handy, that," Selene said, taking the little book.

Switching on her flashlight Jill came over to stand at Selene's elbow and peered over.

The book appeared to be a handwritten journal. The lettering was neat and precise, and in a foreign language she did not recognize. One page, however, was covered in tidy red letters that spelled out recognizable English words. She read it through, mouthing the words under her breath.

"Don't," said Selene, giving her a gentle nudge with her elbow. "Wait until Clara gives the word."

"I was only practicing," Jill objected.

"Yeah, well, the great mystical ether don't know that," Selene said with a wry grin.

"Are you ready?" Clara asked. She was kneeling above the bowl, a match in one hand, box in the other.

"When you are, sister," Selene said.

Clara nodded, and struck the match. It flared to life, briefly illuminating her bony face—in the stark light her eyes appeared unusually dark: black pools save where the fire was reflected as a tiny golden spark. She began to speak, and only a little off cue, Selene and Jill fell in behind her.

"Find," they spoke in more or less unison. *"Messenger without message. Out of maker, out of order. Find the doors, find the footsteps.*

Find the flame behind the light. This is what we charge: melohinon elozere."

Jill tripped a bit over the last two words, and feared what came out of her mouth was closer to "melanin-hello-there," but she was drowned out by Clara and Selene's more assured pronunciation. To her surprise the sound of their voices intensified and took on a strange echoing quality—as if there had been nine of them speaking instead of three. Clara dropped the match into the bowl, where it went out with an anti-climactic *puff.*

"That's it?" Jill asked, moderately disappointed.

"It has begun," said Clara. "Now we wait."

Selene brought out her duffle bag and used it as a cushion while Clara stood over the bronze bowl. Jill went and sat in Arcana's back seat, typing up a report of what they had just done. She was particularly intrigued by those last, alien words—which apparently had no English equivalent.

"How did you spell those last words?" she asked, her fingers hovering over the keyboard. "Mellow-high—"

"*Shush!*" Selene and Clara hissed in unison, and Jill bit off the end of the word.

"What?"

"That's a . . . how do you say?" Selene said, waving a hand as if trying to catch the right phrase out of thin air.

"A Word of Power," Clara intoned, so clear and defined that Jill could almost hear the capital letters.

"Which is . . . what?" Jill probed.

"The closest thing you get to *abra cadabra,*" Selene said. "They're um . . . well we actually don't know exactly where they came from."

"They are all that remains of the Language of Making," Clara said.

Jill wrinkled her nose. "Wait . . . isn't that something from a book?"

"It has been alluded to in many books," Clara said. "It is one of the Universal Truths that permeate the human subconscious and often manifest in the stories you think of as . . . well, as fairy tales and fantasies. There was a Language of Making, but it was lost a long time ago. I do not think it was originally *words* as you or I understand them. It was something else. What we used was only a fragment of it, but like a drop of dye cast into clear water it will have a profound effect."

"Basically those aren't words you want to risk saying lightly," Selene said. "I mean, they *might* do nothing . . . or they might do *anything.* Without the proper context to guide their actions—the bowl, the lavender, the oil, the chant—it's almost completely random whether it has any effect or not."

"Like getting radium from thorium decay," Jill said, nodding sagely. "I see."

"Getting what from *what now?*" Selene said.

"Radium," said Jill. "Specifically, one of its more unstable isotopes. You can get radium when thorium decays, but it doesn't *stay* radium for very long before *it* decays into something else. So you can have a lump of, say, uraninite, which *may* or *may not* have any radium in it, all depending on what is happening at a nuclear level."

Selene put her head on one side, digesting this. "*Yeah,*" she said with a sort of half shrug. "I guess you could put it that way. Just imagine if you could also, I dunno, find a way to make *sure* there would be radium in that lump of ura-whatever at a given time. And if that radium could then make *really weird* things happen."

Jill opened her mouth to begin expounding upon all the weirdness radium was capable of, but thought better of it. She returned to her computer, and Selene and Clara returned to their silent vigil.

The night slowly crept by: one by one the dark figures in the neighboring site left their bonfire, and the conflagration itself burned down into a pile of dimly glowing embers. Jill finished entering her report and went to sit on the cold ground next to Selene. Clara shifted occasionally from foot to foot, but never actually sat. Jill's knees grew stiff from sitting in a folded position, so she uncrossed them and sat with her legs stretched out until her rear began to ache. Then she went and lay down across Arcana's back seat.

She had thought herself too wound up to sleep, and she doubted she ever properly drifted off, but she was in a slight doze when she was roused by a word from Clara.

"M-wha?" she mumbled, pulling herself upright and lowering her feet to the ground.

"I said: it begins." Clara's voice came drifting through the darkness.

Jill checked her phone: it was fifteen minutes after midnight. Slipping it back into her pocket she made her way over to where Selene had gotten to her feet and was standing opposite Clara across the bowl.

The bowl, which now contained a faint purplish glow. It lit the faces of the two women from beneath, casting vague shadows up around their eyes. For a moment Jill felt a wave of disorientation as she saw different features highlighted in what she had come to think of as familiar faces: the tense lines around Selene's mouth and brow, the sharp planes of Clara's cheekbones and the flare of her nostrils. They stared intensely down at the bowl and made no move to acknowledge her as she came to stand between them.

The glow turned out to be coming from a single ball of light that was slowly growing as little drops of light condensed on the rim of the bowl and slid down to pool in the bottom. As they watched, it grew in intensity until it was so bright Jill had to avert her gaze.

She was aware of it still; in her peripheral vision she saw it begin to rise up out of the bowl, and there was a subtle pulsation in its radiance that suggested rotation. Up, up it went, until it hung at about head height. Then it went out abruptly.

Jill blinked, trying to rid her mind of the afterimage left by the light. Instead of fading, however, the negative image only intensified, and to her amazement began to move again—as if whatever was creating the light was *still there.* It rose high above their heads, and Jill had to crane her neck back so she could track its motion.

When it reached a height of about fifty feet it halted—and then began to grow, throwing out arms that twisted as it slowly spun, forming a shape that put Jill in mind of a spiral galaxy. As the arms of the negative light passed over them, Jill thought she felt a chill settle on her skin.

The strange form hovered above them, rotating majestically against the starry sky, and after a while she began to see faint traces of lights at the tips of the arms, like dimly flashing stars. Once, one flashed brightly, far out at the very tip of the longest arm, and then the whole thing slowly faded from view. The chill left Jill's skin, and the gentle murmuring of the wind picked up in her ears, sighing across the campground.

"What . . . " she began. "What was that?"

"That was the Celestial Gunn Sweep," said Clara. "It read nothing in the vicinity either in the near past or future."

"But . . . but there was a flash," Jill protested. "I *saw* it, out on the end of the arm."

"That was somewhere far away from here," Selene said gently. "And at least two weeks in the future, I'd say."

"Colorado, at the closest," Clara added. "Maybe Kansas."

"So . . . no angels have been around here?" Jill asked, stamping down on her disappointment.

"Not in the last year," said Selene. "Or the next."

Jill sighed and helped Clara pack up the bowl and the remains of the ingredients. They put them in Arcana, and Jill drove them back to the motel. They fell into bed—even Clara—tired and deflated.

They were woken in the early morning by the trill of both Jill and Clara's phones ringing at the same time.

"Arrrgggh!" cried Selene, fumbling in Jill's coat, even as Clara rolled out of bed and flipped open her phone.

"Nordstern," Jill heard her say, and then her face went perfectly blank.

"Yellow," said Selene, putting Jill's phone to her ear. "Yeah," she said. "Yeah, she's right here. Phone call for you, boss," she said, passing the phone to Jill, who took it and peered at the name on the display before bringing it to her ear.

"This is Jill Hamilton," she said. "How can I help you, Dr. Carlston?"

"You can tell me what you were doing in Sarah Wightman's room last night," came the clipped voice of the doctor, in a mix of anger and hysteria.

"I . . . *what?*" said Jill. "I was never *in* Sarah Wightman's room last night."

Behind her, Clara was speaking into her own phone:

"I assure you I have no knowledge of—they said *what?*"

Jill put a finger in her other ear and turned up the volume on her phone.

"I was at Green River campground until past midnight—ask the volunteer patrol," she said. "What's *happened?*"

"What do *they* say happened?" Clara asked.

"What's *happened?*" repeated Dr. Carlston over the phone, the anger subsiding and the hysteria growing to fill in the gaps. "Sarah Wightman has *completely* recovered, *that's* what's happened!"

"Really?" said Jill, blinking in disbelief. This was a far more dramatic result than she had dared hoped for. "Then my treatment worked?"

"That's just the *thing,* Hamilton," Dr. Carlston said. "When the nurse came in this morning the bandages were all stripped off. She found them in a pile next to Wightman's monitor with a *note* on top. I thought *you'd* left it."

"What—a *note?*" said Jill. "No, no I never . . . wait, what does it *say?* And what does *Wightman* say happened?"

"Girl was under the influence of painkillers and sedatives," snapped Dr. Carlston. "She's saying an *angel* came and healed her. Needless to say, her *mother* is having a field day."

"I can imagine," said Jill, dropping the phone to her shoulder. "*Selene,*" she hissed. "The reading from last night . . . are you *sure* it was from out of state?"

Selene nodded. "Nowhere closer than a hundred miles. And not due for another two weeks."

"So no chance it could have indicated activity, say, at the hospital *last night?*"

"What?" said Selene, sounding almost offended. "Naw, no way. What's happened?"

"I don't know," said Jill. "Doctor, I need to see Sarah Wightman. No, no, I *assure* you I had *nothing* to do with this."

She hung up.

"I need to get to the hospital," she explained. "Something happened in the night and Sarah Wightman's been healed." She stopped. Clara had also gotten off the phone and was looking like she'd been hit by a truck and hadn't quite accepted it yet.

"What's wrong?" Jill asked.

"Amar and Desta Dresner," Clara whispered. "They're back."

Jill nearly dropped her phone in shock.

"*What?*" she cried.

Amar and Desta Dresner turned out to be amber-skinned children with vigorously curly black hair and large, almond-shaped eyes with dark lashes. They were the most enchanting children Jill had ever met, and they were entirely unharmed. Indeed, they were in high spirits, running wild over the large house, when they arrived.

Clara, who'd gone ahead, ushered them downstairs while their mother hovered protectively above them.

Martin Dresner, even taller and somewhat bulky, rambled around the kitchen making coffee while Jill tried to interview the children. They regarded her with serious dark eyes, and did not seem inclined to answer her questions.

Where had they been?

"Exploring," Amar said firmly.

"Castles," said Desta. "Big castles, small castles, cloud castles, star castles . . . "

"Desta has been in a castle phase for the last three months," Martin explained self-consciously.

"Yes," said Jill. "But *where?*"

Amar shrugged. "Around," he said.

"We saw a . . . we saw a *giraffe-bird,*" said Desta, raising her hands to illustrate. "It cackled and carried me on . . . carried me on its *shoulders.*"

"Was it the giraffe-bird that took you?" Jill asked.

"No, *silly,*" said Desta, grinning. "*Amar* came and got me."

"Amar, you came back *home*?" his mother asked.

"I didn't want Desta to be left out," he said. "So after waffles I brought her along. We didn't fight or make any messes," he assured his parents.

"How did you get out of the outhouse?" Jill asked.

Amar shrugged and looked up at her with the perfect innocence only a seven-year-old could manage. "I went somewhere else," he said, and that was all she could get out of him.

"They seem *perfectly* fine," Ayana told them as they left. She sounded like she was still trying to convince herself of this fact.

"And they just appeared in their beds this morning?" Jill asked.

The woman nodded. "They must have sneaked in through the back door. They were horribly dirty—but fine. They must have been off playing make-believe for the past few days. I can't imagine how they weren't seen . . . but here they are."

"Do you have any intention of making a statement to the police?" Clara asked.

Ayana Dresner looked ready to throw them bodily out of the house, but her husband stepped in and said, with a good approximation of a soothing voice:

"Only to tell them to call off the dogs, as it were. I mean, we have them back, and that's the important thing."

"Let's hope Sarah Wightman is a bit more forthcoming," Jill grumbled as they pulled into the hospital parking lot.

"Don't count on it," Selene said, putting the truck in neutral and setting the parking brake. "This is looking more and more like a GOA to me."

Jill, distracted with her briefcase, didn't question this. She hopped out and fairly pelted up the steps to the main lobby and into the restricted-access corridors before anyone could stop her.

Dr. Carlston was hardly surprised to see her when she burst into his office.

"If you're hoping for a clear explanation," he said heavily, "this is the *wrong* place."

"Sarah Wightman doesn't remember what happened?" Jill all but wailed.

"Oh, she *does,* that's the problem," Dr. Carlston said bitterly and spun his open laptop around so Jill could see the web page displayed there.

"'Roosevelt teen cured by miraculous angelic visitation,'" Jill read in the blog's headline. "But that's *wrong!* We *checked!* There were no angels around here!"

"You checked," said Dr. Carlston blankly. "For *angels?*"

"I need to see her. Can she receive visitors?"

Sarah Wightman was sitting up in bed eating yogurt from a plastic cup when Jill was shown in. Her mother fairly bounced to her feet and shook Jill's hand in both of hers.

"It's a miracle!" she cried, her eyes shining. "Thank *God!*"

Even to Jill's skeptical mind it looked pretty miraculous. Sarah Wightman's hands, uncovered and clearly useable, were the healthy brownish pink of healing skin, and apart from a few minor discolorations there was no sign of the burns or the horrible necropsied tissue. The girl herself was vibrantly pink and smiling blissfully.

"Sarah," said Jill seriously, sliding a chair up next to the bed, "Sarah . . . what happened?"

Sarah Wightman sighed rapturously. "I was *visited,*" she said. "By an *angel.*"

"Can you *describe* this angel?" Jill asked. "What did it *do?*"

Sarah Wightman swallowed a spoonful of yogurt and stared airily over Jill's head.

"I was lying in bed, praying for forgiveness," she said conscientiously. "When suddenly there was this blinding light and an angel stepped out of it. I could tell he was an angel because he had this glowing halo around his head. Anyway, he came and undid the bandages on my hands, and he told me everything would be all right, and I *knew* it would be, so I went to sleep—and when I woke up I was healed!" She set down her yogurt and waved her hands.

"Has Amar been returned yet?" she asked, suddenly concerned. "I need to apologize to him."

"Amar Dresner is fine," Jill said. "As is his sister. They reappeared at approximately the same time you had your . . . visitation."

"That's *good,*" said Sarah, leaning back in her pillows.

"Is that true?" Dr. Carlston asked as Jill made to leave.

"Yes," she replied. "Their parents believe they were off playing somewhere."

Dr. Carlston shook his head. "Oh," he said, picking up a small box from a trolley in the hall. "Here are the wrappings we found on her table this morning. They appear to be the dressing you applied yesterday."

Frowning, Jill opened the box, and there sure enough were the stained pads and medical tape. There was also a scrap of paper, clearly torn from a corner of Sarah Wightman's treatment record. Taking it out and holding it up Jill peered at it.

"And there is the note . . . " Dr. Carlston said unhappily.

In sloppy, blunt pencil was scrawled a single line:

Good try, but look harder.

"I was hoping you could tell me what that meant," the doctor said.

Jill, who'd stopped in her tracks to read the note, practically shuddered with frustration. "Apparently," she said, stuffing the note back into the box, "*apparently* I need to *look* harder."

Selene and Clara were waiting in the parking lot, standing between Arcana and the motorcycle, Unicorn, when Jill stormed out the doors and down the steps.

"I take it Wightman was not a perfect witness . . . " Selene hazarded.

Jill practically growled as she stuffed the box into the back seat and then thrust the scrap of paper at Selene.

"*Someone* was there," she said. "They healed Sarah Wightman, took off her bandages, and left *that.* I think they left it for *me.*"

Squinting rather, Selene read the note. Then she let out a low whistle and passed it to Clara, who read it in turn and responded with one of her inverted shrugs.

"Well?" said Jill. "What do *you* make of it?"

Clara looked up at her, then over at Selene, and said in tones of mild wonderment: "It's a GOA."

Selene put her head on one side and nodded. "Yep," she said. "I'm calling GOA."

"*What,*" said Jill, "is a 'gee oh ay?'"

Clara dipped and raised her shoulders again. "An initialism," she said. "It stands for God Or Aliens."

"Basically," said Selene as Jill groaned and rolled her eyes. "It's something we don't know what it was and there's no way of finding out. Might as well be God . . . or aliens. *We don't know.*"

"*Ugh,*" said Jill, snatching the piece of paper out of Clara's gloved hand. "That is *not* an acceptable answer."

"It isn't an answer," said Selene. "It's just a way of admitting that *we don't have an answer for this.*"

"It happens sometimes," Clara said gently. Then she said, in a rhythmic way as if quoting someone: "Does the trapped spider understand the human intervention that frees it? We, as humans, must accept that there are beings in this universe that are so far beyond our understanding that their actions are as incomprehensible to us as ours are to the spider."

Jill glowered at them and climbed into Arcana.

"Hey," said Selene, putting her head in after her and grinning. "It could have been a lot worse. At least nobody *died* this time!"

Jill sighed, and though she was still stewing in her own impotent frustration, she found she had to admit that Selene was right.

Still, she couldn't help muttering under her breath: "But I *will* figure this out one day . . . "

"Whatever lets you sleep at night," Selene said amiably, climbing in beside her. "Now, if you'll give this a break, maybe we could get something to eat? I'm *starving.*"

Jill felt her stomach grumble, and decided this was something she agreed with whole-heartedly.

*

Did you see that?

My child, this might be a disaster
Young lovers, watch out for the blaster
See that flash from the sky, it's
God or aliens!

That's right, you choose one or the other
Tonight, do your best to discover
What's that sound that you hear? It's
God or aliens!

If you pick one you can bet some people will get quite upset,
But you've nothing to fear.
Look up into that blue sky, say you've got big fish to fry
Your intention is clear.

All ways, they lead you in a circle
What now? You act like it's a surprise.
Don't you see it's got to be
God or aliens!

If allowed to have your say, we could be stuck here all day.
It's getting harder to hear.
All the crazy in this verse, still your courage won't disperse.
Immolation is free—so is this:

God or aliens!

A ship no ship a door no door oh how
Can you figure out this big mess now?
Things you can't explain, might as well be
God or aliens!

You've got no lines of inquiry just magic and some wizardry.
Cooperation is key.
I don't know why you reject all the things that I expect
But now all we have is
God or aliens!

God or aliens!

—God or Aliens, *The Laughing Hands*

The Arcana crew will return in
"Missionary Man"

Complementing the preceding "God, or Aliens," "Amar and Desta's Big Day Out" follows Amar past the outhouse door, and explains how his sister Desta went missing as well. It also offers some clues as to the identity of the mysterious person who cured Sarah Wightman. It was written in the first week of November, 2013, at the same time as "God, or Aliens."

Amar and Desta's Big Day Out

Amar had not been enjoying the camping trip. It was cold and wet, and he did not like the other children. He had not wanted to go into the outhouse. It was dark and dirty and smelled strongly of fermented urine. Once he was inside, however, the smell vanished, and he found it was not as dark as he first supposed. Dim lights of red and green and blue and gold twinkled somewhere above him, and putting his hands out, he felt the shape of stairs, soft and springy with carpet.

Thinking what an odd sort of outhouse this was, Amar began to climb the stairs on his hands and knees, careful so he wouldn't trip and fall. When he reached the top he found it was a much bigger place than he had expected. The lights came from a high wall full of twinkling bulbs and glowing tubes and cables, which made a soft humming sound as the lights went on and off. They reminded Amar of the Christmas lights people put up in his neighborhood, all soft and dim and multi-hued. Amar had always thought those lights made a place look magical, and had been slightly disappointed when such places turned out to be boring and ordinary.

This place, however, looked like it might actually *be* magical. It reminded Amar of the inside of a spaceship, or perhaps a submersible—though he had never been inside either. To his left and right were swivel chairs bolted to the floor, and in front of each was a big, square monitor—like the one belonging to his father's computer—which glowed a bright, sky blue. By their light he saw the rest of the ship: long and narrow with windows placed along the walls on either side. These had cream-colored lace curtains, drawn aside to let in the starlight, and the wallpaper was a dusty pink with rose patterns on it. The floor was metal at first—one reason it had put Amar in mind of a ship—but further in, it changed to hard, polished wood. When Amar bent down he could just make out his reflection in it.

Most of the room, he now saw, was taken up by a giant wooden table, like the one in the dining room of his own home. It was covered with a pink-and-green floral cloth that hung down in drapes on all four sides, and there was a person asleep on it.

They were a grown-up, Amar could tell by their length (they lay curled on their side with their knees bent and yet still took up most of the table), but they were the strangest-looking grown-up Amar had ever seen. They wore a bright green coat that went all the way down over their legs and tied in the back with a cloth belt—like his father's overcoat—and they wore red-and-purple striped socks. As Amar came around to their head, he saw it was a woman with whitish, peach-colored skin and hair the color of pale gold. She lay with her head resting on one arm, her eyes closed, and her mouth partly open. A quiet snore escaped from it.

"Excuse me," said Amar, reaching up to touch the sleeve of her nearest arm. "*Excuse me,*" he tried again, when this had no effect.

The woman stirred. Her shoulders stretched, she wrinkled her nose, and then opened her eyes and raised her head to look at him.

She had big dark eyes, with pupils so huge they reminded Amar of a cat. They reflected the lights from behind him, and seemed to twinkle in the dark.

"Hello," said this strange person. "Can I help you?" Her voice had an accent to it, sort of like his mother's but not. It was easy enough to understand, however.

"I'm looking for the bathroom," Amar whispered, not having lost sight of his main goal.

"Up the ladder and to the right," said the woman with the cat eyes and shining hair, and pointed.

There, Amar saw, was a ladder, with little blue lights shining along its sides and rungs, and he climbed up it easily. This let him off on a narrow walkway that extended around the place like a balcony. There were doors set into the walls instead of windows, and the first one on his right was indeed marked with a little pictogram of a man, like the ones on public restrooms. He pushed it open and felt around for a light switch.

He needn't have bothered. The light came on automatically; low and orange and pleasantly soothing, it illuminated a room with sandstone-colored tiles and a wavy mosaic on the wall. There was a toilet with a fluffy pink cover, a sink with soap and a towel and a mirror above, and a little three-legged stool just the right height for Amar to stand on to reach the taps. There were two more rooms extending off the far end, and after Amar had used the toilet he stuck his head in to find that one contained a big, deep circular bath, and the other a wide, walk-in shower. More towels hung just outside: the long, fluffy kind, perfect for lying on or bundling up in. Amar was tempted to experiment in the bath and the shower, but he worried that the woman below might be bothered, so he went out again.

In the main room the lights were brighter now—though not bright enough to illuminate the ceiling, which stretched on up into the dark beyond Amar's vision—and he saw the woman had got off the table and was now sitting in one of the swivel chairs by the monitors and lights, peering at something on the screen. When she saw Amar descending the ladder, she switched off the screen and stood up.

"I was about to get breakfast," she explained, straightening her hair. With a jolt Amar realized it must be a wig. "Are you hungry?"

Amar, who'd not been able to finish his dinner of cold potatoes and canned peas, and had only eaten half his burnt marshmallow, said: "Oh, yes. But it's actually dinnertime."

"Dinner for you, breakfast for me," said the woman with a shrug. "It won't be a problem. Well, what would you like? I still have an ostrich egg, we could split that."

"Just an egg?" Amar asked, a little disappointed.

"Or we could go out," said the woman. "Do you like pancakes? Waffles?"

"With syrup?" Amar asked hopefully.

"Syrup and fresh fruit and powdered sugar too, if you like," said the woman.

"That sounds good," said Amar.

"Excellent," said the woman. "Take a seat, this won't be long." She indicated the other swivel chair.

Amar climbed into it, noticing the seat belt hanging off to one side. He put it on.

"I'm Amar, by the way," he said.

"I'm Odd," said the woman.

Amar laughed. He thought the woman was making a joke.

"Nice to meet you, Odd," he said.

But instead of correcting him the woman just grinned.

"All right then, Mr. Amar," she said. "*Hold on.*"

What happened next was the most marvelous thing Amar had seen since New Year's Eve fireworks. Perhaps even more awesome than that.

All the lights around the little console blinked and flashed, making quiet humming noises and *tinking* sounds. It was like the most complicated display of Christmas lights ever, and Amar watched in stunned amazement. At last all the lights flashed—it was nearly blinding—and there was a deep, loud, *bonnnng* like a church bell.

The woman Odd pulled a lever with a red knob at the end and spun out of her seat.

"We're here!" she announced.

"No, we're not," Amar said, unbuckling and climbing out of his seat. "We're in the same place we were before."

"*Technically,* yes," Odd said, waving a finger. "But *that* place is now in a different, bigger place. Go open the door, you'll see."

So Amar went back down the stairs to the door. He had thought this should be the door of the outhouse, but when he got there he found it was a neat, clean wooden one, painted a dull but pleasing blue. It smelled crisply of wood polish, and it had a brass doorknob, which turned agreeably under Amar's hand.

Instead of the dark and foul-smelling night he was expecting, Amar felt a cool breeze on his face that smelt of wet stone, mostly, with a hint of car exhaust and a waft of fresh baking pastry. Pulling the door the rest of the way open he found he was looking out onto the stone steps of a house which led down to a cobbled lane. Sunlight was shining in at such an angle that he guessed it must be morning, casting the houses opposite him in bright golden light. These were tall, narrow buildings which looked old but well cared for. They had steeply tilted roofs and lots of square windows, reflecting the bright blue sky, and were made of brick mostly, except where they were made of plaster painted in various cheerful colors.

"What happened to the campground?" Amar asked.

"It's still where it was." Odd had appeared behind him; she had put on a pair of dark circular glasses and wrapped a fuzzy scarf around her neck. "I told you, I just moved the place *we* were in. Well, *technically* I moved your universe a bit—but not so much that anyone would notice. Had to jump forward a bit as well, so that the shops would be open. Brussels is *much* more fun with the shops open."

Amar, who only knew the term "brussels" as it applied to the vegetable, felt his heart sink. Then Odd was out the door and trotting down the steps.

"Coming?" she asked when she reached the bottom, and Amar decided that no one as fabulous and whimsical as Odd would ever feed anyone something as terrible as brussels sprouts. He tramped down the steps after her, closing the door behind him.

The street they were on was very narrow, and the street signs were all a bit different than Amar was used to—smaller and rounder all over. He was confused by them, until he realized they were written in a foreign language.

"Two foreign languages, actually," Odd said. "Well, foreign to *you.* This is *Belgium,* after all, so *we're* the ones speaking a foreign language, really. See, *Zeehondstraat?* That's the name of this street in Dutch. But here it's *Rue du Chien Marin.* That's in French."

"Don't Belgians speak . . . um . . . " Amar thought of what the word would be, then said it. "Don't they speak Belgish?"

Odd, beginning to walk down the double-named street, laughed. "You'd think so, wouldn't you? But no, in this narrative it's French or Dutch, and honestly sometimes they can't make up their minds between the two. There are some versions where it's *mostly* French or *mostly* Dutch, but very few indeed where they have been able to develop their own language—and then they call it *Belgian,* just like the people."

"They should just speak Belgian," said Amar, hurrying to follow her. The narrow street was not long, and soon they emerged onto a wide promenade lined with trees and street vendors under blue umbrellas selling things that smelled delicious.

"It would be simpler," Odd allowed. "But then, *you're* American and you speak English."

Amar was silent, for this was a discrepancy that had bothered him before, and in the end he decided he was in no position to dictate what language other countries should be speaking when his didn't even have a language of its own. Besides, now Odd was approaching one of the vendors, and Amar could see that the cheerful round man behind the counter was indeed selling waffles.

They were not like the waffles he had had at Wendy's or McDonald's. They were a thousand times better. Big and square, with deep pockets perfect for filling with syrup, they were cooked to a crisp golden-brown and slightly darker around the edges, making the powdered sugar they'd been dusted with stand out like a gentle frosting of snow. Amar inhaled deeply, rejoicing in the smell of sweet, fresh-baked dough.

"How many would you like?" Odd asked him.

Amar, who was accustomed to being told how many sweets he was getting, and always the number too low, said, experimentally: "Ten?"

Odd didn't even remark on his request. She spoke to the little man in a strange language—Amar couldn't tell if it was French or Dutch, but it certainly wasn't English—and ten crisp waffles were delivered into his arms, wrapped in paper and with little packets of jam and syrup and lots of napkins tucked in around the corners. Odd also got one for herself, and paid the man with many small gold and silver coins.

They walked down the promenade together, slowly, eating the waffles—which were perfectly crunchy on the outside and soft on the inside, light and sweet like cake but just the right amount of chewy—and admiring the façade of what looked like a church at the far end. It had a big dark archway and a circular window above that, with spiky little turrets on top that put Amar in mind of a castle.

Between them and the church-castle was a wide, shallow, green pond, and in front of that was a low stone pedestal with a strange metal sculpture, like a wheel and part of a gear, laid across it. People were sitting on the edge of the pedestal around it, and Amar and Odd sat on a corner as well, while Amar ate waffles until he felt a little ill. There were still three left.

"May I have them?" Odd asked politely.

Amar, who felt he would be sick if he took another bite, gratefully shoved them into her lap and wiped his sugary hands down the front of his jacket.

Odd ate the waffles carefully, in big sharp bites. Afterward they were both thirsty, so Odd went over to another vendor and came back with steaming paper cups: coffee for her, hot chocolate for Amar. It was a darker, more bitter hot chocolate than the kind his mother made from powder, but it was the perfect thing to follow the sweet waffles. Amar sipped it carefully as they walked down to the very end of the promenade and stood looking up at the church.

"My sister would like that," Amar said. "She likes castles. Lots of castles."

"Would you like to show your sister this castle?" Odd asked. "We could go and get her. We can visit lots of castles."

Amar, who shared his sister's fascination with castles more than he would admit, pretended to give this due sober thought while inside he twisted with delight. At length he said: "I think she would be asleep by now."

"True," Odd allowed, nodding. "But we'll just be sure to visit when she will be awake. How is that?"

"That sounds good," Amar said, and handed her his empty cup.

Odd took the cup and disposed of it and her own in a brown metal trash can as they walked back down the promenade and through the narrow alley. Amar recognized the door they had come out of and bounded up the steps to it, hauling it open.

They did the same thing with the lights again, sitting in the swivel chairs with the seat belts on, and this time Amar felt a definite *thump* and *shift* before the deep *bonnnnnng* went off.

"Not bad," said Odd, dusting off her hands. "That door should lead out of your sister's closet now."

Excited and still partly disbelieving, Amar unbuckled himself and hopped down the steps. Sure enough, that was the inside of his sister's closet door, with the little broken hook in the center from the time they'd both swung on the sleeves of Desta's winter coat at the same time. Carefully he pushed it open and stuck his head out.

To his surprise it seemed to be afternoon now, but there was Desta sitting despondently on her bed, her knees pulled up into her chest and an unhappy pout on her face. She lit up when she saw him, and jumped down.

"Ammer!" she cried, which was her name for him. "You're back! I was *lonely!*"

"We're going to see some castles," Amar said, suffering to be hugged.

"Cas—"

"Shh!" Amar cut his sister off. He knew, deep in his bones, that galavanting off with strange women to see castles was not the sort of thing his mother would easily agree to, and he decided it would be better all around to skip that conversation entirely. "Grab your boots. Come on then!"

Desta's boots were bright pink rubber things, but they were sturdy and comfortable with fleece lining. They were slipped on, and Amar bundled his sister back into the closet.

"Why the *closet?*" Desta asked.

"It's not a closet!" whispered Amar excitedly, closing the door behind him. *"Look!"*

Desta did look, and her big brown eyes grew even wider as she took in the twinkling lights and the unusual figure of the woman Odd sitting on the swivel chair.

"Hello there," she said with a big grin. "Now, which castle would you like to see first?"

Desta wanted to see a princess's castle, so Odd made the door open onto a magnificent corridor with a painted ceiling and views of pine-covered mountains. Desta ran up and down the hall, shrieking with delight. She was so loud that some rather unfriendly looking men in black jumpsuits came to see what the matter was, at which point they all dove for the special door and slammed it shut.

"Somewhere less well occupied?" Odd suggested, and this time made the door open onto a deserted courtyard. This castle was mostly ruin, and Amar liked it much better. It had chunks of walls and bits of tower that broke off in jagged edges, and staircases that had once led up to higher floors but now crumbled away to nothing. A thick bed of green grass covered the ground, and Desta spent most of the time picking clover flowers and making Odd tie them into strings. By the time Amar had finished exploring—and gotten his trousers nice and dirty—Desta and Odd between them had made three circlets of clover flowers; the one Desta had made herself was sloppy and tended to come apart, but she wore it anyway. Odd had put one on her own head, and offered the third to Amar.

"I don't want to wear *that,*" he said in contempt, pushing it away. "Flowers are for *girls.*"

"Boys can wear flowers too," Professor Odd said, but she took the circlet away and put it in her pocket.

This didn't sound quite right to Amar. He knew that any boy who showed up at school wearing anything remotely pink or floral would be teased mercilessly. After a time, however, he realized that there were no other children around to pick on him, and he did feel a bit left out being the only one without a crown.

He went back to Odd and pulled on the tail of her coat.

"I changed my mind," he explained.

Professor Odd beamed at him and settled the little crown of flowers snugly within his curly hair.

"Now we are *team!*" Desta announced.

"Are you ready to go home?" Odd asked.

"No!" cried Desta and Amar together, and Desta added: "I want to see another *castle!*"

"Oh, what sort of castle?" Odd asked, adjusting her circlet of flowers.

"A *big* one. A castle in the *clouds!*" Desta said, throwing out her arms to illustrate.

Amar scoffed, and was about to point out that there were no such things, but Odd just smiled and nodded and said: "All right. We'll have to go a bit farther to find that, but it shouldn't take long."

She was as good as her word. They'd hardly been sitting in the place with the blinking colored lights for two minutes when Odd announced they had arrived at "Cloud Fortress Eight" and gave them both scarves to wrap around their shoulders and necks. "It's very high up and rather cold," she explained.

It was cold, but it was also *marvelous.* The door opened onto a wide hall, at the far end of which people were scurrying about. Odd hurried them into a lift, and they rode it all the way to the top of a tower, where when they got out, they were able to look down on the towers and pillars of a castle that looked as if it had been made from blown glass. And beyond it, instead of grass or hills or mountains or even a city, there were only distant, puffy pink clouds. In between them Amar could glimpse a land, far below, with the twinkling lights of cities and the hard edge of a coastline glittering in the slanting light. It appeared to be sunset, and they watched as the world below them slowly sank into the darkness. The castle, however, remained in sunlight long enough for Desta to explore the top of the tower. When that too had fallen into shadow, and the electronic lights inside had come on, Odd asked once again whether they were ready to go home.

"Nooo," said Desta, though Amar wished she hadn't; he was beginning to get sleepy. "I want to see a *star* castle!"

"You mean like a castle in outer space?" Odd asked, impressed.

Desta nodded exuberantly.

"Okay," said Odd, and took them back down the lift and through the special door.

This time when they opened it again, after having waited out another set of flashing lights and a loud *boonng,* they were not in a castle at all, but in a tiny space pod. Amar felt like his tummy was rising in his chest as he stepped out, and with a thrill of excitement he realized he was *weightless.* All the tiredness left him at once, and he and Desta had to spend several minutes hurtling themselves back and forth across the little cockpit, while Odd handed herself along the ceiling and strapped herself into a chair.

"Eyes ahead," she told them. "Or you'll miss the best view."

Reluctantly Amar and Desta stopped their play and slowly crawled over to where they could see out the windshield-like window.

And there . . .

There . . .

"Star castle!" shrieked Desta, and squealed with laughter.

Amar said nothing, but his mouth was silently open in wonder and awe.

"Star castle" described what lay before them very well. It was an immense construction of dark gray metal ramparts and curving tongues of steel, in the center of which rose a thin silver dome studded with spine-like rods from which ran strings of lights. All along the gray metal skin were little windows which glowed blue and purple, like tiny stars imbedded in a silver sky.

The whole thing appeared to Amar to be floating in space, for there was nothing beneath, behind, or above it but a blank black sky speckled with distant real stars. Then the little ship they were in swerved around as they made a huge circuit of the place, and a planet—deep and swirling blue—came into view to their right.

"It's a *space station,"* whispered Amar.

"Star castle!" Desta insisted.

"Actually, you're *both* right," said Odd cheerily, taking them in closer so they could get a better view of one of the great gray arms—of which Amar guessed there were at least a dozen—that sprouted out of the main dome and went curving out into space. It made the whole thing look a little like a giant spinning top. "This is the Palace of the Premier of Amphitrite," Odd went on. "But as *Amphitrite*—that's her over to your right—is an uninhabitable gas giant, all the people living here stay on what are, in effect, *space stations.* The Premier's Palace is just the most fancy of them. I borrowed this shuttle, for example, from one of the

Regimental Office Stations. You can see it behind us, there . . . " she made the little ship turn, and there sure enough was *another* top-like construction—albeit a plainer, less attractive one.

"Can we go *inside?*" Amar asked.

Odd shrugged. "The Premier *does* owe me a couple of favors," she allowed. "Which part would you like to start with?"

"I want to see more of the *outside!*" Desta insisted.

"We can take a complete fly around, see all of it, before we dock," Odd assured her, and thereby neatly avoided what Amar and Desta's parents called a "critical mass event."

She was as good as her word: they circled around the whole place in an ever-tightening spiral, and Desta spent the whole time with her nose pressed to the glass. Amar had to admit, it *was* pretty cool. They passed fans with blades made of blue metal that glittered ("Photovoltaic generator panels," Odd explained) and little turrets with bulging domes at their tops. Once they even passed another shuttle, like their own. At last they came in close to the main dome—which Amar now saw bulged *down* as well as up—and threaded their way neatly into a little opening like a square mouth. Here they had to wait for a while so that Odd could explain what they were doing to the frowning man in the box outside. This didn't take long, however, and soon they were able to open a hatch and float out.

There was a pole there, and Odd had them clip themselves to it with ropes that attached to harnesses they wore around their shoulders, almost like backpacks.

"*Why?*" asked Desta.

"Because there is no gravity," Odd explained in her cheerful way. "And you don't have any jet propulsion on you. So if you let go of the pole and floated away you wouldn't be able to do anything about it, and you might float into a ship's engine and be incinerated."

"What is *incinerated?*" Amar asked.

"It means to be burned to death instantaneously," Odd told him.

Amar and Desta clipped themselves to the pole without any further protest.

It was actually great fun shinnying up the pole. Amar was reminded of rope climbing in the playground, only instead of a bristly rope that scraped his palms, the pole was smooth and cool, and it took only a little effort to drag his weightless body up it.

They eventually passed through a circular hole which closed behind them and into a small room with padded walls.

"This is the Gravity Lock," Odd explained. "Try to stay right-side up."

This was harder than Amar expected, even though he stayed clipped to the pole along with Desta. Odd pushed herself away and floated effortlessly with her legs crossed.

"*Now* what?" Desta asked.

"Now we wait," Odd said.

The gravity came on gradually. Amar felt it first as a gentle tugging on his insides, and then he noticed he was slowly sinking toward the padded floor. It reminded him of his swimming lessons, when he'd learned to float underwater without the help of a life preserver. Only here he kept getting heavier and heavier, until his feet touched the ground, and he felt all the bits of himself settle into their usual place.

"Aw," said Desta. "We've gone back to *normal.*"

"Actually, the gravity here is only seventy-five percent that of Earth," Odd said from where she was now sitting on the floor. She popped up, like a jack-in-the-box toy, and clapped her hands. "*Now,*" she said, "who's hungry?"

They all were, it turned out. The waffles seemed very distant now after running over all those castles, and Amar found himself dragging behind Odd and Desta as they made their way out of the padded room and into a long hall lined with shops. Amar tried to read the signs as they went past, but found that the letters were all strange shapes that he didn't recognize. Instead he looked at the other people; there were quite a lot of them, milling along the hall. Some of them pushed carts or strollers; others walked arm in arm. It put Amar in mind of the town mall where his mother sometimes took him shopping, only the people were much stranger.

They were human shaped, for the most part, but a few of them had strange faces that did not seem quite right. Either their noses were odd shapes or their eyes slanted disconcertingly. Many of them had brightly colored hair. Then, drifting through the crowd like a sailing ship, Amar saw the most extraordinary creature: tall as a horse, with a long neck bedecked in rings of beads, its bird-like face covered in feathers. It had long spindly legs and carried its arms tucked up by its sides.

Even as Amar stared, this magnificent creature spotted them and dove through the crowd in their direction.

For one terrible second Amar thought it was coming after him, but then the creature changed direction and came to a sliding halt in front of Odd, who gave a little cry of delight and threw her arms around its thin neck.

They began talking to each other then, in a high babbling language that Amar did not understand at all. He began to feel left out, so he came up under Odd's elbow, opposite Desta, and yanked her sleeve.

"Ooodd," he said, "I'm *hungry."*

"Yes, yes of course!" said Odd, and said something to the bird-like person, who in turn looked down at Amar out of wide orange eyes. It chittered in a friendly way and offered a thin, scaly hand. Amar shook it gravely.

"Do you mind if Kaklee comes with us?" Odd asked, indicating the bird-person.

Amar had no trouble with this. Desta wanted to ride on Kaklee's shoulders. When Odd explained this, Kaklee made the chittering noise again and lifted Desta up. This made Amar feel left out, so Odd picked *him* up and carried him piggy-back.

Like that, they made their way along the hall and up a moving flight of stairs until they came to a wide area with lots of tables set out in front of a huge window from which they could look out and see the arms of the space station and the little ships coming and going.

The place turned out to be some sort of restaurant, and they sat at a high table with Odd and Kaklee on either end and Amar and Desta across from each other between them. They ordered off of menus with little pictures of food from a man with skin as white as paper and bright blue hair, who peered at Amar and Desta curiously. He seemed to know Odd, however, and shook her hand before he left.

Lots of people seemed to know Odd. So many people came up to talk to her that she barely managed to eat any of the bright orange, cheesy noodles she had ordered. Amar and Desta ate them for her.

Kaklee ordered a bowl of black soup with shiny crunchy bits in it and ate it with careful slurps of its long, prehensile tongue. Amar had almost as much fun watching Kaklee eat as he did eating his own dinner—which was a pile of pancakes topped with mountains of mildly sweet whipped cream.

After that, full and satisfied and monumentally tired, Amar felt himself leaning forward on the table. Desta had already gone to sleep against Kaklee's side.

He felt Odd pick him up again—he pretended to be fast asleep so he would not be made to walk—and carry him away from the loud restaurant. He opened an eye briefly to see Kaklee carrying Desta in its wiry arms. The creature winked at him.

They arrived at the gravity lock again. He heard Odd say something about "Leaving it in dock seven. Must get them home, you see . . . " and the next thing he knew he was weightless, and then the next thing after *that* he was back in Odd's very own ship. He blinked his eyes against the colored lights and looked around.

Kaklee was gone, and so was the station. He was sitting in a comfortable armchair with Desta tucked in beside him. Odd was sitting a little ways away at her console.

"Ready to go home?" she asked.

Amar stretched, careful not to wake his sister.

"Sounds good," he said.

"All right then," said Odd, and flipped a lever. With the gentlest flicker of lights and a low thrumming sound that Amar felt more than heard, the whole place shifted around him, and the next thing he knew Odd was propping open the door at the end of the hallway by his room.

Odd carried Desta down the stairs and into his house, but Amar insisted on walking. He saw that Odd tucked Desta in the way she liked, with her favorite stuffed dog up under her chin, and then at last he tottered across the way and into his own room. He kicked off his shoes and crawled into bed, curling up halfway on top of his pillows. He was so tired every part of him hurt, his face was dirty, his fingers still smelled of dinner, and he had never been happier.

The last thing he heard, before he drifted off completely, was Odd's voice saying, "Good night," and the click of his door as it shut tight behind her.

"The Monster's Daughter" is composed of two stories: "The Detective" and "Subject 0-D"—which are presented here back to back. "The Monster's Daughter" is the sixth Professor Odd *novella and marks a turning point in that series. Though you need not have read the first five (available individually from Heliopause), it helps to know that, despite being the titular character of that series, little is actually known about Professor Odd. What she is, where she came from, even how she got her name, has remained a mystery. "The Monster's Daughter" attempts to change that, a little. It was written in the summer of 2013.*

The Monster's Daughter

It was decided, after much discussion, that they would visit London.

"Yes, but *which* London?" Elo asked. "We have a choice of an almost infinite number."

"Rapid Gregorian," Professor Odd replied brightly.

"Which one is *that?*" Alister wondered aloud.

"Why, the one that suffered the least damage in World War II," Professor Odd said as she twirled the levers on the Oddity's control panel.

"Technically it's a series of universes, not a single one," Elo amended. "But they are similar enough it doesn't much matter which one we get."

The lights of the cockpit flashed, sparkling on and off, while the Oddity emitted a series of musical hums and beeps. At last there was a deep *bonnnnng* from within the ship (machine—place—*thing* . . . Alister still wasn't sure what it was) and a slight tremor went through the floor. Something shifted, and the lights changed subtly.

Professor Odd pushed her chair back and frowned. She reached up under her wig—deep ultramarine blue today—and rubbed her hairless scalp.

"Something wrong?" Elo asked.

Raising a hand for silence, Professor Odd got up and walked down the stairs to the Oddity's front door. Now that they were tethered to a universe, it appeared to be a solid wooden door with an old-fashioned latch. Professor Odd opened it and put first her head, then the rest of her body, outside.

Coming up behind her, Alister saw a dull gray sky cut by the horizon of a city: craggy old spires mixed with turn-of-the-millennium arches and glass domes. There was a smell of wet pavement and rubbish—such a familiar combination to Alister that he went fearlessly out the door, hopping briskly down a set of steps to the street.

Professor Odd was an incongruous splash of color in the otherwise grayish landscape: her blue wig and green coat standing out sharply against the black asphalt of the road and the subdued tans and browns of the houses to either side.

To Alister, who had spent the better part of his life living in a big, old city, it felt breathlessly, achingly familiar. Right down to the rubbish bins set out on the pavement and the antennas and power lines strung overhead. He took a deep breath of the thick, city air, and quietly rejoiced even as his heart broke a little inside. He had not known until then just how much he had missed his old home. Even so, he felt an immense calm engulf him. If he closed his eyes and forgot about the inter-dimensional portal just behind him, he could imagine he *was* home.

Professor Odd, meanwhile, was anything but calm. She marched to the end of the street and looked both ways. She strode back, her coattails flapping behind her, and stopped by the nearest rubbish bin. She lifted its lid and looked inside. She knelt and stroked a finger over the wet pavement. She held it up. She opened her mouth and stuck out her tongue—Alister noticed it was mottled pink and greenish, not unlike her bare scalp.

He and Elo watched her, curious, but not alarmed.

Not alarmed until Professor Odd came at them, arms wide, and shooed them back into the Oddity.

"Inside," she said sharply. "Back inside, quickly, don't say a word. Go."

They went, tripping over each other, and Professor Odd slammed the door behind them.

"Wrong universe?" Elo asked.

"Wrong series," Professor Odd said. She sat down at the control panel, tapped a few buttons and pulled a lever.

The Oddity let out a deep, mournful groan. Professor Odd chewed a finger, then tapped out a longer string one-handed while she slowly began turning a hand crank under the desk of colored buttons.

Alister felt as though every atom in his body was being pulled apart. He screamed. Elo howled in pain. Dave, who had been maneuvering his panvironment suit down the ladder from the second floor, plummeted and hit the ground with a sickening *thud.*

Professor Odd quickly back-wound the crank and pressed a large yellow button.

The pain stopped as abruptly as it had begun, and Alister blinked the tears out of his eyes to find Professor Odd stroking the Oddity's cockpit and murmuring apologies.

"*What* was *that* about?" Elo demanded.

Without a word Professor Odd got up and went back to the front door—which was unchanged. She opened it.

The same dull, gray-and-brown street lay outside. She came back up the stairs, her face white as paper and her mouth pressed into a thin, humorless line.

"Professor?" Alister asked. "What's wrong with the Oddity?"

"WE HAVE BECOME WOVEN TO THE UNIVERSE," Dave announced, making them all jump. "WE WILL NOT BE ABLE TO LEAVE UNTIL WE UNTANGLE OURSELVES."

"Yes, but *which* universe?" Elo prodded. "Professor, *what* is out there?"

Professor Odd raised a hand and chewed nervously on a fingernail. She wrapped her arms tightly about herself and looked at them with wide, jaguar eyes.

Alister felt a cold dread grip his insides as he realized that Professor Odd, who had faced down killer robots, flying whales, dinosaurs and giant sea monsters . . . Professor Odd, who grinned like a maniac in the face of imminent death . . . that *Professor Odd* was scared.

"It's the wrong universe all right," she said in a dry, hoarse voice. "Out there . . . that's *my* universe. And we're *stuck in it.*"

Part One: The Detective

ALISTER STARED OUT THE WINDOW in fascinated horror. Where there should have been nothing—the vast black-blue emptiness between universes, pricked with the lights of distant worlds—now he looked out past the lacy curtains and the thick panes to the water-stained brick wall of the house next to them. They were separated by a narrow footpath in which a broken ladder sprawled despairingly. The sight scared him almost as much as the nothing had the first time he'd looked out the Oddity's window.

"Okay," he said, swallowing down a bubble of panic. "How did this happen?" He preferred to think about that—why was the Oddity, which normally attached and detached from universes with the flick of a switch, now so thoroughly embedded in this one?—Rather than the more distressing question: *why did Professor Odd not want to be in her home universe?*

There were a number of reasons why Alister did not want to return to *his* home world—unfriendly men in hazmat suits working for a sinister corporation called the Canary Company chief among them. If there was something similar in Professor Odd's world . . .

"Someone . . . " Professor Odd was scanning a scrolling wall of code in a language Alister could not decipher on one of the cockpit's little screens. "Someone . . . *called* us here. Called the *Oddity* here, I mean. It's the strongest working of transdimensional adhesivism I've ever *seen.*"

"Does your world have that technology?" Alister asked. "Is that how they built the Oddity?"

"The Oddity doesn't come from my world," Professor Odd said. "And no, they *don't* have this kind of tech—I made sure—" she cut herself off. Alister and Elo looked at each other uncertainly.

The mutant wolf rubbed her paw-hands together. "Uh, Professor—" she began nervously, when Dave interrupted them.

He rolled his panvironment suit around the table and came to a halt at the Professor's elbow.

"WE NEED TO COMMUNICATE," he said in an even more abrasive tone than usual.

Professor Odd blinked at him. "I'm listening," she said.

"I DID NOT MEAN VIA AUDIBLE SPEECH," Dave said meaningfully. "TAKE OFF YOUR HAIRPIECE."

"Oh," said Professor Odd.

"Oh," said Elo. "I'll go get some towels."

Dave was not psychic. Professor Odd had explained this to Alister before. Rather, he communicated through psychoactive slime that he secreted from the fine, anemone-like tentacles that grew from the back side of his disk-shaped body. It was a somewhat more efficient form of communication, since the words were transferred directly into the recipient's head without having to be translated by the ears. Because of this, more information could be exchanged within a shorter period of time. The disadvantage was that it made a mess.

Which was why Professor Odd spent the next half hour sitting in the kitchen alcove with her head in the sink, Dave visible only as a couple of twining, green tentacle-arms dangling over the side.

Elo busied herself at the Oddity's console, pushing buttons, listening to the unhappy beeping noises, and occasionally swearing under her breath in a language that sounded like growling.

Alister sat by the window and watched what he could see of the street. His view was mostly blocked by a cracked and splintering wooden gate with a rusty latch, but beyond that he could glimpse the upper stories of the houses across the main road. These were a block of uniform, cream-colored houses, each with rusty brown trim around the windows. Alister wondered if their front doors matched, or if residents were allowed to express their individuality by painting them different colors. He suspected not. The whole street was so drab and uniform, any creativity would likely be treated as a sign of rebellion.

Was his own world this depressing? It wasn't as colorful as the Oddity, of course, and perhaps not as vibrantly strange as some of the worlds they had visited, but surely it wasn't as bad as this place.

Was it?

Alister was a little shocked to discover how little he remembered about his own world. Perhaps because, when he was in it, he simply thought of it as *the* world, with no possibility for alternate realities. Would he even recognize it if he ever returned? Or, like the Professor, would he know immediately by some inner instinct? He hoped so.

Something passed by on the street beyond the fence. It was difficult to see, and Alister couldn't hear anything through the thick window pane, but he thought it was a car.

"There it goes *again,*" Elo said.

Alister got up and went over to her console. She had gotten one of the Oddity's screens to display a view of the street equivalent to looking out their front door. From there Alister could confirm that all the houses opposite had the same color doors. The only way to tell them apart was their number plates and the different curtains just visible peeping around the edges of their front windows.

"There went what again?" he asked.

"The same black car. I don't like it." She wrinkled her nose. "I think they're scanning."

"Scanning for what?"

"With our luck? *Us.*"

"They're looking for me," Professor Odd said from behind them both.

She had a towel draped around her neck and was using a corner of it to wipe the last of Dave's slime out of her ear.

"What are we going to do?" Alister posed the obvious question, rather dreading the answer.

Professor Odd shrugged unhappily. "We have two choices," she said. "We wait here until Dave and I figure out a way to get the Oddity untangled—which I have no idea how long it will take and they may find a way of getting inside in that time—or . . ." she finished wiping her head off and looked thoughtfully at the screen.

Elo turned right around in her seat. "Or *what?*" she demanded.

Professor Odd looked up at them and put on a bright, humorless grin. "Or I go out and *see what they want.*"

So saying she whipped around and scrambled up the ladder to the catwalk that ran the circumference of the interior. There was a clatter as she pattered along it and a slam as she disappeared behind the door with a brass O-D bolted to the center.

She returned a few minutes later looking . . . well, not looking very much like Professor Odd at all. She had somehow convinced the Oddity—which supplied their clothes—to make her a mousy gray overcoat and a similarly mousy brown wig. Her blue pinstriped trousers had been replaced with dull gray ones, and she carried a black umbrella. With dark, round glasses covering her eyes and a thick, charcoal-colored scarf around her neck she looked alarmingly *normal.*

Alister and Elo stared in horror.

"What are you *doing?*" Alister blurted out.

Professor Odd shrugged. "There's no running from some things," she said with a sigh. "You best sit tight while I get it sorted out. Shouldn't take too long. Be back before you know it."

She strode down the steps to the front door and there stopped.

"Is it clear?" she called back up.

Elo bounced over to the screen and examined the view of the street.

"Deserted," she replied.

Professor Odd came back up the stairs at once and went over to one of the windows. With a deft tap and shove, she pushed it open.

The smell of wet concrete, car exhaust and a faint hint of rubbish flooded into the Oddity.

"They want me to come out the front," Professor Odd explained, throwing a leg out the window.

The rest of her soon followed. They were so high up she had to hang by her hands in order to drop to the ground. Alister tossed the umbrella down after her. He saw why she wanted it: outside, the gray sky had opened up, and it was beginning to rain.

Professor Odd caught the umbrella one-handed and grinned at him.

"Keep the windows closed," she said. "Don't go outside."

She opened the umbrella and promptly disappeared under it, moving swiftly down the alley in the opposite direction from the street. Alister watched her go, feeling deeply unsettled.

No sooner had he and Elo got the window shut again than there was a knock on the door. Alister nearly jumped out of his skin; the Oddity's door was somewhat detached from reality, and he'd never heard someone knock on it before.

If it startled Elo she didn't show it. She went over to the console and checked the screen.

"Oh dear," she said.

Alister came and leaned over her shoulder.

A tall, dark-haired man in a neat black suit wearing dark gloves stood outside. He was pale-skinned, with a long, delicate nose and a high, arching brow.

Something about the shape of him jostled uneasily in Alister's memory. He'd seen that profile before, surely, a long time ago and very far away.

There was a hiss and rumble as Dave came up behind them in his panvironment suit.

"IT WAS HIM. I THOUGHT SO," he said through his translator.

"Him? You know him?" Elo demanded, turning around.

"NOT YET," said Dave. "HE IS ANOTHER TRAVELER."

Alister didn't bother to ask was that meant. He had a pretty good idea.

They sat and watched the dark figure on the screen until, with a little shrug, the man turned and walked away down the steps.

What came after was something that had rarely occurred since Alister had come on board the Oddity: boredom. Quite literally, nothing happened. Dave opened a panel beside one of the cockpits and began pulling out the wiring using little claw-like appendages that sprouted from the front of his panvironment suit. Elo sat in the other cockpit, watching the readout on one of the monitors and saying things like: "Nope, nothing," or, "Wait, I think that made it worse . . . "

Left with nothing useful to do, Alister went and sat by the window with the best view. This overlooked a part of their neighbor's garden, and Alister could see a ratty lawn and some washing hung out to dry. The sun appeared to have come out, and a breeze blew, flapping the towels and shirts and trousers pinned to the line.

There was an unhappy buzzing sound from where Dave worked. Elo gave a yip of triumph.

Outside, the world suddenly grew dark. There was a flash of white and gray that distorted the view, and then it was past. The laundry was nowhere to be seen, and everything was soaking wet.

Alister blinked.

"What did you just do?" he asked, turning around in his seat.

"I HAVE MANAGED TO EXTRICATE US FROM THE NATIVE TIME STREAM," Dave intoned. "THIS WILL GIVE US MORE TIME TO FIGURE OUT A SOLUTION."

"Uh . . . " Elo said, squinting at her screen.

Outside, Alister saw the shadows lengthening, stretching into twilight. Night fell, streetlights came on. Then the dark sky turned gray, and another day dawned . . . only to rush by at the same speed. It was like watching an extremely long, extremely boring time-lapse video.

"I think you pushed it too far the other way," Elo remarked. "Time is moving faster out there than it is in here."

"It's been at least two days out there." Alister blinked. Was it speeding up? "Or . . . three?"

"OH . . . BUGGER," Dave said.

They watched a few weeks flit by. Eventually Alister drew the curtains, since the days and nights were flashing past at such a speed it was almost like a strobe light.

"So, is this a good thing or a bad thing?" Alister asked.

"Depends," said Elo, scratching behind one ear. "It's good that Dave's managed to make some progress separating the Oddity from this universe. But . . . "

"But weeks—maybe *months*—have passed outside," Alister pointed out. "Where's the Professor?"

"THE TEMPORAL DISCREPANCY SHOULD NOT INTERFERE WITH THE ODDITY'S DOORWAY," Dave said.

"In other words," Elo explained hastily. "Just because the time-synch's messed up, it shouldn't prevent Professor Odd from re-entering the Oddity."

This, Alister decided, was not at all comforting. The way she had been acting, he'd expected her to be back in a day or so. But outside the Oddity (or, inside the universe) weeks had been flashing by for several minutes. *Where was she?*

"Something's gone wrong," he said tightly.

"You got *that* right," Elo said dryly. "This whole debacle smells funny to me. Why'd she go out *alone* anyway?"

Dread gripped Alister by the stomach. He swallowed hard. He had been too relieved at being left behind to wonder *why* Professor Odd had neglected to drag her companions along. What had she said? *Don't go outside . . .*

She was trying to protect them.

From whatever was in her native universe.

In which she was currently trapped. Alone.

Alister groaned as he realized what he had to do.

"She's in trouble," Elo said decisively. "She needs help."

"IT WOULD BE UNWISE," Dave said, "TO INVADE A UNIVERSE OF WHICH YOU KNOW VERY LITTLE."

"We're not doing her any good in here," Alister pointed out glumly.

"*YOU* ARE NOT," Dave said. "I AM ATTEMPTING TO SAVE US ALL." And so saying he turned back to the gutted control panel.

Alister looked down at Elo. Elo looked back up at him out of her soft, furry face, but her eyes were dark and grave.

"We'd better go in after her," he said.

"She probably needs help," Elo agreed. She pulled aside the curtain and peered out. "Looks like a fairly standard Britannia Class III. I'll go get my harness."

While Elo went to assemble her disguise as a seeing-eye dog, Alister returned to his own room to see if the Oddity had given him any clothes that would not stick out like a sore thumb in the Professor's drab, ordinary world. He slid open the door to his closet, and stared.

Where there should have been rack upon rack of vibrantly colored shirts, coats, and trousers, there was only his original outfit—the clothes he had been wearing when he had first come on board the Oddity. They were a little crumpled and depressingly flat compared to the wardrobe Alister had become accustomed to, but they fit perfectly with the dull world outside.

What made Alister stare was that there was nothing else. In fact his closet, which before had seemed like a whole room of its own, was now hardly bigger than a broom cupboard. Now he looked around, did his room also look shrunken?

Alister changed his clothes, noting that his window now looked out onto a water-stained brick wall. A bird had left droppings on the sill.

"I think something's wrong with the Oddity," he said when he emerged.

"Tell me something I *don't* know," Elo snapped. She was standing outside her room having difficulty with one of the buckles on her harness. Alister came over and did it for her.

"Did you notice anything . . . em . . . *wrong* with your room?" he asked.

Elo gave him an arch look at that, but she didn't have to look as far as her room: the shriveled, shrunken effect was now visible in the walls and floor of the main area. The table, which even under normal circumstances was piled with junk, looked ready to collapse. Its edges were also noticeably closer to the walls.

"Dave!" Elo shouted, sliding down the ladder.

"THE SPATIAL MAINTENANCE STABILIZERS HAVE BEEN SABOTAGED—I *KNOW*." Dave had several tools and two of his tentacle arms (safely encased in metallic cloth) buried in the Oddity's wiring. There was an angry, humming sound.

"What does that mean?" Alister asked with a nervous glance at the table, where it looked like a tricycle was about to tumble off.

Elo heaved a sigh. "Basically?" she said. "It means the Oddity has to jettison nonvital spaces in order to keep its systems running."

"Nonvital spaces . . . like my *room?*"

"Like our living area," Elo muttered. "Come on, we don't have a lot of time. Help me get this window open." She'd gone to the side and was heaving at the frame. It seemed stuck. Alister came over and hit it. It came loose with an ominous creak.

"Hang tight, Dave," she said, sliding nimbly outside. "We'll be back in a jiff." She dropped out of sight.

"IF YOU ARE NOT," Dave said, "I WILL COME FIND YOU."

"Will you be all right . . . here?" Alister asked, pausing with one leg hanging over the sill.

"I WILL MANAGE," Dave said. "I POSSESS RESOURCES YOU DO NOT."

And that seemed to be all. It was not a very large drop to the path on this side of the house, and Alister let himself down gradually by his hands so he had only a few feet to fall.

As he straightened up, rubbing his palms where they had chafed against the sill, he heard the window slam shut above them.

"Think he'll be all right?" he asked Elo.

"Better worry about *us,*" Elo replied, handing him a pair of dark, round glasses. Professor Odd's glasses. The ones she had been wearing the first time Alister had seen her. He took a deep breath and put them on.

"Hold the handle attached to my harness," Elo instructed, dropping to all fours. "Right there—yes. Oh, and you can talk to me, but I won't reply unless no one can hear. Crazy blind people talking to their dogs is all right. It's when the dog starts talking back that people notice."

"And we don't want to be noticed," Alister hazarded.

For answer, Elo put her nose to the ground and began leading him down the narrow alley.

The short man with russet-brown hair sat in a dark room filled with computers. The hum of their hard drives was a soothing rumble, and the heat they gave off served to make the room the only decently warm place in the whole building.

It was dark; the only light came from the bank of monitors arranged on the wall opposite the man. By their wan light he pulled open a drawer and got out a packet of crisps, which he opened with a satisfying *rip.* He pushed a hand inside, and for a few moments thereafter the sound of the computers was joined by the crack and crunch of crisps being eaten. Then the crunching slowed. Finally it stopped altogether.

The man had forgotten to chew. Indeed, had probably forgotten all about the half-full bag of crisps still in his hand—even though he was the sort of man who would never forget about food in the normal course of things.

This, though. This was so far outside the range of normalcy that it eclipsed everything else.

To an untrained observer it did not look particularly alarming. One of the computer screens was now displaying a flashing red dot on a matrix of blue and white lines.

The short man with russet hair, however, was not only trained, but trained extremely well. He knew exactly what a flashing red dot on that screen meant, and the thought made the last of the crisps take on the importance of something rather less than dust.

With shaking hands he reached back into his desk drawer and removed a telephone directory. He opened it to the back page where someone had scrawled a number in black marker, along with a suggestive message. Then he reached into his coat pocket and removed a slip of paper. On it was written another, shorter number in neat pencil.

The man picked up the handset of the landline and carefully dialed the number written in the back of the phone book. When a breathy female voice asked him what sort of experience he was looking for, the man repeated the number off the slip of paper. He was careful to enunciate.

"Just a moment," the voice said, suddenly going clipped and businesslike. Then there was a *click* and the line filled with the roar of static. Then there was another *click* and absolute silence.

Out of the silence a smooth male voice said:

"What is it?"

"Er, yes, hello?" said the man. His voice was high and crackly, mostly from nerves. "Parsons, from Greentower. Yes, well, I was told to call this number if I ever had a breach."

"Please don't waste my time, Philip Parsons," said the voice out of the silence. It was rich and resonant, but at the same time icy cold. The way it dropped in the "please" implied that it didn't think such a word was necessary, but that it knew that the more words it said, the longer you had to listen to it, and the longer you listened the more time you would have to imagine all the terrible things that would happen to you if you upset its owner.

"How'd you know my name's Philip?" asked Philip Parsons, agitated beyond reason.

Silence.

"Because I know you, Philip. I know you very well. Consider this fact, alongside the fact that you do not know me at all, before you answer," said the voice. And added: *"Please."* The word sent shivers down Philip Parsons's spine.

"It's . . . er . . . the probability on Napswitch Road," he stammered. "There's been a breach. Class 6, easily. I think two bodies got through."

"I . . . see," said the voice, a terrible gap between the two words.

"Shall I send the coordinates over to you, like last time?"

"No." The voice was clipped now, as if its owner were walking briskly. "We do not know which lines the Professor has compromised."

"Oh? Don't we . . . er, sir?"

"I will retrieve the logs," said the voice. "Manually."

"Very good, sir," said Philip Parsons.

"You've done well, Philip," said the voice, though its tone suggested the opposite. "Your shift is almost over. You will be . . . relieved."

"Yes sir, thank you sir," babbled the poor man. "It's been an honor working with—working *for* you, that is. Sir . . . Detective, sir . . . "

Nothing. The silence now was only the silence of a dead line. Philip looked at the receiver in his hand and shuddered.

They had, all of them—his whole team—been briefed on the Detective. Lots of smoke and mirrors, Charlie had said. But it took a lot to impress Charlie, and none of them had ever met the Detective. Until now, none of them had even spoken with him.

Perhaps *that* would impress Charlie, Philip Parsons thought. On further consideration, however, he imagined she would just roll her eyes at him and say *"Yes* Philip, but how d'you *know* it was him?"

Wait. Hadn't the voice on the phone said *he* was coming *here?* All of a sudden the only thing Philip Parsons could think about was how he had managed to spill crisps all over his chair. *That* would never do. He shuffled around, trying to find a hand broom.

On the computer screen, the red light flashed.

An hour later, Philip Parsons walked down the street outside his building, his head pleasantly empty. The last few hours seemed rather blurry, but this did not concern him. When your job consists primarily of watching nothing happen, blurry memory can be a mercy. He did feel hungry, though, as if his snack time had been interrupted. He altered course to take him toward the fish-and-chips shop that he particularly fancied.

His route took him through a small alley between two tall buildings. To someone observing him from afar, it would have appeared that Philip Parsons—short, brown-headed and rather round—walked in one side . . . and nothing came out the other. Closer inspection would have revealed the alley to be quite empty.

To Philip Parsons, the world went a bit dark and uncertain for a while. He felt sick and confused—and also frightened around the edges.

When his world firmed up again he was sitting in a squeaky leather chair in a cool, dark room. The light this time was provided by a single paraffin lamp placed directly before him. It had a stained-glass shade with dragonflies on it. Philip Parsons noticed this because this was all he could see: the room beyond was lost in glare and shadows.

"Mr. . . . *Parsons,*" said a raspy voice from beyond the light. "Please, don't agitate yourself. I'm not going to harm you. I simply wish to know what happened to you at work this afternoon."

"C-can't . . . remember . . . " Philip Parsons forced out through an uncooperative mouth.

The person behind the light chuckled. "I thought as much. Fortunately I wasn't counting on you being able to *tell* me, so we're going to go about it a slightly different way. Do you know why you can't remember this afternoon, Mr. Parsons?"

"Boring job," said Philip Parsons, trying to sit forward and see around the lamp. There appeared to be restraints on his hands and something on his head like a soft bicycle helmet. He began to panic then, his heart thudding in his chest.

"Don't upset yourself, Mr. Parsons," said the scratchy voice. "I'm trying to help you. Look, see, I'll tell you why you can't remember what happened this afternoon. You want to know why, don't you?"

"I want to go *home*," said Philip Parsons petulantly.

"You met the Detective, Mr. Parsons. You spoke to him. You *saw* him."

That triggered something in Philip Parsons's mind. Not a memory per se, but rather, it made him aware of an empty patch in his head where a memory *should* have gone.

He'd spilled his crisps, and he'd been worried about the mess. Because the Detective . . . the *Detective* . . .

"L-look," he stammered. "If he made me forget, it was for a *reason*, right? So I wouldn't give away . . . give away . . . " he gulped, realizing the enormity of what he had just said, and just who it implied was sitting on the other side of the kitschy lamp.

"*I* don't think that was very nice of him," said the voice. It was hard to tell; was it male or female? He'd heard a rumor that the Professor was a woman. And Philip Parsons was becoming more and more certain that it *was* the Professor who sat opposite him.

"Relax, Mr. Parsons," said the voice soothingly. "I could extract this knowledge from you without your cognizance, but that, I believe, would only compound your problems. Watch and learn, Mr. Parsons. Watch and *learn*."

It then appeared to Philip Parsons that a screen was lowered before his eyes, and he saw there a vision of his day, beginning with the breakfast of eggs and bacon he'd had that morning.

"A bit early, this is," said the voice, and then the images appeared to go on fast-forward like a videotape. They slowed down again when he got to work, then sped up through his morning, his lunch, and into the afternoon. They came crashing back to normal speeds when a red light started flashing on one of his monitors, and Philip Parsons watched in astonishment as he reviewed his actions—saw his hands drop the packet of crisps, saw himself get out the phone directory and his passcode. Saw himself pick up the phone and dial a number.

He listened to himself call the Detective and the halting conversation that followed. In the silence after he hung up, the images sped up again.

"Interesting," said the voice of the person he was almost certain was the Professor.

Then things slowed down again. Philip Parsons watched himself get up and turn at a noise from the back of the building. He saw two people enter: one was a dark-skinned woman in a severe gray suit, while the other was a tall, pale man with black hair wearing a long black coat. His eyes were like chips of obsidian, and their gaze bore into Philip Parsons's head both in the past and present.

In his memory he watched the tall man stride over, neatly stepping across the bundle of cables that crossed the floor. He thought the man was coming to talk to him, but instead he was ignored and the man bent forward to examine the monitor.

In the present, the Professor made a little sound like *"Ah . . . "*

In the past, the woman in the severe gray suit said: "Shall I relieve Mr. Parsons, Detective?"

The Detective turned away from the monitor and looked at him. Up close, he decided, his eyes were more like black wells. He felt like if he looked at them for too long he might fall in. So he looked away.

"Yes, that would be just as well, Gretchen."

Things got rather blurry after that, but he thought he saw the Detective copy something off the computer onto a small mobile drive. Then the woman in the gray suit took his place, and he was steered out of the room by the man in the black coat.

"I think that is all there is worth seeing," said the voice beyond the light, and the screen before his eyes was lifted.

Philip Parsons blinked, wishing he could rub his eyes. "I don't understand," he whined miserably.

"That's all right," said the Professor soothingly. "Very few people do. Relax, Mr. Parsons, it will make this all so much easier . . . "

Philip Parsons saw a shape rise behind the light, and an arm reached forward. He opened his mouth to scream and then his world went dark and uncertain again.

And then . . .

And then he was walking down the street outside his building, his head pleasantly empty.

The city they had emerged into frustrated Alister no end. It had bits that reminded him of London and bits that reminded him of Oxford. Then he remembered that, in his native universe, he'd never *been* to Oxford. All his memories of Oxford were from a version created by a sentient machine on a world where humans survived by going into suspended animation while their minds lived out lives in a constructed reality.

In any case, this city had bits that reminded him of *that* Oxford.

There were also bits that reminded him (eerily, achingly) of his own home. It was there in the little things: the underground signs, the trains, and the shape of the cars.

And there were things that were like nothing he'd seen on any world.

The skypods, for one thing.

These were small, circular objects large enough for two people to sit inside that whizzed by overhead on a wire suspended high above the treetops and most of the roofs. At first Alister had mistaken them for power lines, until the first pod came through. He'd started so suddenly that Elo had growled at him.

"You're *blind,* remember?"

So Alister had reined in his gawking, and made a point of fixing his head skyward so he could watch the pods race by without appearing to be looking at anything in particular. Like this he tripped several times on uneven pavement, which to his mind rather authenticated the disguise.

This city, he soon deduced, was called Londinium, which he assumed meant it was indeed this world's version of London. Elo seemed to be leading him—if his fuzzy memories of his own London were any indication—toward Trafalgar Square, and the streets were becoming increasingly crowded.

The people of Londinium seemed as drab and ordinary as the world they lived in. The only patches of color were on the gold lapels of couriers in uniform and the rare punkish teenager. Grays and browns and muted blues seemed to be the most popular clothing colors, and faces were all pale and a little sagging.

It was strangely liberating, pretending to be blind. In the ordinary way Alister was very conscientious about eye contact, but from behind the shield of his dark glasses he found he could stare at people quite blatantly.

He saw young people, old people, and people in the middle. He saw people with dark hair, fair hair, and even a few redheads. He saw people with no hair at all. He saw people hidden under large, floppy hats, and people hunched over, reading things on their small tablet mobiles. There were even a few people reading newspapers.

Elo stopped. They were at a strange sort of intersection where the road they were on joined another fork. While waiting for the walk signal, Alister noticed a little stand selling magazines and newspapers. The headline of one was so big it was readable, and what it said grabbed his attention at once.

PROFESSOR STRIKES BACK

And then some smaller text that was cut off at the fold. Alister nudged Elo with his knee.

"Read the paper," he muttered.

Elo looked. She read the paper. The light turned, and they walked on.

A few blocks later Elo stopped by a table outside a cafe. At first Alister did not understand why, and then he saw another copy of that same paper abandoned on a chair.

"You're clear," Elo growled through her teeth. "Grab it."

Alister did. He even had the presence of mind to tuck it inside his coat. Because what could a blind person want with a paper?

They walked on until Elo found a small alley and darted into it. After carefully checking for cameras and inconvenient windows (there were none), she stood up.

"Let's see it then," she said.

Alister removed the paper and handed it to her, then took off his dark glasses. Like that he could read the story over her shoulder.

It went:

> *Gravesend, Londinium.* A new batch of secret cables has been publicly released by the notorious hacker known as the Professor. These details contain, among other things, the complete correspondence between the American Union and its embassy in Persia, as well as several dossiers it keeps on Persian citizens. The Persian government . . .

Here the article went on at length about the political ramifications of said information becoming public, which made almost no sense to Alister. Elo skipped over it anyway, flipping to an interior page where they read:

> This counts as only the latest in a string of acts by the Professor to force transparency on international governments. The Professor, whose current location and identity are unknown, has stated that they are not partisan, but that they intend to provide common people with the information they need to make informed decisions. Though it is rumored that the Professor is a single person, experts believe it to be a small group of close-knit hackers, crackers, and informants. The Professor has been labeled a terrorist group by the American Union and the European Council, and anyone with information as to their whereabouts is requested to contact their local law enforcement. The local hotline is . . .

Alister didn't bother to read the number that followed. He blinked at Elo, trying to clear his head.

"Sounds like *she's* been busy," he said in a stunned voice.

"This makes no sense," Elo mused, folding the paper over. She frowned at the headline.

"Not like her?" Alister queried.

"Not like her . . . *in this circumstance,*" Elo said. "If this even is our Professor. It's not like she has a trademark on the title."

Alister had to agree. "What do you mean, 'in this circumstance'?"

"Well," Elo sighed, sitting down and leaning back against the wall. "She said she was going to see who brought us here and why. This? This doesn't look like her collecting information. This looks more like . . . like . . . " Elo scratched under her ear nervously.

"Like *what?*" Alister burst out.

Elo looked up at him, a nervous crease between her eyes. "Like she's in it for the long game. Like she thinks she's *stuck* here."

There was a screech of engines, and a dark car pulled up at the mouth of their alley. It was the large sort with tinted black windows and a humorless, professional exterior. It looked so much like the sort of car that serious men in dark suits drove in certain kinds of American films that Alister almost wasn't surprised when a tall man in a black coat got out of the passenger seat and walked down the alley toward them. He was pale-skinned with short black hair, and his hands were hidden inside dark leather gloves. He was undoubtedly the same man who had knocked on the Oddity's door earlier that day—or several months ago, depending on the universe. Just as assuredly, he was the same man Alister had seen somewhere before.

It was the walk that did it—a particular, powerful sort of walk that took a person places. At the same time the man was so self contained and confident that he almost appeared lazy, as though he were strolling through a park.

The last time Alister had seen that walk, he'd been halfway out of his wits with fright in a virtual reality constructed by a sentient machine.

Now he stood and stared.

"You—" he began.

"Run you fool!" Elo barked, and grabbed his sleeve in her teeth.

This jerked some sense into Alister's brain. He noticed the other two men who had also gotten out of the car while he was staring. They were not as tall as the first man, but half again as wide and just as serious looking.

Alister ran.

The alley they had taken refuge in dead ended in a ten-foot brick wall. Elo bounded toward it, leapt, grasped the top with her long paws, and then kicked her hind end up and over. She reached back down and grabbed Alister by the arm.

Elo was a large canine, but she was still smaller than a human. There would have been no way for her to haul Alister up the wall had not his foot found a hold where a brick had been knocked out. Using it as a step Alister was able to get his own hands over the wall, and Elo helped him along, pulling at his jacket.

Even as he flung one leg over he felt a hand close on his dangling ankle, and he kicked out blindly. Then he was over and falling down the other side.

Luckily, here someone had pushed a large dustbin up against the wall, and Alister was able to break his fall with it.

Dazed, his hands and knees stinging, Alister limped away from the wall—he had landed awkwardly and now his left ankle was complaining. Elo was by his side on all fours.

"Come *on!*" she growled.

Alister had just the presence of mind to grab hold of her harness before she took off. Like that he was able to keep up as they tore down the alley toward the bustle of the main street. As they reached it, Alister chanced a glance back.

The men had also scaled the wall. One of them was talking into a radio.

Alister and Elo ran down the street. They went faster than Alister would have, favoring his left leg and uncertain where to go, but they also went much slower than Elo could have gone on her own. Alister was sure of this. He was also just as sure that, going the pace they were going, the men would catch them. Every time he chanced a glance back they were a little closer. There was a large black car following them, and would, Alister was certain, catch up with them once it sorted out the traffic.

They couldn't escape together, but on their own, one of them might.

"Elo," Alister gasped, wincing at the pain in his ankle. "Elo, you've got to leave me."

"Not an option!" Elo barked, making a sharp turn that was nearly the end of Alister. They were on a straight road filled with traffic now, beyond which Alister could glimpse a wide, gray river. They had lost the car, but now the three men were in sight behind them and had been joined by another two.

"*Think!*" Alister gasped. "You could drop these guys in an instant—*you* could get away. But not with me hanging on to you!"

"And where does that leave you?" Elo growled, making a nearby pedestrian jump.

"I'll manage," Alister panted.

"No, you won't," Elo snapped. "You'll get taken."

"Better me than you!" They had to jump out into traffic to pass a slow-moving couple with a stroller and nearly collided with an oncoming car. Alister grunted at the pain in his ankle.

They ran on a few more strides while Elo thought over the implications of this. On their own she could escape, Alister could not. Of the two of them, she would be better able to survive in this world; she would be better able to forage for information, and she could provide Professor Odd, when found, with all sorts of help involving sharp teeth, claws, and if need be, technical assistance. Whereas Alister could do none of those things.

What Alister could do was be an ordinary person who wouldn't excite the natives of this universe by being an unknown animal.

"We'll come back for you," was all she said.

"Oh aye," said Alister. "I'm counting on it."

He let go of her harness.

Relieved of her burden, Elo darted away up the road. Alister saw her disappear up a side street before his view was blocked by two heavyset men coming down the pavement toward him. Alister limped to a stop. He watched as they ambled past the road Elo had taken.

Alister took a breath and turned to check behind him. The three original men and their two new friends were within shouting distance. They would be on him in less than a minute.

Alister tested his bad ankle, which twinged ominously. He didn't have many options.

Still, it seemed rather a waste to let them catch him so easily.

Alister darted out across the road, aiming for the path on the far side.

The oncoming car—one of the ubiquitous black cabs—saw him and slammed on its brakes. This was why, when it hit him, it was only going about fifteen miles per hour. Which was why Alister was still conscious when he hit the asphalt ten feet away. He was conscious of the fact that he could not breathe, and of how very hard the road was, and of something wet running down the side of his head.

Then things got a bit muddled.

For clarity's sake, it shall be explained thus:

The woman riding in the back seat of the cab that hit Alister heard the driver's shocked exclamation and saw a body flying through the air. She thought: a body that goes *up* after being hit by a car has a chance of still being alive when it comes back down. She unfastened her seat belt and got out of the car almost before it had stopped moving.

"Wait here," she told the stunned driver, and went around to the front where there was a man lying in the street. Even from this distance she could see his eyes—wide and dark brown—flit to her. She pulled out her mobile and speed dialed the hospital's front desk.

"Yes, this is Dr. Watterson," she said, marching up to the stricken man. "I'll need an ambulance to King James Road, just south of Knightsbridge. Pedestrian hit by car. He's still conscious." She snapped the mobile shut as she arrived at the man's side and thrust it into her coat pocket.

"Easy there son," she began. "Looks like it's your lucky day."

"Not . . . really," mumbled the man.

"Can you tell me your name? I'm a doctor, I'd like to help you." As she spoke she was already assessing him: a head wound, probably cracked ribs. He'd landed hard on his back, which worried her. She was on the point of asking him if he could feel his legs when he said, very suddenly and with surprising clarity:

"They are bad men. Please don't let them take me."

Dr. Watterson looked up. There were indeed a great number of men—and women—gathered at the side of the road. Seven in particular stood out to Dr. Watterson as the sort that you didn't want taking you. They stood at the front of the crowd, silent, somber, and dark-clad. The one in the center—a tall man with a sickly pale complexion and short black hair—looked intently back at her as she scanned them. He smiled faintly, in a way that put Dr. Watterson off, and raised a hand. He had what looked like a small camera in it.

Dr. Watterson ducked her head just in time as a flash of light went off. When she looked again, all the men were gone. In the distance, there was a sound of sirens drawing near.

On the ground, Alister had passed out.

The first thing Elo did was get out of her seeing-eye-dog harness. It was helpful when she was working in tandem with a human, but on her own it was better to enact the role of lovable stray. She stashed it on a rooftop in the lee of an old air conditioning unit. From this same rooftop, lying flat out along the edge, she watched the aftermath of Alister's accident. She waited until she saw him safely loaded into the ambulance, and then set about the rather difficult task of getting down.

Once this was accomplished she set off at a trot, her nose to the ground. She moved with such purpose that no one looking thought to stop her. Indeed, it was likely they didn't even remember seeing her. Which was just the way Elo liked it.

For Alister the world was dark for what felt like only a moment or so, but it must have been much longer. At first he was confused as to why he was still in bed, for he distinctly remembered climbing out the Oddity's window and into the Professor's universe. Then he tried to move, and his whole body protested. He didn't hurt exactly, but only because everything felt muted and numb. Another part of his brain was aware, however, that things were very wrong indeed.

Voices. There were voices in the next room. Not voices Alister knew, but voices he seemed to remember. One of them, anyway. A woman with a thick, northern voice was speaking.

"... and you'll have to show better identification than *that.* I don't care if you represent the Union and the Council and their grandmothers, I'll not release an unidentified, *unconscious* patient to *you.*"

"Please think about what you are saying, doctor," replied a smooth, cultured voice. It was the kind of voice that made you *want* to trust it, and for that Alister was instinctively distrustful. "You won't do anyone any good by being stubborn."

"You don't seem to understand me, Detective . . . er . . . "

"Just Detective, madam."

"Detective. I have refused to release patients to very unhappy men carrying large guns. You, with your neat black card, are a *long way* from convincing me . . . "

The female northern voice sounded incredibly determined, which Alister thought was a good thing. He felt cold inside and tired. He wanted to skip to a part of his life where he felt better, so he went to sleep.

This time Alister dreamed. These were vague, muddled affairs, in the way that dreams tend to be. He dreamed of detectives in long black coats, shadowy figures called professor, and doctors with military bearings. It all seemed familiar to him. In his dream he was on the verge of grasping it when someone came into his room.

He opened his eyes. Before him stood a wide, barrel-chested woman of indeterminate race. Her skin was light coffee colored, and her hair was only a touch darker shade of brown. She had muddy hazel eyes and a crooked nose. She wore the white coat of a doctor but something about her bearing said "fighter," and she looked evenly at Alister from under bushy brows like caterpillars. She was not a handsome woman; she clearly didn't feel the *need* to be handsome.

"Oh good," Alister mumbled without thinking. "You must be Dr. Watson."

The woman's mouth twitched to one side. "It's Watterson, actually," she said, confirming that she was the owner of the thick northern voice from earlier.

"It's all gone back to front," Alister said. "I think the *detective* is the bad one this time, and the *professor* is the good one. Where does that put the doctor? Hmm?"

Dr. Watterson laughed shortly and shook her head. "I've just come to see you all right," she said. "I was only riding in the cab that hit you, but it still feels like you're my responsibility. By rights you're Dr. Jacobsen's patient now. How are you feeling? Can you tell me your name?"

"I feel like I've been hit by a car," Alister said, then he realized. "That's what happened, wasn't it? I got hit. Thought I could make it across the street. Trying to get away . . . "

"Get away from whom?" Dr. Watterson asked. If she was impatient at all she didn't show it.

"The men in black. One of them was here earlier, wasn't he? That detective fellow . . . "

"He's gone now," Dr. Watterson assured him.

Alister wanted to nod, but a twinge in his neck told him he shouldn't.

"That's good," he said instead.

"*Can* you tell me who you are?" the doctor asked.

Alister tried to think about this, but his brain started shutting down again.

"Don't think I should," he said at length. And that was all Dr. Watterson was able to get out of him.

It is a difficult thing to build a telecommunication scanner. Building one with scavenged parts is harder. Building one with scavenged parts while living out of trashcans and in alleys while on the run from an unidentified enemy in a unfamiliar world would have been impossible for most people. In fact, there were probably only three or four people in that particular universe who could have done it. The first two were Dave and Professor Odd.

The third was Elo Marhütz.

It took her two days and a lot of trial and error and one last-minute move when the storage shed she had commandeered was suddenly invaded by its rightful owners. Nevertheless she kept at it, with the determination of dogs digging tunnels under their fences or scratching holes in wooden doors, only Elo applied herself, not to dirt and wood, but to wires and soldering, batteries and frequency filters.

In the end she had a construction that resembled a complicated radio remote attached to an old television she had lugged out of a dumpster. Once it was up and running, the screen showed, not video, but lines of information. Elo's eyes, accustomed to the much more dense and complicated language of the

Oddity, had no problem decoding this into individual phone calls, radio transmissions . . . even wireless internet signals.

She spent the third day just scanning.

On the fourth day she narrowed her frequency range.

On the fifth day she had a piece of paper filled with scribbled notations tracking origin points, bounces, and redirections. And, at the bottom, a set of coordinates.

On the sixth day she dismantled her operation and left.

What Elo hadn't picked up on was a conversation between two parties who, for all appearances, did not technically exist. Both sets of signals were encrypted and untraceable, they existed only in the static surrounding the busy highway of ordinary, law-abiding information, and the only recording was written on a heavily protected drive that was itself stored in a heavily protected location.

Had there been someone with the right equipment, however, and had they taken the time to splice the messages together, the conversation would have sounded like this:

"I know you're listening," said the first voice. It was smooth and rich, with an educated accent. "You're always listening. So I won't waste your time with pleasantries. I have your accomplice, Professor. And, do not mistake me, I *will* use him in any way I can to . . . *encourage* you to cooperate."

"Interesting," said the second voice. It was lighter, scratchier, and probably female. "You know, you're not a very *good* detective."

There was an unfriendly silence.

"I have traveled," said the first voice. "I have traveled across universes and galaxies. I have walked patiently down the ages and over the rise and fall of empires . . . hunting *you*, Professor. And I *found* you. I *brought you here.* What, may I ask, would it take for someone to be a *good detective* in your illustrious book?"

"Oh, no," said the second voice. "You're good—*very* good—at detecting things. You're probably the best detectoring detective I've ever met. What I *meant* was . . . you don't sound like a fundamentally good person. If you don't mind my saying so."

"From what *I* have heard, your definition of good and evil is perhaps not the same as most people's," the first voice retorted.

"And what *have* you heard, exactly?" said the second voice eagerly. "Because *I've* been hearing some *very interesting* things about *you.* And I must say, really, you're perhaps the coldest personification of the Holmesian Paradigm I've ever seen."

"Excuse me?"

"The Holmesian Paradigm! You're a transuniversal traveler. You know how character archetypes repeat across worlds? Well, the Holmesian Paradigm is when a person exhibits characteristics similar to that of Sherlock Holmes, the fictional detective created by Sir Arthur Conan Doyle in—"

"I *know* who Sherlock Holmes is," said the first voice, sounding intensely bored.

"Have you got a Watson?" asked the second voice.

"A what?"

"A Watson!" the second voice sounded downright enthusiastic now. "Because I can tell you, I've met a *lot* of Holmesian Paradigms, and none of them needed the Watson Effect more than *you.*"

"Listen," said the first voice through gently clenched teeth. "You know how to find me. I would recommend you do so, before I become *frustrated.* I want to remind you, your accomplice . . . "

"Detective?" asked the second voice.

"Yes, Professor?"

"Just one question, Detective."

"And what, pray, is that?"

"The persons you are working for—I have some idea who they are—I was just wondering, how *much* have they paid you?"

"That can't possibly be relevant."

"Well, I just wanted to say, however much it is . . . "

"You cannot buy my cooperation, Professor."

"*However much it is . . .* " the second voice continued, a hard edge behind the light tone, "it cannot possibly, in all the realms of probability, ever—*ever*—be enough to cover the trouble you will get into hunting *me.*"

There was a *click* and then silence once more.

The Detective hadn't bothered to answer.

* * *

Philip Parsons was *not* having a good day. Even though work had been going smoothly—no beeps, no flashing red lights—he couldn't shake the feeling that he was being watched. He also kept getting flashbacks to what he could only assume was an uncomfortable dream. In what else but a dream could he have been kidnapped by the Professor and then forced to watch a memory of himself interacting with the Detective? He had never met either of those people. He was sure he would remember that.

Wouldn't he?

There was a faint clacking of claws above him. Philip Parsons thought it was a rat in the ceiling. He thought this because his brain refused to allow for the possibility that it could be exactly what it sounded like: a dog in the ventilation duct.

To distract himself from the sound that was definitely *not* a dog, Philip Parsons reached into his desk drawer for a packet of crisps. This was something he found himself doing more and more often of late, and the bag he pulled out was the last of its kind.

He ate them nervously, and the crunching sound easily covered the faint *whish* of a furry body leaping through the air, and the soft *whump* as it landed.

On the other side of the room, hidden behind banks of computers and a wall, Elo stood up. She was wearing a strange harness pieced together from bits of webbing and straps torn off old backpacks. It held a number of handy items including a flashlight, knife, screwdriver, lock-picking kit, a small drive with some very interesting software on it, and a water bottle.

Elo took a sip from the bottle. Then she went over to the small monitor set in the bank of computers and turned it on.

Instead of entering the password as prompted, Elo plugged in the drive she'd brought with her and watched the software work.

The first password fell in seconds. The second in minutes. The third took a little impromptu reprogramming, but she got through just the same. She accessed a database of monitored calls and began going through them, her thumb claw tapping at the down arrow on the monitor's attached keyboard.

Then her thumb stopped.

She had come to the conversation between the Detective and the Professor.

She pressed play.

To Philip Parsons, it went something like this:

He heard a voice say, *"I know you're listening . . . "* and he nearly jumped out of his skin. For that voice he had only heard in his dream, the half-remembered nightmare. It went on, the dulcet tones sending goosebumps up his arms.

Then a new voice answered. The *other* voice from his dream. Slowly, Philip Parsons realized that they were not speaking in the other room, as he had first thought, but that he was listening to a recording. A recording which, by the sound of it, no one in their right minds would play.

On shaking legs Philip Parsons got up and came around the bank of computers.

"From what I have heard, your definition of good and evil is perhaps not the same as most people's," said the voice of the Detective, so close it made Philip Parsons pause instinctively. He took a few deep breaths. The conversation continued.

" . . . you're a transuniversal traveler . . . "

"I know who Sherlock Holmes is . . . "

"Have you got a Watson?"

Philip Parsons couldn't stop listening. He was fascinated.

"You cannot buy my cooperation, Professor."

" . . . it cannot possibly, in all the realms of probability, ever— ever—*be enough . . . "*

Philip Parsons came around the bank of computers, and stopped.

A large golden dog with sharp triangular ears looked up at him. It was wearing what looked like a climbing harness, and its hand-like paws were spread over a keyboard.

They stared at each other for a moment. Then the dog neatly unplugged a drive from the computer and placed it in a small pouch on its harness.

Then the dog stood up.

Philip Parsons found himself backing away. The dog was as tall as a short woman, but that is still a lot higher up than you want a dog's face to be.

Then the dog spoke. It said in a light, female voice:

"You might want to find a new job. Or go on holiday. Things are going to get a little messy around here."

Then she stopped. Her nose twitched. Abruptly she rushed forward and grabbed Philip Parsons by his shirt front. She sniffed at his collar, at his—*gulp*—throat, at his hands and his legs. Then she let go.

"I don't *believe* it," she said. "You *met* them. Met *both* of them."

With that she dropped to all fours and bounded out of the room, her nose skimming the ground.

Philip Parsons wobbled a bit on his way back to his desk. He picked up his phone.

He should report this. Verily, he should. But he had the niggling certainty that getting out the phone directory and calling *that* number would only give him grief. And more bad dreams too.

Philip Parsons sighed and looked up the number of his travel agent instead.

What appeared to be a golden dog—or perhaps a wolf—bounded down the city streets heedless of the stares and commotion that followed in its wake. It was hot on a scent, running with its nose to the ground. It came to a narrow alley and darted down it.

Many people saw it go in one end. No one saw it come out the other. When a few children followed cautiously after, they found the alley empty.

For Elo, the world went dark and confused for a moment. Then she blinked, shook her head, and things came back into focus.

"Ah," she said. "A local portal. *Very* clever!"

"Thank you!" said Professor Odd, looking up from over a desk covered in wires, monitors, and strange humming cylinders. It smelled strongly of metal and grease.

Despite thousands of years of evolution and a few jumps sideways from her domestic counterparts, Elo had to resist the urge to wag her tail wildly and jump up and lick the Professor's face. She contented herself by coming around the table and hugging the tall woman about her midsection. For a moment Elo felt herself enfolded by those strong, bony arms, and then she was being gently pried away.

"Now, tell me why Dave evicted you and young Mister Alister," Professor Odd said, pushing a chair forward. "Speaking of Alister, what possessed you to leave him in the hands of the *Detective?*"

Elo gave a deep sigh, sat down, and began to explain. As she did, her eyes adjusted to the dim light, and she got a better look at the Professor's lair.

They were in a small, circular room with no windows. The walls were made of stone blocks, and there was a bundle of wires that ran up one wall and disappeared through a hole in the ceiling. Beside this hole was a tiny ventilation duct, from which a cold stream of air blew, wafting scents of evergreen trees into the room. The floor was covered in layers of throw rugs, all in different styles. Aside from the desk with the computers and the chair, the only other piece of furniture was a small camp bed pushed up against one wall, and a rather frightening contraption that reminded Elo of the chairs used by human dentists. Back the way she had come was only a blank wall with a doorway formed of a metal frame, with small circular nubs and gas jets at regular intervals bolted to it. A wooden door with a crescent moon cut in it was the only visible exit.

"So, how long has it been for *you?*" Elo asked when she had brought the Professor up to speed. "And . . . *where is this?*"

"Technically it's an unused dungeon, heavily remodeled," Professor Odd said cheerfully. "I had to have some place . . . secluded. There are people in this world who would very much like to capture me."

"So I've gathered," Elo said, rubbing an ear. She cast an appreciative glance at all the equipment over the desk. "You've been busy."

"Less so than I'd have liked," the Professor said, walking over to a small table near the camp bed. There was a little gas stove there and a battered kettle. Professor Odd lit the stove and put the kettle on. She was wrapped in many layers of scarves and coats, and there was a fur cap planted firmly over her head, its earflaps down and tied together under her chin. "Oh, it was fun in the beginning. A lot of running. Narrow escapes. Getting all this set up took me the better part of three months."

"Professor," Elo prodded.

"What? Oh, yes. I'd say it's been about a year. Not that I was worried," she grinned. "I thought a temporal discrepancy was likely. I'm sure Dave will get it fixed in no time. Well, no time for *him.*"

"Huh," said Elo. She went over to the not-a-human-dentist-chair and inspected the bit that hung down from the ceiling. It appeared to be a holographic projector of some kind.

"Not that I'm not *absolutely delighted* to see you," Professor Odd said kindly. "But it *was* rather stupid for you to leave the Oddity. Once Dave gets the discrepancy fixed and the place untangled he'll be able to move his next portal time backward so it will have been less time for us. If you'd waited for that, you could have come through not long after I did . . . "

"Maybe," said Elo. "We were worried. Alister felt like he was doing us no good sitting in the Oddity. And"—she fiddled nervously with a clamp—"it's shrinking. The whole place is shrinking."

Professor Odd looked up from pouring hot water into a chipped mug. Her jaguar eyes were open very wide and the pupils dilated so that they looked like deep black pits. "What?" she said, her voice like a knife dropped on ice.

"Dave said the spatial maintenance stabilizers had been sabotaged," Elo said miserably.

"Oh," said Professor Odd, her voice making a U-turn and chugging back toward its normal, optimistic tone. "Oh dear." She handed the steaming cup to Elo and rubbed her chin. She was wearing knit fingerless gloves, Elo saw, her fingertips protruding like curious, pale fish heads. "I didn't think he was capable of *that,*" the Professor went on. "Really it's quite remarkable. I'd congratulate him except—*you know*—entrapping the Oddity and sabotaging her. *Tsk, tsk, tsk.*"

Elo came away from the chair. "Him? You mean the Detective?" She lapped hot water from the mug. It tasted faintly of tea.

"Oh, so you know him," Professor Odd said cheerfully. She had removed the kettle and was now heating water in a small saucepan. "Ramen?" she asked, holding up a packet of dried noodles.

Elo shuddered. "Pass. And not really. He came to the Oddity moments after you left. And then later, he found me and Alister. He chased us."

"And he let you get away?" Professor Odd asked in some surprise.

Elo shook her head miserably. "No, Alister insisted I go. He caused a . . . a distraction. It's okay though, an ambulance picked him up. I saw."

"And the Detective let you get away?" Professor Odd repeated in surprise.

Elo frowned. "Give me some credit. I can be quite slippery when I want to."

"You don't know the Detective," Professor Odd said, ripping open the package of ramen and gently easing the brick of dried noodles into the boiling water. She turned the heat down and began stirring it.

"Just who is this Detective anyway?" Elo demanded, sitting down on the camp bed. "Dave called him a *fellow traveler.* Does that mean he's not from this universe either?"

Professor Odd chuckled. "Dave would see it that way. He is, after a fashion, just a fellow traveler. And no, this isn't his native world. I'm not sure if he even *has* a native world at this point. He's . . . troubling." She turned off the heat and began stirring in the little packet of seasoning. The smell of over-salted pork filled the room. "I confess I *had* heard of him before. I just didn't realize this was the *same* Detective. He's an odd-jobbing private investigator bounty hunter sort of person, from what I can tell. Tracks down fugitives across the multiverse. But he's not just limited to the multiplicity-aware worlds. Go into any sufficiently advanced universe, and you'll find someone—or stories of someone—who can find things no one else can. Who can solve problems that seem unsolvable. Who doesn't work for any government or agency, but chooses cases based on their own personal interests. That's the Detective."

"A Holmesian Paradigm," Elo said. "I hacked into his data center and heard your conversation," she explained to the Professor's questioning glance.

"*Good* girl," said Professor Odd, taking the pot and blowing on it. She took a pair of chopsticks from her pocket and grabbed a bundle of noodles. She tasted them.

"So . . . if he's a free agent," Elo pondered. "It's not really *him* that's after you . . . it's whoever he's working for."

Professor Odd, her mouth full of noodles, nodded.

"Who is that, exactly?" Elo perked her ears and stared expectantly at the Professor.

Professor Odd swallowed slowly. She made a face. "No matter what, it never tastes as good as it smells," she sighed. "Given that he's brought us to my homeworld that does narrow the field a bit. I *know!*" She looked up, grinning widely. "Let's ask *him!*" And she took her bowl, still mostly full of hot water and thin, slimy noodles, and tossed its contents at the chair by the desk.

The liquid flew through the air and splattered across the face and chest of the tall man who, until that moment, Elo was sure had *not* been sitting there.

Now the Detective stood up. He took a handkerchief from his breast pocket and carefully wiped the soup off his face. He plucked a stray noodle from his hair and gazed forlornly at Professor Odd.

"That was uncalled for," he said.

"*You* shouldn't have involved Alister," Professor Odd snapped, and Elo saw for the first time just how angry she was about that. She was *furious,* the rage that had been simmering below that icy exterior now rising to the surface. Elo actually felt a little *sorry* for the Detective. But only a little.

The Detective smiled. A long thin smile that made Elo wish she had accepted the Professor's offer of ramen, just so she could have her own pot of it to throw at him.

"Professor Odd," he said, somehow managing to appear suave even with ramen water dripping from his hair. "I have come to take you into my own personal custody, for the acts of technological and practical terrorism you committed here in this universe in the local year eighteen hundred and—"

Professor Odd didn't let him finish. She grabbed Elo by the paw and hauled her toward the wooden door with the crescent moon cut in it. She kicked it open and, withdrawing two carabiners from her pockets, clipped them onto a hidden rope.

"Hold onto me," she hissed, and Elo felt the soft length of her tentacle wrap around her upper arm. She reached up and threw both her paws over the Professor's shoulders and jumped.

The Detective, leaping after them, closed his hands on thin air.

Elo and the Professor fell a long way, the dark air whistling past them. Elo kept expecting them to land in a lake of sewage—or worse, a puddle, because then they'd break their backs—but they met no resistance. Eventually Professor Odd closed the carabiners, creating friction on the rope, and they slowed, and slowed, and eventually came to a halt. The Professor let go of the carabiners and they dropped a foot or so to land on clean, dry stone.

"Professor, what—" Elo began, but the Professor was scrabbling at a nearby wall, and a moment later a section of it rolled back and daylight flooded in.

Elo blinked out onto a winding stone stairway. There were long narrow windows in the wall, letting in a cool stream of pale daylight.

"I thought you said it was a *dungeon!*" she exclaimed.

"Didn't say where the dungeon was, did I?" Professor Odd replied with a grin. "I was counting on him being too excited about following you through the portal to bother to check the destination. Had to throw him off just a *little.* Now stand clear."

Elo scurried out of the little alcove and stood on the stairs as Professor Odd took a small radio transmitter out of yet *another* pocket.

No wonder she wears all those layers, Elo thought.

Professor Odd pressed a button. There was a distant explosion, and the rope they had descended fell in a shower of rock dust at their feet.

"That should slow him down a little," she remarked. "No rope, no more local portal device. And now comes the part where we run."

"My favorite," Elo said dryly, and took off down the stairs, the Professor hot on her tail.

They appeared to be in the tower of a castle. Elo caught glimpses of forested mountains out the narrow windows, with a picturesque little town on a distant hilltop.

The stairs led out into a wide hall, deserted and dusty. They sprinted across it, through a high arch, and then across an overgrown lawn studded with crumbling stone walls. It was a treacherous place, with hidden rabbit holes and stone masonry liable to give way. Elo leapt from block to block, nimble and sure-footed, with Professor Odd, her scarves trailing in the wind, only a little way behind.

Through a hole in the towering outer wall they went, and then they were in thick forest, ducking through undergrowth and jumping over fallen trees.

"North!" shouted the Professor. "Train tracks!"

Elo altered course, dropped her speed so that the Professor could catch up, and together they moved away deeper into the woods.

The Detective stood in the circular room, examining the empty shaft that had until recently contained a rope. He had been only partway through his copy of the software stored on the computers when the tiny charges blew, removing his means of pursuit and destroying the portal framework. He sighed. It was a little frustrating, but the Detective was nothing if not patient. And persistent.

He looked around at the disheveled little room that had been the Professor's headquarters for almost thirteen months. He shrugged. There was nothing left for him here. Nothing he did not already know. Besides, now that he'd been here once, he could easily come back.

He rolled up his sleeve and pressed a button on the pad strapped to his wrist.

And then he was not there anymore.

"How did he do that?" Elo asked. They had slowed to a walk and were now moving casually through the woods. "The way he just *appeared.* I mean, I couldn't see him, hear him, *or* smell him."

"The Detective has fewer scruples about what sort of technology he brings with him from world to world," Professor Odd said. "Some of it's not strictly conventional."

"I see," said Elo, who knew something of the *un*conventional that was implied here.

"From what I gather, there are two devices he makes use of," Professor Odd continued. "One is best described as a perception modifier. It redirects your attention around him, like a sort of mirror. It is easily circumvented, however, by direct physical contact. Hence the ramen."

Elo couldn't help a small snort at this.

"The other, and the one that troubles me more," the Professor went on, "is his STC manipulator."

"STC?" Elo repeated. "You don't mean Space Time Continuum?"

"That very one," Professor Odd said grimly. "Albeit, he can't use it to full effect in a temporally fixed universe such as this one, but it does allow him certain advantages. The appearance of instantaneous travel, for example. It behaves something like the Oddity, only not as powerful."

Elo shook her head. "I can't believe I haven't heard of him before."

"But you have," Professor Odd insisted. "Or at least a version similar to this individual. The Holmesian Paradigm is not uncommon."

"I meant *this* individual, *this* person. *The* Detective."

Professor Odd shrugged. "It is not so surprising when you think about it," she said. "The multiverse is filled with extraordinary people we haven't met yet. I expect there is quite a queue. Ah, here's our station."

Their station was in fact a layover for freight trains. Elo and the Professor picked a boxcar half filled with bags of grain and made themselves comfortable.

"Now explain to me exactly what problems Dave was encountering," Professor Odd said, arranging the bags around her like a throne. "Because, working together, there *may* be something we can do to help him out. In which case the temporal discrepancy will actually work *in our favor.*" She grinned at Elo, showing her white, square teeth.

This time, Elo grinned back.

A few hours later the train pulled out of the yard and began gathering speed, leaving the ruined castle far behind.

* * *

When Alister woke up he felt *much* better. His chest still hurt, and he still felt tired, but the deep cold ache had vanished, and his head felt much clearer. He could wiggle his toes. He could lift his head and look down at his hands, which were folded neatly over his stomach. There was a white sleeve over one finger with wires coming off it, which in turn led to a monitor by his bedside that showed a steady, even heartbeat.

Alister felt good. Despite his questionable position he was optimistic as to his prospects, considering he had been hit by a car while trying to escape . . .

. . . the Detective.

The Detective. That tall, dark-haired man in the long black coat. Alister remembered him perfectly. Which was why he knew the man sitting across from him in the hospital room was exactly that person.

All the good feelings went out of Alister like water down a drain, leaving him a weak, injured person lost in a strange world. He groaned as he laid his head back against the pillow.

"Ah, Mr. *Bane,* I am glad to see you are awake."

He really did have a remarkable voice. Like someone out of an old movie. Soothing, deep and powerful. But Alister knew the man behind that voice was an enemy of the Professor's, and by extension, his enemy as well.

At least he did not seem inclined to drag Alister out of bed. Alister relaxed and shut his eyes.

"No," he said hopefully. "No, I'm not."

"Mr. Bane, I have been to a *great deal* of trouble tracking down your . . . leader . . . I'm afraid to say I'm getting a little impatient."

"Not," said Alister. His mouth was dry and sticky, making it difficult to talk. "Not my leader."

"Professor Odd is not your leader?"

A drink of water. That was what Alister needed. Not questions from this frightening man. "She's . . . my professor," he said.

"Are you a student, Mr. Bane?" the Detective asked.

"Could say that," Alister said.

"What has she been teaching you? Why did you seek her out?"

"Didn't *seek her out,*" Alister grumbled. He got the feeling the Detective wasn't particularly interested in his answers. He was getting answers to *different* questions—ones Alister didn't know—from the way Alister was talking or the way he responded. Since it appeared what he actually said didn't matter, he decided to tell the truth.

"We met by accident. I got tangled up with the Canary Company; she helped me escape. And she doesn't *teach,* not really. She shows you things."

"Things like what?"

"Worlds," said Alister, giving a feeble shrug. "Worlds better—and worse—than this one. Worlds with orange skies and giant flying whales. Worlds with dinosaurs. Worlds without humans."

"And she teaches you about these worlds, does she?"

The manner of the Detective's questions was beginning to get on Alister's nerves. They put wrong notions in his head that he felt obliged to correct, but he could see no other reason to tell the Detective anything.

"I want to see my doctor," he said. "I don't think having you here is aiding my recovery."

"Dr. Jacobsen is on a house call," the Detective said, a little smugly.

"Not him—the other one . . . " *The one that saved me,* Alister did not add.

"Mr. Bane, I have followed you from world to world, across the multiverse. It has been quite exhausting. Now at last we have an opportunity to speak frankly, and yet you persist in obfuscation. Understand me, Alister Bane, when I say there is no place you can run, no place you can hide, where I cannot follow. Now open your eyes and look at me, and tell me, *do you know where Professor Odd is?"*

Alister did open his eyes, and he squinted across his sheet-covered body at the Detective, who had leaned forward in his chair and clasped his hands together. His eyes were black as pits, his cheeks hollow and lean, and his brows like the wings of a dark bird arching up on either side of his face.

"Why are you looking for her?" Alister responded.

The Detective stood up. He really was quite tall, like a long black shadow. He crossed Alister's room in two paces and stood at his bedside, his hands resting casually in the pockets of his waistcoat.

"Mr. Bane," he said quietly. "You are aware Professor Odd is wanted on this world for several counts of terrorism, not least of which is blowing up a Deutsch research facility?"

Alister opened his mouth to respond, but said nothing. He frowned.

"Clearly I overestimated her confidence in you." The Detective sighed, turning away. He picked up a jug of water that was sitting on a nearby table and poured some of it into a little paper cup, which in turn he brought over to Alister. Laying his hand gently over Alister's clasped ones he raised the cup to Alister's mouth.

Alister sipped the cool, clear water. It seemed to come at a mere trickle and disappear into his dry mouth as if it had never been.

"They cleared you for advanced caudata-assisted, stem-cell therapy last night," the Detective said conversationally. "I expect your cracked ribs and other injuries to be almost completely healed, if not by now then in a few hours. After that they will release you. At that point, Mr. Bane, you will have two choices. You can attempt to find your professor, which I would not recommend, as you are technically an illegal alien in this world and will have no means of obtaining food, lodging, or other resources. Or"—here he took a small white card and tucked it between Alister's fingers—"when they release you, ask the receptionist to call that number. I will have you collected."

"Collected?" Alister rasped; his throat still felt dry. "For what?"

The Detective poured another cup of water. "For . . . nothing. For safe preservation until the conclusion of my case. After which I will escort you back to your own world."

Alister shook his head, dislodging the offered cup. "No," he said firmly. "I can't go back. Not yet."

The Detective raised two perfect, black eyebrows. He seemed bemused. "You cannot stay here. Without the Professor you have no means of returning home."

"I don't want to *go* home," Alister said, surprised that he meant every word of it. Apparently all it took to kill his homesickness was the prospect of being delivered into the waiting arms of the Canary Company. "I'm not going home," he said firmly. "I'm going to wait. I'm going to wait, and once they've untangled the Oddity from whatever you've trapped it in, they will come and get me. And then we'll leave. And you . . . you can just keep on following us from world to world." He paused. He was still short of breath. "You have to admit," he added, "she visits some pretty neat places."

The Detective shrugged. He replaced the paper cup on the table and dug his hands deep into his coat pockets. "Ah," he said. "Well, I am sorry you feel that way. You've been through so much trauma already, I did not want to compound the problem."

Alister turned his head sharply to look. Something in the man's expression, the tension in his shoulders and the way his right hand seemed fisted in his pocket, all set alarm bells ringing for Alister.

Fortunately it was at that moment that the door burst open.

Both men turned. For one wild moment Alister thought it was the Professor and Elo and Dave, and the Oddity was working again and he was saved. But it was not the Professor.

It was Dr. Watterson.

"And what *possessed* you to let him in to see the patient alone?" were the words just leaving her mouth as the door bounced off the wall. She stared at Alister. She glared at the Detective. She was wearing a neat plaid vest over a button-down shirt and slacks, her brown hair stylishly coiffed in a masculine sort of way. She looked like she had been interrupted in the middle of an evening out, and was now ready to ream the person responsible.

The Detective turned, palming the syringe he had been holding and setting it on the table.

"Doctor," Alister wheezed.

Dr. Watterson pointed at the Detective. "You," she said shortly. "Out."

"On whose authority?" the Detective asked sweetly.

"Mine," grinned Dr. Watterson.

"Are you this man's doctor?"

"No, but I am *a* doctor—Martha, call security—which is more than I can say *for you.* Out."

The Detective sighed. He glanced back at Alister with a rueful grin. "Sorry about this," he said. He raised his other hand, in which he held a small metal box rather like a camera. It had a little yellow flashing light in the center.

There was a billowing of the curtains over the window, and a squealing as the screen was wrenched off and the pane slid backward. Everyone, even the Detective, turned and stared.

And Elo shot into the room.

Gone was her seeing-eye dog harness. She was dressed once more in her favorite purple jumpsuit, and she carried clutched to her chest a huge gun with bare wires protruding from the muzzle.

The Detective saw it. More than that, he recognized it. He lunged for Elo, but Alister's bed got in the way, and the wolf was too quick.

"Down, Alister!" Elo howled, and fired the time gun.

It was like an invisible bubble spread over the far side of the room, enveloping the Detective (caught mid-lunge) and Dr. Watterson. Within this bubble the passage of time slowed to the point where the Detective was suspended in midair, and Dr. Watterson's cry of surprise was drawn into a long, low moan.

"How are you?" Elo asked, all business, as she holstered the gun in the sling she wore over her back.

"Been better," Alister gasped. His heart was racing, and he felt like he might pass out again.

"Can you walk?" the wolf asked, coming over and briskly unhooking him from all the wires and meters.

Alister tried to sit up, and failed. "I don't think so," he said.

"Well, there's a way around that," came Professor Odd's voice, bright and cheerful and just a little bit manic. Alister rolled his head, and saw her jump down from the windowsill. Gone were the drab overcoat and mouse-colored wig; she was back in her olive-green trench coat and was wearing a particularly vibrant wig of neon yellow. She kicked out her legs as she jumped, and

Alister saw these were encased in a pair of improbably gold pin-striped trousers.

"Professor!" Alister gulped. "It's the Detective, he's after you—he said—"

"There will be time enough for that later," said Professor Odd, briskly wheeling Alister's bed over to the window. "Now, where are your injuries?"

"Fractured ribs, I think," Alister said. "And a concussion. And bruises. Lots of bruises. But they gave me something, said it would help the healing. Caudata-assisted stem-cell . . . something. Mostly, I just feel weak."

Professor Odd paused. She looked at Alister intently, frowning under her wig.

"Something wrong?" Alister asked nervously.

"So that's what they called it," Professor Odd muttered to herself. "Interesting. All right, Elo, if you would—we'll lift him on three. One, two . . . "

They heaved Alister through the window, and there, blessedly, were the steps of the Oddity. They seemed a little more worn and dingy than Alister remembered, but that might have been because his face was closer to them than normal.

With her arms under his shoulders and Elo supporting his legs, they trotted Alister up the stairs and deposited him in a chair. Alister glimpsed the room—noticeably smaller than he remembered—and Dave in his panvironment suit sitting at the cockpit.

"You . . . fixed it?" he asked, breathlessly. His ribs were not exactly hurting, but they were sending him the equivalent of angry notes.

"I HAVE REMOVED ALL EXTERNAL INTERFERENCES," Dave said as Elo came up the stairs. "THE ODDITY INSISTS ON REPAIRING THE DAMAGE ITSELF."

"Give," Professor Odd said to Elo, who handed over the time gun.

"You're going to release them?" she asked, a little startled.

"Fair's fair," said Professor Odd, and marched back down the stairs. "Just be ready to get us out of here."

"More than!" exclaimed Elo, and took her place across from Dave.

Alister watched placidly as Professor Odd's yellow wig disappeared down the stairs. He listened to the muffled *whumph* of the time gun's field releasing, the startled cries resuming, and then the sudden and absolute silence as the Oddity's portal closed for good.

Professor Odd came slowly back up the stairs, turning little knobs and dials on the time gun so that it could not go off accidentally. She was frowning, and seemed to be feeling none of the triumph and relief that was currently coursing through Alister.

"So . . . that's it?" he asked hopefully. "We're completely disconnected . . . no more entanglement or spatial stabilizer sabotage?"

"WE HAVE SEVERED ALL CONNECTIONS WITH THAT UNIVERSE," Dave said. "OBSERVE FOR YOURSELF." One cloth-covered tentacle rose, pointed out the window. There, to Alister's intense joy, was the deep blue-blackness of the void, pricked by the distant lights of far away worlds.

Funny, Alister thought to himself. *The first time I saw that, it terrified me. Now, I couldn't be more relieved.*

The sight of the void was better—far better—than the dull brick walls, for it meant they were no longer trapped in that bitter and unfriendly world. For the first time in days Alister felt his body relax completely.

"Well, I don't know about you," he said. "But I'm *starving.*"

"I could eat," Elo said, unclipping the holster and throwing it on the table. "Let's see what the kitchen can manage."

The kitchen, it turned out, could only manage a kind of dried, salty noodle mix that Elo called ramen. For some reason this sent her into fits of laughter. So Alister agreed to the ramen, which was oily and salty and tasted vaguely of chicken, and ate it with a fork while Elo told him her side of the adventure: about finding the Professor, escaping the Detective, building a separate portal to link directly with the Oddity . . .

"It allowed us to move the portal about within the world," Elo explained. "So we were able to find and infiltrate the installation where the Detective had been broadcasting the signal used to interfere with the Oddity. And disable it."

Alister paused with a fork full of noodles halfway to his mouth.

"You . . . *disabled* it?" he said.

"Oh yes, it is *very* disabled," said Elo smugly.

"Define 'disabled.'"

"We didn't hurt anyone!" she assured him. "Well, maybe one. But he'll only have a headache for a few hours. Anyway, with the interference gone Dave was able to get the Oddity up and running in no time. We detached long enough for it to repair itself enough that we could open a portal in a different place seconds after we left the world—and that one was into your hospital room. And not a moment too soon! I insisted on bringing the time gun because I thought the Detective would be after you. Did you know *he's* got off-world tech too? And a lot less restrained about using it than our Professor."

"A little thing, like a camera," said Alister. "And I think he can mess with people's memories."

"He can do a lot more than that," said Professor Odd wearily. She had pulled up a chair and was idly spinning the rear wheel of the bicycle that lay across half the table. She had propped her head up against one hand and seemed to be lost in thought.

"Oh, no," said Alister, pushing the bowl full of broth over to Elo. "You're not happy. Something's gone wrong. What's gone wrong? Has he got a fishing line attached to us or what?"

"THERE IS NO LINE," Dave said indignantly. "THERE IS NO TRACER. WE ARE AS FAR FROM THAT UNIVERSE AS ANY OTHER. HE HAS LOST US TO THE INFINITE MULTIPLICITY."

Alister turned back to the Professor.

"Then . . . *what*?" he asked.

Professor Odd looked up. She stared blankly over the table piled with junk, and said in a flat voice: "I have to go back."

Elo jumped to her feet. "No, no, *no,* you do *not!*" she said.

"I have to go back and *explain,*" Professor Odd went on as if she hadn't heard.

"Explain *what?*" Alister said. "Professor, you can't go back there. He thinks you're a *terrorist.*"

"Yes, and I know why he would," Professor Odd said. "Which is why I have to explain."

"I nearly broke my back getting you out of there," Elo snarled. "Dave worked his tentacles to the bone—"

"I DO NOT HAVE AN ENDOSKELETON," Dave pointed out.

"Shut up," barked Elo. "Alister got *hit by a car.* We finally get free of that place—we're free to go *anywhere* we want . . . and now you want to go *back?*"

For the first time, Professor Odd looked at them. Her eyes were very big and dark, and reflected the rainbow lights of the Oddity like little gems. She smiled sadly.

"I don't want to," she said quietly. "But I know I should. And it's because I *can* . . . I can leave. I can make the Detective start his game all over again. That's why I have to go back now. Because now he'll *listen* to me."

Alister sighed—cautiously—and shook his head.

"Well, can it wait a day or so? I don't feel up for much as it is, and I *am* going with you this time, don't argue."

"Me too," Elo joined in.

Professor Odd looked at them. She seemed touched, and saddened.

"It's not going to be pleasant, what I have to say," she said softly.

Alister thought about this.

"Would you prefer we didn't hear it?" he asked.

Professor Odd leaned back in her chair and stared at the black emptiness that passed for the ceiling for a while. "I suppose you deserve to know," she said. "It's just . . . difficult to talk about. To tell the truth, I would appreciate the moral support."

Elo and Alister exchanged glances.

"Well," said Alister, hitching himself up on his chair. "Consider yourself supported."

The Professor rolled her head to one side and looked at him; a faint smile ghosted across her face.

"I WILL REMAIN HERE," Dave announced. "IN CASE OF . . . TROUBLE."

"That," said Elo, removing the bowls and standing up, "sounds like an excellent plan."

* * *

The doctor was becoming a problem. The Detective paused with his key halfway to the lock of the flat he'd rented in middle Londinium and sighed inwardly.

First she had possessed his target. Then she had interfered with questioning—and worse, distracted him at a critical moment. He might have thought she was another agent of the Professor, except she seemed too simple for that. Then again, Alister Bane had seemed simple—but he clearly had experience of the multiverse, and the Detective suspected that superficial naiveté hid a formidable intellect. But the doctor . . . she confused him. She knew about his methods—maybe didn't understand them but she knew—and after the inexplicable reappearance of the Professor and her damned dog she had refused to be brainwashed and led away. She had . . . *hounded* him, that was the word. Hounded. And like a hound she had sniffed out his scent and followed him here. He could sense her by the tense shadow in an alley two doors down.

The Detective unlocked his front door, and stepped back.

"You won't get any answers shivering the night out there," he told the alley.

A brief movement, and the doctor appeared on the pavement. She had added a camel-colored overcoat to her ensemble and a matching fedora, and looked rather like a 1930's wiseguy until she opened her mouth and spoke, her northern accent pronounced in her agitation.

"And if I go inside?" she asked, her face like a stone wall.

"If you come inside the very least you'll get is to ask the questions I know you want to," the Detective said. He shrugged. "You might get an answer or two in return."

The doctor took a step toward him down the pavement. She wore patent leather shoes and seemed to favor her left leg.

Scar tissue in the knee, thought the Detective. *Not a bullet, but an injury. Maybe running away from a bullet?* She had seen military service, that was for certain.

"And I expect then you'll use your handy flasher to make it all go away. Drive me home and set me up with a snifter or two so when I wake up I'll just think I dreamed it all. I've had my head messed about in before, and I'm not in a hurry to repeat it, thank you very much."

"I can assure you there will be no 'messing about' of any kind," the Detective said. "On the contrary, it is my wish to *clear up* messes. You can reassure yourself of the fact that I have never actually harmed anyone—it was *your* cab that struck poor Mr. Bane—but you will have to trust me. Trust me, doctor, or stand outside and wonder."

He turned away and opened his door. Slowly. By the time he'd finished he could feel her breath on his neck. Her steps had been almost silent. He approved.

"Listen," said the doctor, radiating menace even though she only came up to his shoulder. "I know that you know that I've served time in our armed forces. That's good. I *wanted* you to know. I also want you to know that, though I may be in civilian practice now, I haven't let go of my military . . . training."

The Detective looked over and glanced down, to where her hands were still in the pockets of her overcoat.

"Duly noted," he said. "Then I trust you to know when . . . and when *not* . . . to use this . . . *training.*" He smiled. "My dear doctor, won't you please come in?"

Together they entered the flat. Together they ascended the stairs to the Detective's apartment: a large airy living room with an attached kitchen, a bathroom and two bedrooms. One of the bedrooms was covered in papers and clippings and some very interesting wire constructions. The other was empty. The living room was, by contrast, impeccably furnished with a sofa and two deep armchairs arranged tastefully around a vintage fireplace.

When the Detective and the doctor stepped through the door from the hall they found the two armchairs already occupied: in one was a tall man with short-cropped dark hair in an eye-splitting pink-and-chocolate three-piece suit, while the other held a large golden dog in navy-blue overalls. Behind them stood another figure, her long green trench coat thrown open to reveal a crisp white shirt under suspenders attached to a pair of pinstriped, forest-green trousers. She wore a thick, sky-blue scarf wrapped loosely around her neck, round dark glasses, and a wild, neon-yellow wig.

The Detective stopped. He felt the doctor bump against his shoulder and heard her gasp. Inclining his head to glance behind him he saw that the doorway they had just passed through no longer led to the hall, but to a flight of stairs leading up a narrow passage. In the middle of this passage sat a thing like an oil drum with tractor treads around the midsection and a blue glass dome on top. It had many arms encased in cloth that emerged from round holes and stretched across the doorway like a spiderweb, effectively blocking their exit.

The Detective turned back to the people in his living room. "What is the meaning of this, Professor?" he asked coldly.

"Ah, *Detective,*" said the Professor in that increasingly irritating voice that reeked of smug self-satisfaction. She came forward between the two chairs and took off her glasses. Her eyes looked a little big for her face, and the pupils were the wrong shape. They were not human eyes. She folded her dark glasses and handed them to the wolf. Then she began unwinding her scarf. "I know this must seem like a terrible intrusion," she said, looping the scarf over the back of the man's chair and shrugging out of her trench coat. She had a tall, slender body that seemed to disappear under her clothes. "But the fact of the matter is, Detective . . . " and here she slid a hand up under her wig and pulled it off in one smooth motion.

She was completely bald. More than that, her pinkish-white skin was mottled with pale green spots, like a leopard's, and extending from the base of her skull was a long, puckered, flesh-colored tentacle, similarly mottled. She gazed at him evenly out of those eerie cat eyes, while her tentacle rested, curling, over her shoulder.

"Detective," she said. "I think it's high time you and I had a little chat, *face to face.*"

Part Two: Subject 0-D

DR. JANE WATTERSON WAS HAVING a *very* strange day. Strange days had happened to her before, in the way of patients with unusual injuries, lucky or unlucky coincidences, and that exciting day in Persia when someone had tried (and very nearly succeeded at) shooting her.

None of them, however, could hold a candle to this day.

First there had been her John Doe patient, who had lingered in her mind even after he was no longer technically her patient anymore. Perhaps that was why she'd left a lovely woman sitting at a restaurant when she'd been paged about the man's unexpected visitor—Dr. Jacobsen being absent. She'd gone only to find the man called the Detective haranguing him. This would have annoyed her on anyone's account—the caudata-assist meant people healed faster and more completely, it did not make them instantly better!—but the poor man had looked so wretched. He clearly didn't want the Detective there. Dr. Watterson didn't know their history, or whose side she should be on, but as a doctor her sympathies defaulted to the person in the bed, and she'd gone about getting rid of the Detective until . . .

Until a large golden wolf wearing a purple jumpsuit had hurtled in through the window holding a *very* unusual-looking gun and shouted *"Get down!"*

And then it had seemed like things sped up for everyone except her and the Detective. She saw a tall figure in a neon-yellow wig help the dog carry her patient away, all three of them moving at super-speed. Then the yellow wig was back again, and the gun was pointing at them.

Dr. Watterson's heart didn't even have time to leap into her throat before the gun fired . . . but all that happened was the outside world slowed back down to normal.

The Detective leapt over to the window . . . but it opened onto empty space, and a thirty-foot drop to the roof of the building below.

That had been strange. Strange enough to cause Dr. Watterson to utilize some skills she'd thought she'd left in India in order to track the Detective back to his house. Then she'd stood outside uncertainly, watching the man fiddle with his keys, wondering whether to approach him.

Eventually the choice was taken out of her hands when he spoke to her. It was uncanny, but Dr. Watterson was nothing if not adaptable, and her tolerance level for the strange had been climbing all day.

She came forward. Words were exchanged. For her part, she made her position clear. She didn't expect to need to shoot anyone—she certainly hoped not—but the weight of her old army piece in her pocket was comforting. It allowed her to ascend the steps to the Detective's flat with some semblance of composure.

The person—Dr. Watterson was reasonably certain it was female—in the neon-yellow wig was standing in his living room. In one armchair beside her was the John Doe—Bane, the Detective had called him—and in the other was the golden wolf, sitting upright like a human with her tail neatly folded over her lap.

When Dr. Watterson turned instinctively to reassure herself of a safe exit, it was only to find the way blocked by a thing like a barrel with a blue glass dome on top. Cord-like, cloth-covered arms stretched from the barrel and fastened on the door frame.

Other people might have panicked at this point. There is only so much strangeness one can take in a single day. But when confronted with the unusual, Dr. Jane Watterson did not reject it—rather she rearranged her perspective to define "normal" as containing a good deal more strangeness.

Even so, this was pushing things.

Then the woman—the Professor—had taken off her coat, scarf and wig, and Dr. Watterson felt the strangeness overcome by her professional curiosity.

The woman was clearly a splice, exhibiting features of many different animals. Dr. Watterson had never heard of a splice getting so large or—apparently—living so long. Never mind possessing humanlike intelligence, as the Professor clearly did.

She must have noticed Dr. Watterson's stare, for those cat eyes darted to her and lingered.

"I see you've found your doctor." The splice smiled, showing large, white, square teeth. "Excellent. Well, I won't waste your time with pleasantries. To be frank, I know you can leave anytime you want, and you know *I*"—she indicated the eerie doorway behind them—"can leave anytime *I* want. The conversation that I'm proposing is, therefore, *entirely optional.* You can leave, if you like, and then I will leave, and then I promise, Detective, *you will never see me again."*

"Are you all right?" Dr. Watterson asked the man in the chair, cutting under the Professor's words. Clearly the Professor and the Detective had history together, but her prime concern was her former patient, who was sitting very still and looking strained.

The man—Bane—looked at her. Recognized her. He smiled and mouthed *I'm fine,* then pointed at the woman with the tentacle growing out of her head. She had gone on talking.

" . . . if you stay," she was saying. "Well, if you stay, then *I'll* stay. And I can give you . . . not an explanation exactly. Let's say . . . a *story.* A series of facts that may help you make an informed decision as to whether you *really want* to pursue this case any further. What do you say?"

The Detective turned to Dr. Watterson and smiled ironically. "Well doctor," he said. "It appears you are in luck: you shall receive many answers tonight."

The Detective made tea. Dr. Watterson sat on the sofa eyeing the guests cagily.

"Can you tell me your name *now?*" she asked the young man.

He smiled weakly. "I suppose so. I'm Alister, Alister Bane. This is Elo." He indicated the golden wolf. "The one with the tentacle is Professor Odd"—Professor Odd bowed—"and the thing in the doorway that looks like a robot is Dave."

Dr. Watterson twisted around in her seat to get a good look. Behind it, through its web of arms, it appeared another room had been slotted in behind the door, with stairs leading up to a dim cavern twinkling with many colored lights.

"HELLO," intoned the barrel-shaped object.

"You're *not* a robot?" Dr. Watterson asked. She had hoped it was. After everything, a *robot* would have been comparatively normal.

"QUITE THE OPPOSITE," said Dave.

"Everyone," said Alister Bane, bringing her attention back around. "This is Dr. Watterson. She's . . . em . . . "

"I was in the car that hit him," she explained stoically. "I took a professional interest."

"I'm glad you did," said Professor Odd, giving her a keen look. "Will you be taking notes?"

"I hadn't anticipated—"

"Please do." Professor Odd removed a notebook and pen from the pockets of her trench coat, which had been draped over the back of a chair, and handed them to Dr. Watterson. "For my sake."

"What are you planning to do?" Dr. Watterson asked, taking the implements.

Professor Odd looked up sharply; the Detective had returned, carrying a tray bearing cups and a pot. He set it on the ottoman and began pouring. He too had taken off his overcoat, underneath which he was wearing a tidy black suit over a dark, gray-blue shirt. Dr. Watterson found this little splash of color reassuring; it made him look more like a person and less like a caricature.

"I am going—*thank you*—" the Professor took an offered cup, "going to tell you my story."

The Detective came and sat at the end of the sofa, a polite distance from Dr. Watterson, and crossed his legs. He shut his eyes and steepled his hands, leaning back into the cushions.

"You may begin," he announced.

Dr. Watterson saw Professor Odd give him a look of part annoyance and part amusement. It rather raised the doctor's opinion of her.

Professor Odd took a sip of tea and drew in a deep breath, as though she were preparing to dive under water. Then she let it out, long and slow. She set her teacup on the mantelpiece, and went to stand behind one of the low lamps that was the room's only illumination. Like that, partly lit from below, she appeared even more alien.

"I suppose I should begin by asking if you've ever heard of a place called Entdeckungfeld? The Detective has, I know, but you, doctor?"

When Dr. Watterson shook her head, the Professor shrugged.

"I might as well start there, since neither Elo nor Alister know what it is either . . .

"To put it simply, Entdeckungfeld was a place in the country you know today as Deutschland—Germany, to Alister—which is . . . well it's not there anymore. Many years ago, however, Entdeckungfeld was the home of a complex, advanced, and utterly secret research facility run by a collegium of scientists from around the globe. Ostensibly they had gathered together to conduct medical research with the aim of improving the quality of life for people the world over. Which they did. They also conducted practical experiments. The results of some of these have been made public knowledge—though they've been attributed to different institutions. They had to be, you see, because of the *other* things that went on at Entdeckungfeld, the place could not, legally, exist."

Professor Odd went to one of the tall windows that looked out on the street below. She stared out it for a few moments, her tentacle curled tightly at the base of her neck.

"There were twenty-one of us, in the beginning," she said quietly. Turning back to them her eyes were very dark; her pupils blown wide. "I remember that. It was the name I was given for all of us. Twenty-one. We were divided into four groups: A B C and D. Within each group were subjects, and we were numbered: Subject 1-A, Subject 2-A, etc., 3-B, 4-B, etc., 5-C . . . There were five subjects in each group, except group D. Group D had a sixth subject added a little after the rest which, for . . . *accounting* purposes—that is to say, for the purpose of *cheating the accountant*—this sixth subject was given the designation *0-D*. It is the story of Subject 0-D that I wish to tell, but to understand the enormity of what happened to her you must also understand that there were *twenty other subjects* who cannot, for reasons that will become apparent, stand before you now and tell their own stories." The Professor clasped her hands behind her back and smiled. "It falls to me . . . Subject 0-D, the late addition, the last living subject of Entdeckungfeld, to say the things that by rights they should have said themselves.

"It began as a quest to develop medical treatments to promote healing and regeneration. Scientists had discovered that members of the *caudata* family—salamanders and their cousins—could regenerate body parts better than any other vertebrate. They wanted to develop a treatment that would allow human amputees to regrow lost limbs—or even to regrow whole limbs where before they had been malformed due to genetic defects. Members of *caudata* were chosen as the basis for the Entdeckungfeld experiments because of their relative similarity to humans—as opposed to planarian flatworms, for example.

"The Subjects, as we came to be known, were created to serve as a genetic bridge between *caudata* and *homo sapiens.* Each Subject began as an artificially created embryo which was then spliced with different kinds of DNA. There were countless numbers of these embryos. Many never got beyond a few hundred cells. Of those that did, most were spontaneously aborted. In the end, only thirty survived to full gestation, and nine of those died in the first week. A tenth wasn't expected to survive much longer, and so was not counted in the initial sorting. The twenty live infant subjects were divided as I have explained, and the twenty-first added to group D about a month into the live portion of the experiment.

"Each group concentrated on a different mix of genetics designed to translate the *caudata* regenerative abilities into a form useful to humans. Group A was primarily aquatic—I remember I was able to see their tanks from my cage—while Group B incorporated insect DNA. Group B did not live long. By the time I was old enough to understand these things all that was left were a couple of bodies suspended in preservative fluid. Group C was the most human, and perhaps that is why they suffered from autoimmune diseases. None of them survived past puberty. And then there was Group *D.*

"Group D was an almost random mix. Of Group D, 1-D died in the first year when he began growing a second stomach in his left lung, 2-D had a pair of horns and they called him Little Devil, 3-D had scales and looked like a humanoid lizard with feathers, 4-D had a third arm growing out of her chest, 5-D looked like a human but acted like a rabid animal. He was euthanized after he mauled one of the scientists. Finally, there was 0-D.

"They called me Odd almost from the beginning. I don't think they meant to name me. They didn't name any of the others except for Little Devil. I think it happened because I was the odd one out, and because in their notes they shortened our designations. Five-hyphen-A became 5A. So Zero-hyphen-D became 0D, which looks a bit like OD, and so it was pronounced *Odd.* However it happened, that was the first word I learned to recognize, because it usually meant something was about to happen to me.

"Early on all that happened was they would take me out of the cage and put me on a cold metal thing and shine bright lights in my face. I later learned the cold metal thing was a *table,* and a lot worse stuff happened on it later. But when I was very young all they wanted was to study my development. They had lost enough subjects that the survivors in Group D were precious. They measured us, monitored our growth, and tested our reflexes. None of the other D's fully developed mentally—partly because they were never given any stimulation beyond being poked and prodded and carried from cage to table and back again, and partly because they were all lobotomized at the age of four when it became apparent they were developing high-level intelligence—but the scientist who was in charge of me—the same scientist who, in the first week of my life, decided not to flush me out of the incubator and who added me to Group D under designation 0—was curious about how my brain would grow. So instead of carting me about in a travel cage he would carry me over his shoulder. When he shone lights in my face to get a look at me he would say things like 'Here comes the light,' or 'This will be very bright.' And he wouldn't let them lobotomize me. I was always 'in the middle of an experiment' and couldn't be disrupted. After a while I think they just gave up. This was the way my scientist did things: he never said no, but he wouldn't say yes to anything he didn't want either; he would just do what he liked, and do whatever it took to get what he wanted.

"Some of my earliest memories are of crawling around a room with a springy, prickly floor. There were pillars and caves made out of a mottled brown substance that gleamed. These were the desks and chairs of his office. He would take me there once a day to study my behavior, or whenever the other scientists were running group experiments that he didn't want me to be a part of. Once I spent a whole week there. That was the week they performed surgeries on Little Devil, 3-D, 4-D and 5-D to disconnect the two hemispheres of their brains so they would be more docile. That was also the week I learned how to use toilets, and what 'Go hide in the closet' meant. I got to eat food that was different colors, shapes and textures than the paste we were given in the cages. That was a good week . . . until it ended.

"I have some memories of my cage. Most of them are influenced by what I found later, when I went exploring, but I have a few genuine memories. I remember the tanks of the Group A subjects, when the oxygen tubes still sent bubbles up from the bottom, and they had little lights behind them. I remember how, one by one, they went dark. I didn't understand until much later that they had died, and I didn't find out what had happened to them until even later than that.

"My cage was . . . hmm . . . about the size of that table, and maybe two feet tall. It had a mesh floor covered in soft shavings. Urine trickled through and down a drain below, but feces had to be cleaned out manually every day. There were two bottles with rubber teats on the end that stuck in through one side. One dispensed water, the other was filled with the nutrient paste which was our only food. I understand they changed it every day so we received the correct balance of vitamins, protein, fiber, fats and so on. But it always tasted the same.

"I lived in that cage for the first three years of my life. When I got too big I was moved to a room, but it was really just a bigger cage. Only now the walls were made of a white substance that I couldn't see through. I felt very lonely in that room.

"Then, one by one, the other subjects were also moved into the room. First was Subject 4-D. She spent the first day huddled in a corner and wouldn't talk to me. I later found out this was because she couldn't. But we became friends anyway. We would talk with our hands instead of our voices, and she kept cheating and making up words I couldn't say because she had an extra hand. We made a game out of it. I liked that. It was fun. After a while Little Devil and 3-D joined us. So did 5-D but they took him away again after he tried to bite 4-D's third hand off.

"I think it must have been only a year I spent in that room with the other subjects, but it makes up a lot of my early memories. I think because I learned so much. 4-D and I taught our sign language to Little Devil and 3-D, and from then on we all talked like that. The others only knew verbal speech as this noise that meant they would be carted away, poked with needles or put on a cold, uncomfortable surface, so they didn't like it when

I talked out loud. After a while I stopped, and when we were alone together I would only make the simple, animalistic noises that they did. I got very good at our sign language though. I remember a few words even now."

Professor Odd held up her hands, palms forward and fingers splayed out. Slowly she brought them together and wove her fore and middle fingers together, with her thumbs overlapping at the bottom and the pinkies sticking out to either side.

"This is the sign we'd make when the scientists would come and take one of us away," she said. "I'm not sure how best to translate it. It means 'be strong,' and 'things will be all right,' and 'we are together in this.' It was our way of recognizing that we cared about and supported each other."

Slowly she took her hands down and cupped them together in front of her. "It was the last thing I said to them, before my scientist took me away. Then I spent a week in his office eating human food and learning to use the little chamberpot in his closet. I did a lot of verbal talking that week, because he couldn't understand our sign language. I remember I had a lot of fun.

"Then at the end of it he put me back in the big cage. I thought the others must have been very worried about me by this time, but when I got there all they would do was sit and stare off into space. They wouldn't respond to anything I did. They didn't care where they defecated or urinated anymore, and the scientists had to come in and feed them by hand. It was like the part of them that was *them* had gone away, leaving me with only the shells.

"I hated it. I shouted and yelled at them, trying to get them to wake up. I thought they had gone to sleep inside their own heads, you see. But they weren't afraid of my shouting anymore, and after a while I realized they weren't sleeping. They were dead inside.

"That was when I learned about death. Before then I hadn't been aware of these book-ends to existence. I thought I was and would always be. It never occurred to me that I would ever not exist, even though I surmised that there was a time in the past when I did not exist. Before, death hadn't been *death,* really. The lights in the tanks went out. 1-D went to sleep in his cage and the scientists took him away and never brought him back.

Things *went away* all the time. It never occurred to me before that sometimes it was because they stopped working.

"Sometimes the insides stopped working while the outsides went on.

"I couldn't be in the room with the others anymore. I threw fits. I screamed. I banged myself against the walls. Scientists came and took me away. My scientist came and took me away from the other scientists. They set up a cage for me in his office, but he would let me out of it whenever no one was around.

"He never explained what had happened. He only offered to teach me things. He was fascinated to discover that we had developed a whole language between ourselves through hand signs, and wanted me to show him so he could write them down.

"I didn't understand what writing was at the time. I just thought he wanted to become like the other subjects, and I didn't want that. He was my scientist, and he could never replace Little Devil or 4-D. I hid under his desk and refused. I wish now I hadn't. Except for a few words I managed to remember, that language died with the other members of Group D.

"One thing that came of it—it convinced my scientist that we did possess humanlike intelligence, and it made him all the more determined to protect me. I started seeing the other humans less and less, and my cage door was left open more and more.

"He taught me about writing and reading. He taught me about beds and about fruits and vegetables and meat. That was how I learned about the other part of death. How our outsides can stop—both naturally and by the interference of others. I didn't want to eat the meat for a while after that. But he was patient: he explained about biology and physiology and nutrition, and after a while I started eating meat again. He explained about a lot of things, mostly because he would talk to himself while he worked, and I would ask him what this or that meant, and he would tell me. He seemed impressed by my ability to absorb information, though to me it felt like I was at the bottom of a mountain made of things I didn't know, and I was impatient to get to the top.

"Those were the good days. I got to eat real food, I got to learn things, and my scientist would sometimes take me out into a little courtyard at the back of the complex. We caught insects together, and once he took me out in the middle of the night and showed me the stars.

"That was something. He had explained the solar system and the galaxy before, but until then they'd just been abstract concepts in my head. Being able to actually look out and *see* what he was talking about made me realize how much I hated being shut up inside all the time. I wanted to get out. I wanted to see the world. More than that, from the moment I looked out on all those stars, I wanted to see *other worlds.*

"I was insistent. I didn't understand that I was the product of a lot of advanced science and a good deal of money and that to them I was as much a piece of property as my scientist's desk or chair—albeit an incalculably valuable piece of property. I did not understand why I was not allowed out, and I kept asking. And for the first time my scientist wouldn't give me a straight answer. He would say things like 'you're too young,' or 'maybe some other time.'

"That was when I discovered I could see in a person's face when they were lying. My scientist's face would twist and change when he said things that weren't true. This was rare, so when it did happen the difference was remarkable. I had learned to watch all the scientists closely, to see if they were going to stick me with needles or just measure me with tapes and rods. They would always move carefully and cautiously, but I found I could figure out what they intended by looking at their faces. Now I found myself watching my scientist very carefully indeed, and to my surprise I caught him in several other, smaller lies.

"When I asked how people were made, for example, he explained in frank detail how sexual reproduction worked. But all the time he was talking his face said it wasn't true. I kept pestering him until finally he admitted that this was how *most* people were made, but that I was different. And that was all he would say. It was one of those blocks on his knowledge that he wouldn't tell me about. I thought of them as blocks, because when I asked him something that he honestly didn't know the answer to he'd explain that he didn't know. But there were other things—how I was made, why I was not allowed out—that he simply would not talk about.

"Looking back, I think he was trying to shield me. I wish he hadn't. Things might have turned out differently if I'd been in possession of all the facts. Then again, it might have just made me miserable.

"At the time I didn't understand what I was or what was being done to me. Because of the blocks on my scientist he never said things like 'I can't take you out in public because you are a bald child of indeterminate gender who is clearly genetically spliced with at least two other species, and we would probably be arrested,' or 'the reason the other scientists are taking you away for tests more and more is because all the other subjects have died and you're the last one,' which might have helped me get an idea of the situation. As it was I just thought it was normal: for all I knew, everyone lived out of a cage when they were young and had to get blood drawn and be weighed and measured and urinate into a cup every week. Maybe that was kinder; I certainly didn't worry myself over it. If I had known what they were doing, and what they planned to do with me, I probably would have driven myself mad.

"I mentioned before that my scientist was curious about my mental development. That hadn't been part of the original plan. We were living incubators for the next generation of medicine; intelligence was never the goal, and only occurred by accident in Group D. But as I was clearly intelligent, my scientist wanted to study my brain. I think he intended to dissect it when I eventually died—that was a big reason why he didn't want them damaging it. And while I was alive he wanted to find out as much as he could.

"And what did he find? Well, that I have a very powerful brain. It is mostly human, but there are bits of it that aren't. I have about twice as many neurons per square inch of cortex than the average human, and my scientist was curious about how these affected my learning and behavior. From reading his notes, it appears I learned faster and forgot slower than the average human child of equivalent age. Of course to me, since I had nothing to compare myself to, I just felt normal.

"That's something to remember. That, in the early days, I felt normal. I had a concept of the world with myself in the middle, and I defined everything around me—not the other way around. I was normal—*other people* were weird.

"As it turned out, however, my brain was far more powerful than even my scientist imagined.

"I don't remember much of what happened directly before the incident—everything goes rather vague and fuzzy. It's like my mind got to that part and decided it wasn't worth the energy to repair. Or maybe I decided I didn't want to remember. Whatever the reason, I only learned the details of what happened much later—after I got into Entdeckungfeld's records. That was strange. It was hard to reconcile the clinical notes that had been kept with my nightmarish memories.

"But it is good I read the notes, because from them I was able to reconstruct what happened, and what happened was this: My scientist had forever been something of an outsider at Entdeckungfeld. Nevertheless he hung on and had earned some grudging respect because of his skills. After about twelve years of the grand experiment involving Group D and the others, he decided he wanted to take me out of the project entirely. Maybe this was what he wanted all along, or maybe he finally realized he couldn't treat me as part of a scientific experiment anymore. Either way, it was what he decided, and he must have thought he had gotten to a point where he could pull it off.

"But he couldn't. They rejected his proposal of transferring me to the behavioral studies group, but they did transfer my scientist. The day he left is my last solid memory for quite a while. I remember he was sad and angry and scared. I asked him what being *transferred* meant, and if it would hurt. He explained that nothing bad was going to happen to him, but he was still scared so I thought it was a lie. Now I know he was more afraid of what was going to happen to *me*.

"And he was right to be afraid."

Professor Odd looked thoughtfully around the room. She went over to the little table and poured herself a cup of tea. She had thin, sinewy hands, Dr. Watterson saw when she looked up from her notes. They were perfectly steady as she measured out the milk and sugar.

Stirring her cup with a spoon, the Professor walked over to the chair occupied by the wolf and leaned against the armrest. She sipped her tea and stared back at the doctor.

"You probably know," she said after a minute or so. "Being a doctor, I mean. You probably know what a lobotomy really is. But I'm going to explain it because I don't think everyone here does. I know Dave's species doesn't even have an equivalent.

"First, a lobotomy is *not* a brain scramble. They do not stick an eggbeater inside your head and literally scramble your brains. They don't cut bits off and take them away either. All they do—and it is bad enough—is sever the connections between the different parts of your brain. Specifically, the connections between the prefrontal cortex"—she raised two fingers and tapped her forehead—"and the rest of the brain. This is the most common procedure, and is what most people are talking about when they say 'lobotomy.' Because the prefrontal cortex is where most of our empathic, judgmental and social control abilities are located, cut the connections and it becomes much more difficult—sometimes impossible—to function properly. You become withdrawn, you cannot connect objects with people or cause with effect, past-to-present-to-future. The lobotomy that was performed on Group D was one specifically tailored to inhibit our abilities of cognition, reaction, and decision-making. We were meant to be virtually brain-dead yet still able to function biologically unaided—that is to say, our motor control and digestive systems were not affected."

Dr. Watterson looked up from her scribbling to see Professor Odd smile, wide and mirthless, at her audience. Glancing away, Dr. Watterson saw that the man Bane was looking almost green, while the wolf had her ears laid back along her neck. The Detective sat with utter composure, his legs crossed and his hands clasped around his knees. Dr. Watterson didn't know how he could stand to be so unmoved.

"The scientists," Professor Odd went on relentlessly, now practically glaring at the Detective. "The scientists thought they were being *kind.* They couldn't bear the thought of conducting their experiments on fully aware subjects, so they took steps to ensure we were *not* aware.

"Like I said before, I don't remember much of the time surrounding the incident. I was the last subject they lobotomized, and they had learned from Subjects 2 through 5 exactly how far and where they should go to effect the desired result. Which was . . . " Professor Odd shrugged. *"I don't remember.* My perception of time went a bit murky, and the bit of me that was *me* got tossed around. I don't know if any of you feel this way, but I've always felt like my personality was one big kaleidoscope of little twinkling bits of glass. Well, this felt like someone had come along and smashed that kaleidoscope. Suddenly I was all red, or green, or white with yellow stars. And every time the conscious bit of me jumped from piece to piece I would lose time and memories. It was like I was on the run inside my own head, running from this wave of nothing that would surge up and wash away the pieces of myself.

"Sometimes I caught glimpses of what was going on outside my head. Like passing by windows where each window showed a different view. Sometimes there were people outside, bending over me or shining lights in through my windows. Sometimes I saw pieces of myself. Literally, pieces. I looked out once and saw one of the scientists holding my hand. I mean, *just* my hand. It wasn't attached to my arm anymore, and there was blood on the severed end of it."

Professor Odd looked down at the carpet and twisted her mouth. "I didn't look out the windows for a long time after that," she said.

"What was happening, of course," she said, shaking herself a little, "was that the scientists, now my brain had been compromised, were moving forward with the experiments they had performed on my fellow subjects. These were the same experiments, I later learned, that eventually killed all the others. Because they were looking for the key to regeneration. And how do you find out if something regenerates? Well, first you have to cut it off."

Professor Odd set her teacup aside and raised her arm. With her other hand she rolled the sleeve of her shirt back to reveal a forearm as pale as marble and just as hard looking. The skin was smooth and hairless. The Professor drew a line across her wrist.

"First they amputated here, at the joint. My hand grew back, but it was lumpy and a little wrong. They cut it off again, this time sawing through the ulna and the radius. That time they treated the wound with stem cells encoded with the information for my original hand." She flexed her hand, bending the fingers and making the tendons running across the back dance under the skin. "That's this hand," she said quietly, and rolled down her sleeves. Putting her hands firmly in the pockets of her trousers she continued. "Of course, their success just gave them more ideas. I remember once I caught a glimpse of this arm, and there was *another hand* growing out of it. Just a little hand. I could wiggle the fingers and everything, but the grip wasn't very strong. They had figured out a way to encode cells so that my body would grow a new version of whatever part they desired, whether or not it actually *belonged* there. This went for just about anything from bones and appendages to internal organs. Furthermore, because of my jumbled DNA my body was compatible with cells from different species. You may have noticed this—" Professor Odd waved the tentacle growing out the back of her head, where her skull joined her neck. "I wasn't born with this, you know. The scientists put it on me. It's an octopus arm under human skin. They had to reinforce my neck muscles a bit too, which made it quite strong. According to one report I read, it tried to strangle a scientist when they went to measure it."

Professor Odd grinned at them.

"I actually remember that, but I was stuck inside my own head at the time, and so it felt like someone had just plunked a new addition onto this rambling house, and there were some very strange people in it. After a while I came to realize they were just more fragments of myself. New fragments, with new memories and new ways of looking at things. The first time I woke up as one of these new fragments I knew with perfect clarity that I wasn't in control of myself, that there were people all around controlling me, and that they were going to hurt me. I lashed out and grabbed hold of the nearest thing, which turned out to be someone's neck.

"They cut the tentacle off after that. But I grew it back. That was another thing I'd learned from the new fragments. I didn't *need* the lead cells to tell my body what part to grow back, *I* just needed to know. *I* of course being the fragmented consciousness of my brain, which had been scattered into corners where consciousness doesn't usually go.

"The scientists didn't know about this. They hadn't paid any attention to my brain since they'd cut into it. They thought I was functionally brain-dead. But I was only dead in the ways they knew how to measure, and in all the other ways I was desperately, furiously alive.

"Slowly . . . very slowly . . . my brain began to heal. I told you I have a powerful brain. Well, some of my regenerative abilities got tied up in it as well. As I was regrowing my tentacle, the rest of my brain got busy rebuilding the connections that had been severed. And as more passages opened up, the dark tides of nothing began to recede, and the windows got bigger and bigger, and I stopped losing time. The world came back into focus, and for the first time in years I woke up. That was when things got *really* nightmarish."

Professor Odd tapped her hand restlessly against the chair back, making a soft *thump, thump, thumping* sound. Dr. Watterson's hands were cold, her fingers bent stiffly to hold the pen and notebook.

"You don't know terror," Professor Odd said quietly, "until you wake up on a table, naked, tied down, and someone is *sawing away at your leg.*" She looked sharply at the Detective. "My friends here will tell you I can act a bit nonchalant during a crisis. It is not because I do not appreciate the desperation of those circumstances, but simply because nothing I have yet to experience has been as terrifying as *that.*" She folded her arms, but her fingers kept playing a soft tattoo against her sleeve.

"The really bad part was, I couldn't let them know I was awake. That was crystal clear. So I did what I imagined I must have been doing for who knew how long: I did nothing. I lay on that table for a week, catheterized, with a feeding tube down my throat and a sedative drip in my arm, waiting.

"I passed the time by taking stock of what I knew and didn't know. I knew my designation was 0-D but that everyone called me Odd. I knew I had been friends with a girl who had a hand growing out of her chest, but I did not remember what had happened to her. I also did not remember what had happened to *me* or where my scientist was. When the other scientists came in and changed my dressings I tried to read their faces and found I couldn't. Faces looked like hands or feet: expressive, but not nearly as expressive as I remembered.

"That was bad. I decided I must not be done with whatever I was doing inside my head and went back to sleep.

"I must have slept a long time, because when I eventually woke up I was in a cell, and I had a foot again—though it was small and weak and difficult to walk on.

"This cell was different from the ones I had been in before. The walls were metal on three sides, and one of those sides had a thick, rectangular door in it. The fourth side was made of slabs of stone pasted together with a rough, grainy substance. It was cold to the touch and stayed cold even when I kept my hand on it, unlike the metal walls which would warm if I pressed against them long enough. I stayed away from that wall because it was cold, and it made my body stiff and hard to move.

"I spent a long time in that cell. Scientists came and fed me by sticking a tube down my nose and pumping food paste directly into my stomach. That was hard to sit still for, but I knew I had to make them think I was still brain-dead. As long as they thought I wasn't aware, wasn't thinking, they wouldn't be so careful. And I needed them not to be careful so I would have at least a chance of getting away. I developed this . . . something. Not really an ability. More like a survival mechanism. Basically, physical contact doesn't affect me emotionally anymore. There's this . . . disconnect. Maybe it's something that I developed in order to trick the scientists, but really I think it's leftover damage from the procedure. I'd spent so much time disconnected from my body that there was still a bit of a gap. And it's never really gone away. I *understand* that animals use touch to communicate threats, dominance, or affection, but I don't get any of that. I feel physical sensations like pain, heat, cold, or the pleasure of scratching an itch . . . but none of the emotions that supposedly come with them.

"So even though it was *uncomfortable* getting a tube stuffed down my throat, the sensation didn't make me feel scared or panicky, and that made things . . . easi*er.*

"I digress. At the time I thought that my scientist must still be out there. I thought I just needed to get into his office, and then he would keep me safe.

"So I waited until they took me out of the cell. I waited as I was led down corridors on a leash until we came to passages that I remembered. I remembered walking freely down them with my scientist—what felt like only a few weeks ago.

"The technician holding my lead walked slowly because I still limped on my healing foot—though I made the limp appear worse than it really was. She held her end of the lead lazily in one hand, her fingers lax through the loop. I waited until we were at a juncture with the corridor I knew led to my scientist's office, and then I bolted.

"It was such a shock to them that they didn't give chase immediately. The technician stood and stared for several seconds before she raised the alarm. In that time I had fled down the hall and up a flight of stairs to the level where my scientist lived. I went careening down the corridor, a little lopsided because of my foot, dodging around surprised scientists, until I came to the familiar door that had always meant safety to me. I pulled it open and dove inside . . .

"And it was all *wrong*. The furniture was different, and the carpet was different, and the man sitting behind the desk—who got up as soon as I entered—was the *wrong* scientist. I was still having difficulty with faces, but I could see his features clearly. My scientist had had a dark face with thick black hair, whereas this one was pinkish and bloated with hair the color of straw.

"I started screaming then. I hadn't talked in so long it felt weird to push my tongue into the necessary shapes, and so I just screamed anguish and horror and frustration as loud as I could. Screaming, I dove back into the corridor and started slamming doors open, looking for the office with my scientist in it.

"The place was thick with people. Arms and legs and hands kept getting in my way. I don't think I realized they were trying to catch me; all I knew was that I had to find my scientist, and they were *getting in my way*. I pushed. I kicked. I think I might have bit someone. Eventually stronger arms grabbed me, and they forced a mesh bag over my head and straps around my arms, and then they dragged me, still screaming, back to my cell.

"I started fighting in earnest then. I really, really didn't want to go back into that place. Despite all the confusion I knew with perfect clarity that if I let them put me in that cell I wouldn't come out again. They'd split my brain again—or just kill me completely. I saw the shape of the door open, and I thrashed so hard I managed to kick one away, but the next thing I knew they had thrown me inside and slammed the door behind me.

"It hurt when I landed—more than it should have—because what I'd landed on was angular and pointed. I lay and panted and cried for a few minutes before I realized the uncomfortable things I was lying on were *stairs.*

"That made me stop crying at once. I began noticing other things that were different. It was dark, for a start, and the place I was in smelled sort of like my scientist's closet—whereas my cell smelled of metal and disinfectant. When I reached out and touched the wall it was warm and dry and felt like paper, while the stairs felt fuzzy, like they were covered in carpet. Sitting up I saw them outlined above me by a dome of faint, colored lights that winked in and out of existence . . . "

Professor Odd trailed off, grinning at the Detective with unrepentant glee. The man Bane was staring from the Professor to the doorway with the not-a-robot and back again, his mouth slightly open, while the wolf had a thoughtful expression on her face.

"And that is how I met the Oddity," the Professor announced with a grin.

Dr. Watterson leaned forward to peer around the not-robot, and sure enough, there were the stairs and beyond them the faint twinkling of colored lights.

There was a sigh and a rustling sound as the Detective unfolded his hands and smoothed back his hair.

"Spontaneous portal relocation," whispered Elo. She turned to the man Bane. "Like what happened when the Oddity picked up Kilni."

"And . . . " said Professor Odd with a twinkle, "*you.*"

"Explain," said the Detective.

Professor Odd looked at him quizzically. "I am here to tell you *my* story," she said. "The Oddity has stories and secrets of its own, and they are not mine to tell. Suffice to say . . . " she threaded her fingers together and cracked her knuckles, "it took us a little while to get to know one another. The Oddity was . . . well, it was not then what it is now—and neither was I. We got into some serious trouble together, and went on some pretty marvelous adventures, before I figured out more or less how it worked.

"I learned a great deal in those early times. The Oddity kept moving the portal to different libraries on all sorts of worlds, and it made me a room for me to read in. I'm afraid I was more interested in exploring the worlds themselves—this was where some of the trouble came from—but I learned a lot from both things. Reading and exploring, I mean.

"I learned that there were more different places than I could have possibly imagined, and that most of them were better than the place I had grown up in. I learned about people. I learned about friends. And as I learned new things, I began remembering old things too. I remembered the other members of Group D—and what had happened to them. And though I never did remember exactly what had been done to me, I figured it must have been something similar. It was quite *upsetting* at the time. It still is . . . but not so shocking. Not anymore."

Professor Odd stared out the dark window, frowning. She sniffed, shivered a little, and went on more energetically.

"Eventually I figured out how to drive the Oddity—or the Oddity figured out how to understand me—and I was able to get back to my own world. I wanted to know for certain, you see, what had happened.

"I figured out I could look in on different parts of my world, and that allowed me to watch the events that unfolded following my disappearance. It was fascinating, really, watching the little scientists running around like so many ants. They were quite at a loss as to what had become of me.

"By this point the Oddity and I understood one another well enough that I could tell it precisely where to open its portals, and with some maneuvering I got it to open onto my scientist's old office. I waited until everything was dark, and then I went through.

"I have very good night vision, so I was able to see perfectly. Now that I was more myself I could see at a glance that my scientist had not been there in some time. None of his old artifacts were to be found, and the closet held only lab coats and a spare pair of shoes. The place even smelled different.

"That was an unsettling discovery, and it made me wonder how much time I had lost. Pondering it back in the Oddity, I decided that it was high time I found out just what was going on, and who these scientists were. From my recent experiences I knew that most people did *not* come from test tubes or grow up in cages, and most people did not work in secret laboratories. Things I hadn't questioned all my life were suddenly subjected to the utmost scrutiny, and I found they didn't hold up.

"I used the Oddity to get into Entdeckungfeld's secure records archive. There I found a huge library of files, and I went through them all, piecing together my story.

"That is how I found out that the place was called Entdeckungfeld, that Group D was only one part of a bigger experiment, and that I was the sole survivor. I learned about Groups A and B and C . . . I learned how Subject 1-D had died early, and what had become of the others. That was difficult to read, because the reports were so dry and analytical, whereas I had vivid memories of those individuals. They weren't *subjects* to me, they were *friends.*

"It got even more disconcerting when I read my own file. My scientist's handwriting was all over it, and it was from that that I finally learned his name. No, I shall not tell it to you, nor shall I say whether he is dead or alive.

"His early notes were just as dry as all the rest. He was mostly interested in my brain development, purely for research's sake. But as I grew he developed an affection for me. It looked like he started out just as cold hearted as the rest, but for some reason he connected with me, and that awoke in him a sort of sympathy. Even though he disguised his resistance to my mental scrambling as objections against tampering with a research subject, I could tell what he really cared about was *me.* He didn't want to see *his* subject go through what the others had. And I think the people running Entdeckungfeld figured it out as well: his notes stopped just before the entry stating that . . . 'Subject 0-D has undergone a transorbital leucotomy with the desired result and no noticeable ill effects.'"

Professor Odd scowled. "*Desired result.* That really made me mad. I don't think I'd ever been angry at the scientists of Entdeckungfeld before. Maybe the thought simply hadn't occurred. I'd hated them, surely, but only as an unavoidable part of my life. The way one hates heavy traffic, or headaches. They were something that was not good, but what could I do about it? Until then . . . nothing.

"But now . . . now I *could* do something. I could do a lot of things. My brain had fully healed—perhaps more than fully healed, if you counted the extended consciousness of my spinal tentacle—and thanks to the Oddity, I had experiences that told me exactly what I should do. Not to mention I had the Oddity itself. The Oddity, which the scientists of Entdeckungfeld, for all their research, didn't know about.

"And I was *hopping* mad. Not just on my own account, but on account of Little Devil and 4-D and all my old friends. Even the members of Groups A, B and C, whom I'd never known. I was angry on behalf of my scientist, who had tried to do the right thing and gotten fired as a result. And I was absolutely *furious* because on beyond Groups A, B, C and D, were drafts for proposals of *future* projects. One of them involved cloning me, or 'reproduction via traditional methods'," Professor Odd stuck out her tongue. It was very long and faintly mottled.

"But I couldn't stop myself reading. I wanted to understand *why* this had happened. That's how I discovered what they were driving at in the first place, and it was sobering to realize that they had actually made *progress.* In my file were reports of human patients who had made improbable and swift recoveries after receiving treatments developed from information gained from *me.* Sometimes directly from me, in the form of the amputee who'd regrown a foot after having been treated by a modified form of my stem cells.

"That was something I had to consider. I would destroy Entdeckungfeld, certainly, but how much did I want to leave behind? People would continue to benefit from the knowledge gained at the cost of so many lives, and I was surprisingly at peace with that—I still am—but did I want them to also know the extent of the horror perpetrated at Entdeckungfeld? Did I want to leave enough so people could find out what had happened? Did I want the stories of Subject 4-D and the others to become known? Or was it simply enough to ensure no one else had to endure what they did? What *I* did?"

Professor Odd moved to stand behind Bane's chair, clasping her hands together and staring at them evenly. "Your history, of course, speaks for itself. But for the sake of the off-worlders in my audience I shall explain what I eventually decided—and why.

"It was clear that the research being conducted at Entdeckungfeld, though morally gray, was producing effective and beneficial results. And I guess I felt that that was a good enough thing to . . . not *justify* what had been done to us, but . . . but good enough to *keep*. It was a thing good enough to keep, even if it had been gotten in a bad way. But I had to wonder, if the whole story came out, would people still be willing to use that knowledge? Would they be willing to take advantage of technology that had been developed on living, sentient, *sapient* subjects? And what good would that do anyone if they weren't? It would only rob poor 4-D and the rest of the only legacy their short lives had produced.

"So I decided, very carefully, to destroy Entdeckungfeld and all the records pertaining to it—but not the *results* of its experiments. This was as you can imagine quite an undertaking, since I didn't feel much like killing anyone either. I've never liked killing. Not even in the beginning, when I didn't fully understand what it was. But if my escapades with the Oddity had taught me anything, it was that I didn't want to *kill* anyone—ever. Besides, it was the place and the things that went on in it that I wanted to destroy, not the people who worked there.

"For this reason I decided not to detonate a nuclear bomb in the archive room—which was a possibility I entertained—but instead researched the escape routes laced into the building's structure. I wanted to get everyone out and *then* destroy it, and fortunately for me the people who had designed the place had made it clear how to get everyone to vacate their posts immediately.

"I laid plans. Careful ones. I used a controlled fire to set off every smoke alarm in the place, and at the same time I left a small piece of radioactive material in close proximity to their radiation scanner. It wasn't enough to be dangerous unless you ate it, but it made the warning klaxons go off beautifully.

"It was astonishing to watch how people evacuated—or chose *not* to evacuate, as the case proved. I couldn't understand it until I realized they were trying to *copy down* their research. Some scientists, even in the face of an apparent simultaneous fire and reactor breach could think only of *saving their work.* That was admirable, but it wouldn't do. I'd had enough of Entdeckungfeld, and I didn't want them starting up all over again in a different place. Sitting up in the direct control box (which was so difficult to get to by ordinary means that no one thought to guard it) I cut a few strategic power sources, and plunged the place into darkness. Only then did the last of the scientists leave.

"And then . . . then the whole place was deserted. I locked the outer doors so they couldn't get back in, and took one last walk through what had been my childhood home, my prison, and my torture chamber.

"I remember noticing for the first time how much I had grown, how everything seemed smaller and dingier in the dim darkness. I went all the way down to the basement to see the tanks that had once housed Group A, and found what was left of them strung up in preservative fluid. I took them out and laid them on the floor, covered them with a blanket. I'd read about cultures that burned their dead as a symbol of honor, and though we never had a culture, I thought that was a worthy practice to adopt.

"I walked back up, past the cages where I'd spent my first days—they appeared tiny now, it was horrid to think of anyone living there—and on past the cells. I found the communal room in which I'd played with 4-D and the others, and I found the operating rooms where they'd been tortured and mutilated.

"I lit the real fire in the room where I'd been lobotomized. The fuses led out like a river of wires and dispersed throughout the institution, ending at modest packs of dynamite placed in strategic positions.

"I watched my little pilot light run out of the room and down the hall. Then I stepped through a cupboard door and into the Oddity. I changed the portal so I could step back out onto the roof of a watchtower some ten miles away and watch the cloud of ash, fire and smoke rise over the treetops.

"I cannot say I felt joy or vindication. I did feel a deep sense of relief and a sort of practical satisfaction at executing a complicated and difficult task. I watched the smoke rise over the forest and felt like a dark pond on a cold morning: quiet, still, and blank.

"I went back a few weeks later, just to check on things, and found to my satisfaction that Entdeckungfeld had been reduced to a smoking crater. Everything was either burnt beyond recognition, melted, or blown sky high. I poked around enough to satisfy myself that there would be no attempts at rebuilding the place, and then I left. And I have not been back to this world since . . .

"Until *you* dragged me here, Detective, seemingly intent on my recapture. For what purpose I could only guess, but I assumed that the former Entdeckungfeld scientists had not forgotten Subject 0-D. Subject 0-D, who so mysteriously vanished from under their noses, whose disappearance coincided with the absolute destruction of that—I'll say it this once—that *horrible* place. I thought it wasn't unlikely that some or all of them had gone on to continue their research—in one form or another—and that, should they wish to hunt down their escaped subject, they would eventually contract *you* to do it. When I discovered that I could not leave this world I set about testing these assumptions until I became certain they were indeed *fact.*

"And now you know the whole story, Detective: why your employers want me, and why they call me a terrorist. But you also know *why* I did what I did, and I hope you have a better understanding of the sort of people they really are."

Professor Odd came around in front of the armchairs, her catlike eyes flashing, her tentacle waving. In a defiant voice she said: "The only question that remains to be answered, I think, is *what will you do now?*"

Silence fell in the little room. There was only the scratching of Dr. Watterson's pen as she scrambled to finish writing. The Detective sat like a statue facing the Professor across the ottoman. The man Bane and the dog looked stunned. Dave, of course, was unreadable.

For her part, Dr. Watterson was running over in her head all the treatments that she had come to take for granted that must have been developed from this person's cells. With a slight jolt she realized that the *caudata* stem cell therapy that had benefitted both the man Bane *and* herself must have come, not from salamanders as had been originally reported, but from Subject 0-D—from *Professor Odd.* She glanced across at Bane and saw that he had come to this conclusion as well; he was looking a little green.

The Detective got up suddenly. Turning from the Professor he strode to the door, stopping mere inches from Dave's suit. He bent his long body and stared up into the twinkling lights just visible beyond the stairs. His whole body was tense, like a steel trap ready to spring, and Dr. Watterson had the sudden and worrying idea that he was about to do something mad.

Unconsciously she moved her hand closer to her side.

"You won't need to use that, I promise," the Detective said without turning around. The line of his shoulders sagged, and he gazed down at Dave.

"BEFORE YOU ASK," blared the electronic voice, making Dr. Watterson jump. "WHAT I AM IS NONE OF YOUR CONCERN."

"Perhaps it will be, one day," the Detective said wistfully. "Perhaps, all of this—" he gestured toward the interior of the Oddity "—will unavoidably be *my* business. But . . . for now . . . " he shrugged, and when he turned around he was smiling a little ruefully. With pointed care he stepped aside, leaving the path clear for the Professor and her friends to exit the room. "I find that I must do a little more *research* of my own before I decide whether or not to complete my commission."

"You're not going to drop the case?" Bane blurted out.

"I have heard one side of the story," the Detective said mildly, holding his hands out, palms up. "I need to corroborate it. But I will not pursue you until I do so. And if I find it supports what Professor Odd has told us . . . *well* . . . " He spread his hands expressively. "I may find myself quite unable to complete my commission."

Professor Odd stepped forward. She eyed the Detective up and down, then extended one hand. The Detective reached out and shook it—gently.

She smiled at him a little slyly.

"Tell me one thing, at least," she said. "Was it Allsworth or Vanversen who hired you?"

The Detective started backward, glaring.

Professor Odd laughed. "I relearned how to read faces a long time ago, Detective. So it was *both?* That's *interesting.* Yes, perhaps it would be best if you looked into their *current* projects as well. I'm sure what you find there will be . . . enlightening." She smiled serenely and patted the Detective on his stiff, black shoulder. She bowed to Dr. Watterson and then swept past them to the door, where Dave waddled aside.

With a low groan Alister rose to his feet. The dog jumped down immediately and took his arm. As they passed, Dr. Watterson stood up and the man stopped.

"Thank you," Bane said.

"For what?" asked Dr. Watterson. "For running into you with my cabbie?"

Bane shrugged. "If you like," he said. He glanced past her toward the Detective, who was standing like a pillar in the middle of the room. "Take care of him," he said.

Dr. Watterson glanced at the dark man and frowned. "Why ever should I do that?"

"Because I may have gotten your name wrong, but I *was* right," Bane said. When Dr. Watterson looked mystified he went on: "Look, sometimes life really does imitate art. Or legend. Check the number of this place, if you're not sure. If it's right, though, you know what to do."

"No," said Dr. Watterson, wondering if he had entirely recovered from his concussion. "I'm not sure I do."

Bane smiled encouragingly. "You'll figure it out," he said confidently. "Watson was always smarter than people gave him credit for, too."

They went to the door and passed through. Dave rolled back into the center and, reaching out one long arm, pulled the door closed with a *snap.*

Dr. Watterson was left standing in the middle of a strange man's sitting room, a notebook full of a disturbing story in one hand, with the feeling that she had blundered into a world (or perhaps *worlds*) that was entirely over her head. She wanted to go home—badly—even though home was a tiny room on top of a shop that smelled of mold. Unfortunately her only mode of exit apart from the windows was a door that had, last she'd seen, led anywhere but home.

The Detective solved the problem for her by snaking around the furniture and snatching the door open again.

Gone was the creature Dave in his robotic suit. Gone also were the stairs and the distant colored lights. Now all that lay past the door was the ordinary hallway of the Detective's flat. Dr. Watterson let out an inner sigh of relief and moved toward it.

"What do you intend to do with that notebook?" he asked as she passed him. And though his voice was as soft as ever, something about his tone made Dr. Watterson realize he was intensely interested in her answer. That, more than anything, made her reach a decision.

"I will keep it safe," she replied, surprised at her own certainty.

The Detective didn't react, he only said, "You have no remaining questions?"

Dr. Watterson paused in the hall. "None that you can answer," she said tersely. "In fact, I very much doubt it would be good for me if I knew the answers at all. So, no. No further questions, Detective. And as I do not expect we shall ever meet again, *good-bye.*"

She left him there and made her way down the stairs to the front door, beyond which her normal, frustrating world with all its mundane problems awaited her.

She was at the door when the Detective stepped out of a shadow behind her. This was of interest since Dr. Watterson had not heard him come down the stairs. She ignored him pointedly and began buttoning up her coat.

"Watson," he said, his hard-edged voice cutting through the darkness like a knife.

Dr. Watterson sighed and turned to face him. "Do you know you're the second person in as many weeks to make that mistake?

It's *Watterson,* Detective. And I very much doubt *your* name is Holmes."

"True, it isn't," said the Detective mildly. "But you *were* a military doctor, wounded in action?"

Dr. Watterson felt her lip curl into a sneer. "A few coincidences, Detective, nothing more."

"I am not saying that they are," the Detective said. He put his hands in his pockets and looked at her with his head on one side, as if he were a bird sizing someone up. Then righting himself he continued: "It is only pertinent because, as you are a doctor recently returned from military service, I doubt you have the connections to achieve a desirable position in civilian practice. I do not mean this to cast doubt upon your skills—I am sure they are of the very best quality—but merely that it suggests to me your living situation is likely not as comfortable as you would wish."

Dr. Watterson frowned at the man in the shadows, who only smiled—brief and snakelike—in return.

"I find myself soon to be in a similar situation," he said sympathetically. "The fact is, as you may have gathered, something of a hitch has come up in the job that was keeping me here—and keeping me in such opulent lodgings. I find myself soon to be out of a position, as it were, obliged as I am to take on other jobs with much less promising financial outcomes. What I am getting at, my dear doctor, is that in order to continue living in these comfortable quarters I will require a *flatmate,* much as I despise the prospect, and you seem to be the best available candidate."

Dr. Watterson stared at him in mixed confusion and disbelief. When he only returned her gaze with steadfast assurance she found herself wavering. These rooms were large, well-built, and did not smell of mold. On the other hand . . .

"Does this mean you will not continue your pursuit of Professor Odd and her . . . companions?" she asked straight out.

"I thought I had made as much clear," said the Detective, surprised.

"Well, you hadn't," said Dr. Watterson a little gruffly.

"You must forgive me," the Detective said with a shrug. "I have a habit of speaking in labyrinths. Why, do you think I should?"

"Heavens no."

"Excellent, then we are in agreement," said the Detective, suddenly jovial. He clapped his hands.

"Just one moment," said Dr. Watterson, putting on her hat and pulling the door open. Leaving the Detective inside she went out onto the pavement and looked back up at the house. It was tall, plain, whitewashed brick with four long windows, two of which were lit from within. By the streetlight she read the brass plaque beside the door, and found it similar and yet thankfully different to what she had feared she would find.

Dr. Watterson gave a little shrug, and walked stiffly back up the steps and through the door of 2212 Barker Street.

"Very well," she said heavily. "I accept."

Epilogue

"CUT US LOOSE, DAVE," Professor Odd said as soon as they were all in. There was a fizz from the control panel as Dave's arms flew over the keys. He had replaced the panel, and now the cockpit looked more or less normal. Alister was also relieved to find that the Oddity had finished regenerating the damaged rooms while they were in the Detective's flat, and it had lost the cramped, shriveled look entirely.

Professor Odd dumped her scarf, coat and wig on the table, setting the last at a jaunty angle over the muzzle of the time gun. Then she poured herself a cup of water at the kitchen alcove and after doing so, pulled one of the big armchairs forward and settled into it with a sigh.

Alister and Elo hovered, torn between concern and a sudden, inexplicable shyness. For his part, Alister reasoned that nothing had changed: Professor Odd was still the same person she had always been; now, he just knew more about her.

Like how she had got her tentacle. And why she had jaguar eyes.

Alister found himself looking out one of the Oddity's windows instead of at the Professor. There was a swirl of light out there, slowly fading as the darkness ate away at it from all sides.

The Professor's world. The one she never wanted to go back to.

Slowly Alister sat down at the table. He still felt a bit delicate and weak, although nothing actually hurt anymore. He wondered if the Professor felt the same.

"So . . . is that it then?" Elo asked, breaking the silence.

"Goodness, I *hope* so," Professor Odd said, draining her cup. "Dave, would you be a dear and get me a refill? I am *parched* and *exhausted.*"

"SPEAKING IS A HIGHLY INEFFICIENT FORM OF COMMUNICATION," Dave said, but he rolled over and took the Professor's cup.

"And that's all of it, then?" Alister asked. "Everything you said, that's the truth?"

"Oh, it was all *true,*" Professor Odd said. "It's not *everything,* though. Had to leave him some bits to discover on his own, otherwise he'd never have believed me."

"Do you think he—em, the Detective—will stop chasing us now?"

Professor Odd smiled to herself as she took the refilled cup Dave offered her. "I think," she said with satisfaction, "that the *next time* we see the Detective he will not be our enemy."

Alister was not convinced, but he didn't feel like arguing. Elo, however, frowned and scratched behind one ear.

"Which bits?" she asked suddenly.

"Sorry?" said the Professor.

"Which bits did you leave out?"

Professor Odd smiled. Her teeth really were remarkably square and white. Alister wondered how *that* had come about.

"Well, Elo," she said. "Which bits are you curious about?"

Alister looked cautiously over at Elo. There was one subject he wondered about, but he hadn't felt comfortable asking. Elo, however, had no such qualms.

"Your *scientist,*" she said. "Whatever happened to *him?*"

Professor Odd leaned back in her chair. She seemed pleased to have been asked.

"Ah yes, my *scientist,*" she said with a sigh. "I did quite well not mentioning his name, didn't I? I tell you, it was a challenge. But I really don't want anyone bothering him, goodness *knows* he's been through enough on my account.

"Of course I went and found him, right after I blew up Entdeckungfeld. It wasn't a difficult thing to do with the Oddity. He'd been quite cast down, poor fellow. I found him living in a dingy bungalow outside Bristol *resting on nonexistent laurels* he later told me.

"I remember I came through the door to his parlor, where he was sitting in a threadbare armchair watching the television. At first I thought I'd got the wrong house: he seemed too small and shabby to be the trim man in a starched white lab coat that I remembered. But there was still his smell, and though it had gone a little musty and sour I recognized it.

"The man hadn't lost any of his sharpness either. I'd only stood in the doorway, staring, when he said without turning around: 'I don't get visitors these days. So you're either a burglar or the one person in the universe who would actually *want* to see me. If you're the former you can find what little valuables I have in the breadbox on the shelf above the sink in the kitchen. If you're the other person for goodness sakes come around so I can get a proper look at you.'

"Well, I was so shocked at this that I didn't move, and eventually he roused himself enough to turn and look at me. His trim black beard had grown into a great gray bush, and his hair was pure white and thinning around the back.

"'Come along now,' he said, like we were back at Entdeckungfeld and I was hiding in his closet. 'You've got nothing to fear from me. Rather . . . ' he gestured at the television, where a report of the explosion that had reduced a remote Deutsch castle to a smoking crater was airing, 'I think *I* ought to be afraid of *you.*' He sounded resigned.

"The thought hadn't even occurred to me. I came around and stared at him, like *he* was the escaped biology experiment. He stared right back of course, looking amazed and terrified at the same time.

"'Look at you,' he said at length. 'I'd never have dreamed . . . but I might have hoped.'

"'I'm just here to say good-bye,' I told him.

"'Really?' he said, disbelieving. 'That's all?'

"And do you know, up until that moment I think he really thought I was going to *hurt him.* The realization made me feel cold and tingly all over. But a moment later he got a little of his old character back, and then everything felt better. Normal, almost.

"Thank you,' he said. 'Now, if you'll go into the kitchen and make us a cup of tea I think that would be good. You'll excuse me but my knees aren't what they once were.'

"I did as I was told. We sat and drank tea in his musty little parlor. I asked him about his knees, told him how the research from the Subject D group—namely, *me*—had led to a breakthrough in regenerative medicine. I asked why he didn't take advantage of it. And do you know what he said? *'I haven't the heart, knowing where it came from.'* If anything convinced me I had done the right thing, it was that. I told him I would feel more betrayed if he *didn't* take advantage, and he told me he would think about it. And then I left."

Professor Odd sipped her water and looked thoughtfully at the heap of junk on the table. "I went back, once, a few years later. The place was empty, boarded up. But he'd left a note tacked to the kitchen door: *thanks for the knees,* it said. I honestly haven't a clue where he is now. But I think I would know—the Oddity would tell me—if he had died. I hope so, anyway."

A silence descended gently, but it was a soft silence, underlaid by the constant hum of the Oddity. Alister thought Professor Odd had reached the end of her narrative, but then she looked up and smiled at him.

"You'll like this, Alister. Do you know what his name was? I've never forgotten. First big word I ever spelled. A-L-E-X-A-N-D-E-R. It stayed with me, even during the bad years when my brain was all to pieces. *Dr. Alexander.*"

With that she sighed, and set her cup amongst the clutter on the table. She got to her feet and climbed up the ladder to the catwalk. They watched her go in silence.

After a brief internal struggle, Alister got up and followed her. He found her standing outside her door, staring at the 0-D tacked to the middle of it.

"I took two things from Entdeckungfeld," she said without turning around, and pointed, laying a finger first on the *O* and then the *D*. "That's my name, that's where I came from. I may not like it, but I won't hide it either."

She looked so melancholy, standing there and looking at those figures, that Alister—who was not prone to physical acts of affection—was suddenly overcome with the desire to hug her. He even made an involuntary motion before he remembered what she had said in the Detective's sitting room.

He found himself frozen with his arms at an awkward, half-outstretched angle when Professor Odd looked up at him.

"Sorry," he mumbled, taking his arms down. "You looked like you could do with a wee bit of comforting, but then I was remembering what you said . . . about the gap between," he waved a hand limply. "You know."

Professor Odd huffed a weak sort of laugh. "I don't find physical contact *repulsive,*" she said mildly.

"I know, but . . . " Alister shrugged haplessly. "But . . . what *do* you find comforting?"

Professor Odd looked at him sideways out of one eye, and a slow grin spread up her face.

"What comforts me, Mr. Alister, is waking up and knowing that I can go anywhere, do anything, and there is no cage, no cell, *no bonds* that can hold me. That I can see worlds I was not born to see, and most of all, that I am myself, and I am free. And . . . that I can continue to help people."

She reached out and wrapped her arms around Alister's shoulders. For a moment he felt his frame squeezed by thin, strong, sinewy arms, and then she had drawn away again.

"Of course, just because *I* don't get anything out of it doesn't mean I don't understand why *other people* do." She smiled at him sunnily and pushed her door open. Alister stood and watched her disappear inside with a flick of her speckled tentacle.

Professor Odd will return in
"The Dogs of Canary Island"

Escape Velocity

Apsis Fiction 3.1: Aphelion 2015 will appear in June 2015. In it you can look forward to:

"The Dogs of Canary Island"
"The Moonfoot Problem"
"The Case of Countess Baronia"
"Missionary Man"

and more!

Find the entire library of *Apsis Fiction* issues at

heliopauseweb.com/fiction/apsis-fiction

Apsis Fiction is a Heliopause Production; written, illustrated, edited and designed by Goldeen Ogawa.

More from Heliopause

The Adventures of Bouragner Felpz, Volume I: A Study of Magic

Driving Arcana: Rotation One

Professor Odd Novellas:
#1: The False Student
#2: The Slowly Dying Planet
#3: The Promethean Predicament
#4: The Elder Machine
#5: The Dragons of Geda

Coming soon:

#6: The Monster's Daughter

heliopauseweb.com

About the Author

Goldeen Ogawa is a self-taught writer, illustrator and cartoonist. In her spare time she rides her bicycle and sings. She lives in California.

About the Text and Design

The body of this book was typeset in Elysium using LaTeX.
Cover art and design by the author.

www.ingramcontent.com/pod-product-compliance
Lightning Source LLC
LaVergne TN
LVHW050630100826
845148LV00011B/1806
9780692312766